J. E. MCDONALD

I0524541

Captive Wilderness

GOLDENLACH RIDGE SHIFTERS BOOK 1

MYSTIC OWL

AN IMPRINT OF CITY OWL PRESS

CAPTIVE WILDERNESS

J. E. MCDONALD

MYSTIC OWL

CAPTIVE WILDERNESS
Goldenlach Ridge Shifters, Book 1

MYSTIC OWL
A City Owl Press Imprint
www.cityowlpress.com

Cover Design by MiblArt. All stock photos licensed appropriately.

Edited by Heather McCorkle.

For information on subsidiary rights, please contact the publisher at info@cityowlpress.com.

Print Edition ISBN: 978-1-64898-166-1

Digital Edition ISBN: 978-1-64898-165-4

Printed in the United States of America

This one is for my editor, Heather.
I wouldn't have written it without you.

PRAISE FOR J. E. MCDONALD

"*Ghost of a Gamble* is a contemporary, gothic tale filled with sparkling wittiness, budding romance, thrilling suspense, and scary ghosts!"
— *InD'tale*

"Bree was funny, and quirky, but also independent, which I loved. I enjoyed the quirky atmosphere, the hauntings, and the hot romance between these ghost hunters. A great read for fans of paranormal romance!"
— *J. E. Hunter, author of The Torc*

"I adored *Ghost of an Enchantment*! Fun, magical, and romantic. Stella is everything I look for in a witchy romance heroine, and Wickwood is a delightful setting for these books. The pacing was perfect, and the magical mystery was right up my alley. Well done!"
— *Lisa Edmonds, bestselling author of the Alice Worth series*

"J.E. McDonald comes out swinging with *Captive Wilderness*, the first in a new paranormal romance series featuring shifters, plenty of spice, and forced proximity done right."
— *Gabrielle Ash, author of The Family Cross*

"McDonald's cast of supernatural characters are always impeccably crafted and leave you eager for the next installment of this delightful series."
— *Ashley R. King, author of Painting the Lines and Forever After*

"Bree is utterly charming right from the beginning, and her

dynamic with Zack makes for a wonderfully compelling story. *Ghost of a Gamble* is easy to sink into, with a supernatural plot that escalates all the way to the end."
— *K. Caine, author of A Study in Velvet and Leather*

"McDonald busts this worldwide open and brings it to new heights and dimensions. She easily navigates blending in all of the different plot points and relationships (romantic, family, and friendship) together into a fun and 'enchanting' story."
— *E.E. Hornburg, author of The Night's Chosen*

"A heartfelt paranormal romance about a skeptic teaming up with a paranormal investigator, *Ghost of a Gamble* is sure to make you smile. Bree and Zack have perfect chemistry and their banter is irresistible."
— *Kat Turner, author of Hex, Love, and Rock & Roll*

"Stella is a witch who doesn't trust cops. Unfortunately, Lucas is a cop--and the sexual tension between them is scorching hot, making *Ghost of an Enchantment* a fast-paced, compelling read."
— *K. Caine, author of A Study in Velvet and Leather*

"Transporting readers to a thrilling romance filled dimension, *Ghost of an Enchantment* is a breath-stealing page turner set in the magical town of Wickwood! With characters that provide touches of humor and a plot filled with mystical intrigue, readers will be enticed to move in and peek from their windows in anticipation of what will happen next!"
— *InD'tale Magazine*

"A fast-paced read with a tension-filled romance and high-stakes plot, *Ghost of a Summoning* is a paranormal love story you don't want to miss."
— *Gabrielle Ash, author of The Family Cross*

WORKS BY J. E. MCDONALD

THE WICKWOOD CHRONICLES

Ghost of a Beginning

Ghost of a Gamble

Ghost of an Enchantment

Ghost of a Summoning

GOLDENLACH RIDGE SHIFTERS

Captive Wilderness

Caged Fury

Conquered Betrayal

1

BROOKE

THE WORLD AROUND ME VIBRATED, A LOW, NEVER-ENDING HUM— more than just another hangover. I struggled to open my eyes. A cold, hard surface pressed against my palms, face, and the side of my bare thigh. All around me, it smelled of metal and...manure?

Where the hell am I?

Opening my eyes was a task and a half, like someone had super-glued them together. The constant droning sound made my head throb, like the steady thwack of an ax in my skull. I didn't think I'd drunk that much. Bright, artificial light stabbed at me. Thin metal bars, that's all I could see. They took up my whole line of sight. *A cage.* I was in a cage.

My heart sped up, fear squeezing my ribs. Memories slammed through my brain, making my exhales short and fast. I'd been at the club, my best friend Corey and I dancing the night away. There'd been this guy with tattoos and a nose ring, someone who looked like he knew how to go down on a girl. Someone I could have fun with for a few days and who wouldn't care when I ghosted. I'd been grinding on him without a care in the world. Was he the reason I was in a cage?

No. My sister had been there, too. Sabrina had barged into the club and pulled me away from the tattooed guy. I didn't remember seeing him again.

Pain shot through my forehead and I groaned. The heels of my hands against my temples did little to ease the ache. When I bent my neck, my throat strained against something hard and cold. My eyes widened. I grabbed it with both hands. I was wearing a fucking collar.

I yanked at it. The skin at my nape stretched and twinged like it was connected. Panic swept through me, making me hot and cold all at once. I sat up, my whole body protesting the movement. The world spun around me. I squeezed my head between my hands, trying to make it all stop. *Worst hangover ever.* The spinning kept going and going. My stomach rolled. Bile rose in my throat, acidic and relentless, until I couldn't avoid the need to retch.

Gripping the bars in front of me, I braced myself as my stomach heaved. Last night's supper, an evening of alcohol, the corrosive taste of bile—everything passed my lips in a violent burst. It didn't quit until I was wrung out, my insides all twisted up like a strangled, sopping wet towel. The scent of vomit mixed with the manure smell coming from everywhere. *What the hell is happening?*

My head spinning, I grabbed at the collar again, trying to find a clasp, searching for a way to rip it off.

"Don't touch it."

My sister's harsh voice slapped at me through the mechanical droning noise echoing around me. Swiveling my body, I found Sabrina in a cage exactly like mine—a grid of thin bars thicker than chain link fence enclosing a space about three feet square.

Since she lived five hours away, I hadn't seen my sister in months. I remembered getting a text from her, surprised to hear she was in Detroit. I told her to join me at the club. What the fuck happened?

Gray, curved metal surrounded us in a wide tube shape. We

were in an airplane. Cages and crates lined the compact space. Each cage had an animal inside them—a wolf, a fox, a badger. On the other side of me, a monkey gripped the bars of his little prison, his head bobbing up and down. He chittered at me when I made eye contact.

These were all regular animals, I could tell by their scents. My sister and I were the only shifters, bobcats. A different shifter scent also lingered, a feline one, but I wasn't sure what kind. We were the only cats around that I could see.

I shook the front of the cage with both hands. The padlock rattled. Scanning for a way out, my gaze landed on a matching pile of vomit near my sister's cage.

"The drugs they gave us did that."

They. Who the fuck were *they*?

"What's going on?" It hurt to speak, like someone had taken a weed whacker to my throat, my words garbled. I still wore the clothes I'd chosen for a night out at the club. My jean miniskirt rode up around my hips, the G-string underneath doing nothing to protect my ass from the cold metal of the cage. The sequins from my black halter top dug into the undersides of my arms, and my ballet flats pinched my pinkie toes. Strands of my blonde hair hung limp and tangled past my shoulders.

Music thumping, flashing lights, skin against skin—more memories raced through me. Sabrina had dragged me out of the club, a frantic, desperate expression on her face. Snatches of the things she'd said made me flinch and curl into myself.

Hunters are after us.

They've promised to hurt you and Mom.

You need to come with me, somewhere safe.

I can't get a hold of Mom. They might already have her.

With the memories, panic took hold. Hunters? What was that supposed to mean? My body shook, instincts telling me to shift and fight. The thought hadn't fully formed in my head when a spike of pain went right through my brain and into my belly. I screamed. The drone of the airplane drowned out the sound. My stomach rolled again. I couldn't stop it. This time when I retched, nothing came out but a horrid noise.

"We can't shift with the collars on." Sabrina's voice stabbed at me.

No shit. "Could have told me sooner."

Trying to get rid of the taste of bile, I spat the acidic moisture out of my mouth. The noise of the airplane pressed in on me, making me clutch my head. I just wanted the pain to stop. I hurt all over.

"We need to get out of here," Sabrina said over the engine. "If we don't escape, they'll kill us."

The way she said it disturbed me. *Too calm.* A cold sweat broke out over my body. Did this have something to do with Sabrina's job? It didn't make sense. She was a forest ranger at a national park in northern Michigan.

I didn't understand what was going on, but I was in a cage. I wore a collar. My instincts told me to break free.

Sifting through fragmented memories, I tried to make sense of them. *People are after me.* She'd said that as we'd left the club, stumbling into the parking lot to head toward Sabrina's Jeep. But I hadn't wanted to leave the tattooed guy behind. I'd resisted, shrugging my arm out of Sabrina's insistent grasp.

Don't be childish. This is more important than you getting laid.

Sabrina had said more, but it was hard to remember anything clearly. We'd almost made it to the Jeep when a surge of pain made me fall to my knees. My limbs jerking, my whole body refused to do what I told it to. I'd never felt anything that intense until... I reached up and touched the collar around my neck.

My sister wore one too. The thing looked like something out of a sci-fi movie. Silver and sleek, it was about two inches wide with buttons and lights on it. Despite the collar, Sabrina resembled a model from the cover of a *Backpacker* magazine. Her dark brown hair swept into a ponytail, her blue plaid shirt was rolled up to the elbows and worn loose over jeans. Hiking boots finished off the ensemble.

Sweat beaded Sabrina's brow. I tensed, zeroing in on her movements. What was she doing? Sabrina shifted one claw, trying to the pick the padlock, the curved white of it disappearing inside the mechanism. Holding on to a partial shift with the collar on must be excruciating. Just thinking about shifting again stabbed a spike through my brain.

While she worked on the lock, she kept glancing at the door that closed the cargo area off from the rest of the plane. A gun rack was mounted beside it, but it looked as locked up as we were.

Gripping the cold metal bars of the cage, I held my breath and watched my sister's movements. Even though it wasn't hot, a trickle of sweat ran down Sabrina's brow while she worked. I shivered and ran a hand up and down my bare arm. Urgency kept my heart beating hard in my throat. Seconds, then minutes ticked by as Sabrina messed with the lock. She kept looking at the door, like she expected someone to burst through.

Who put us here? Why was this happening? More questions tumbled through my brain as I squeezed the thin metal bars so tight they made impressions in my palms.

Finally, Sabrina dropped her hand on an exhale. The bar slid out of the padlock and she twisted it open. With another glance at the door, she crawled out of the cage. The animals around us became agitated. The monkey chittered, the high-pitched sound spiking above the noise of the engine.

"Get me out of here." I rattled the bars, wanting to tear them apart.

Sabrina jumped to her feet, swayed, then caught her balance before stepping to my cage. Not making eye contact, she crouched in front of the lock. Concentration puckered her brow. More sweat broke out across her forehead as she shifted one claw, then got to work, her jaw locked tight.

Even though she seemed calm, now that she was up close, I

could see the strain in her face. Her eyes were bloodshot, her mouth pinched. Dark circles made it look like she hadn't slept in a while. Very unlike my usual full-night's-sleep-and-eight-glasses-of-water-a-day sister.

It took less time to pick my padlock. When the bar slid free, I tumbled out of the cage in relief. As soon as I stood, another bout of nausea overcame me, making me press my lips together and clutch my stomach.

Sabrina stepped close with a steadying hand. "Are you going to be okay?"

The nausea subsiding, I nodded.

"Good. Because we're not free yet."

She left me there, heading to an oval door with a circular window. We were on one of those planes that could lower its back end and a car could drive right on up—a cargo plane.

How were we supposed to escape? I knew we were in the air, could tell by how the floor dropped once in a while, giving me that feeling of lightness. Legs shaking, I followed my sister. Sabrina messed with things next to the door, straps and bags, then threw two of the black backpacks on the floor in front of my feet. No, not backpacks. Parachutes.

"You've got to be kidding me." No sooner had the words left my mouth when Sabrina took one of the chutes and forced the straps around my thighs and onto my shoulders.

"This is the only way out."

Buckles snapped in place; straps were tightened. I stood there, numb, as reality set in.

"I've never done this before." The panic of being trapped in a cage was replaced with a new terror. I didn't want to jump out of a plane. I wanted to go home. I wanted to spend the night, or two or three or four, with the tattooed guy. I wanted to sleep in my own bed, drink coffee in the morning, and laugh about the funny nightmare I'd dreamed. Maybe I'd call Sabrina and tell her about it.

Because that's what this was. A bad dream. None of this could really be happening.

"It's easy. I've done this before." Sabrina's voice broke through my chaotic thoughts. "I'm going to clip you into this line." She gestured to the straps above the door. "It's going to pull your chute open for you at the right time, all you need to do is jump."

All you need to do is jump.

A giggle escaped my lips, the absurdity of the situation pressing down on me.

Sabrina stopped in front of me, placed her hands on my shoulders, and stared at me with hard eyes. "You need to pull yourself together. We only have one shot at this. They'll make it impossible to escape if they catch us."

I swallowed. I still didn't know who *they* were but the desperate look on Sabrina's face made all humor evaporate.

With a nod, my sister clipped my cord to the lines above the door then reached for the second pack on the floor. My heart pounded in my chest and head at the same time. I couldn't hear anything except the *boom, boom, boom*. The sense of unreality gripped me, my vision tunneled.

Movement to my left made me turn. Two white men strode through the door at the front of the cargo hold. One wore a black cowboy hat and western-style boots, the other a Metallica T-shirt and a trucker hat. They saw the empty cages first and froze.

Sabrina spun, reaching for the long handle on the door. She pushed down on it.

Everything happened in a blur of movement and sound.

A deafening roar entered the plane the moment the door released. An alarm sounded. A red light flashed above the door. The suction from outside pulled at my limbs and knocked me off balance. I fell to my knees and tried to hold on to the slick, metal floor.

At the same time, the man in the trucker hat moved toward us with inhuman speed. He leaped, shifting mid-jump, clothes tearing away from his body, a cougar appearing where a man had been seconds before.

He landed on Sabrina's back, her chute in his claws, his jaw opened to bite the back of her head. I heard the other one shout, "We need them alive!"

Sabrina didn't have her pack on all the way yet, and it tore loose from her body when she twisted away. The cowboy pulled out a set of keys and turned to the gun rack on the wall.

The suction of air against my body didn't stop, and I could do nothing to help my sister. I screamed her name right before the night snagged me out of the plane and threw me into the sky.

2

BROOKE

A RUSHING OF AIR AGAINST MY BODY. FREEZING, WHISTLING WIND pressed all around me. I fell with no way to stop it, without knowing which way was up and which was down.

I'm going to die. I would hit the ground, *splat.* As a bobcat shifter, I had the potential to live a couple hundred years, and instead, I wasn't going to see my twenty-fifth birthday. Mind-numbing fear enveloped me. *Please be painless.*

Ka-thwap. My body jerked in the opposite direction, my head snapping back so hard it hit the collar at my nape. A groaned shout ripped from my chest. Pain shot through my temples. I stopped moving.

No, not stopped, but fell slower. With the parachute open, I descended in graceful inches, pawing at the straps on my shoulders for something to hold on to.

The freezing air made my teeth chatter. I'd never been so cold. Goosebumps covered my body. I looked up. The parachute was black, almost invisible against the night sky except that it blocked out the stars. Only moments had gone by from the time I fell from the plane to when the chute opened, but it had felt like a lifetime.

I scanned the sky for sight of the plane, its humming sound becoming more distant with each passing second. *So many stars.* I'd never seen such a display in my life. A full moon hung over the world, bright and luminescent, so big it seemed an unnatural thing. The airplane passed in front of it, a bullet shape heading away from me. A small, dark form dropped from it, then disappeared a second later. Another person.

"Sabrina," I whispered into the night, my feet dangling into nothingness.

The last image I had of my sister replayed in my brain, the cougar on her back, the parachute in his claws. Would Sabrina have been able to escape? She would have needed to take care of the cougar, then the cowboy. And if he'd gotten the gun out of the locked cage... On top of that, she'd need to find another parachute. Was there another parachute? I rubbed at my face. Everything had happened so fast. I couldn't remember if there were more.

A sob broke from my lips. Ever since I'd woken up, I'd been living a nightmare. None of it seemed real. I prayed it wasn't. But I was cold, hungry, and nauseous at the same time. Would I really be feeling any of this in a dream? I scratched my nails against the skin of my wrist. They scraped me raw. It felt real.

No matter how much I wanted to believe otherwise, this was happening. I'd jumped from a plane. A cougar shifter had abducted us. Tears froze to my cheeks. I tried to wipe them from my face. My teeth chattered. My whole body shook. I gripped the straps at my shoulders tighter.

Clips hung near either side of my face. I grabbed one, thinking it was the way to control the parachute. When I pulled, I spun to the right. *Too fast.* The stars sped by in a tornado-like blur. My battered stomach rolled and clenched. I pulled on the other side trying to correct the mistake and spun in the other direction. Yanking on both at the same time, I leveled out, but my head whirled, making my stomach heave.

I clenched my jaw and tried to breathe through it. I couldn't see the airplane anymore, the sound of its engines faint. Looking down, the outline of trees speckled the world beneath me, a flat carpet, consistent and never-ending. I twisted back and forth, trying to find some sign of civilization, where I could head once I landed, where I could get help. Nothing. No lights, no roads, no mountains or any other distinguishing landmarks, only the outline of trees upon trees illuminated by the glow of the full moon.

Where am I?

The tree line crept closer and closer. It seemed so far away at first, but as I drew near, time sped up. The trees reached for my toes, greedy and scratching, then my calves and hips. Too late, I realized I was headed straight for a big one. I pulled on the clip. Pine needles scraped my arms and legs, tearing into my skin, making me gasp.

A stretching, ripping sound rent the air. I held the straps tighter as the parachute became tangled in the branches. I jerked to a stop, my head snapping against the collar around my neck.

The ground lay only a few feet away. I was stuck. In a tree. My feet dangled useless underneath me.

Another sob broke free. *This is ridiculous.* I was a puppet with broken strings, trapped. I pulled at the buckles and straps, trying to remember how Sabrina had secured me into the thing in the first place. Maybe I could get the parachute to tear enough to allow me to fall the rest of the way if I kicked my legs.

I dangled there helplessly. It wasn't working. The more frustrated I became, the jerkier my movements. Out of sheer dumb luck, I finally unclipped the correct clasp at my chest. In the next instant, I plummeted, hitting uneven ground with a thud. My ankle buckled beneath me. I gasped. Pain shot up my shin and calf as I fell forward on my hands and knees. My teeth clattered in my head. Pine needles and rocks pressed into my palms.

Shivering, I brushed the frustrated tears off my face and stood on weak legs. My ankle burned and throbbed. God, I wished I could shift. Then all these aches and pains would disappear.

I looked up into the night sky. The fact that someone else had jumped from the plane terrified me. Something told me it wasn't my sister. And if it wasn't my sister, then someone was coming after me. Deep-seated instinct told me to move. I turned around and limped in the opposite direction from where the plane had gone, the moon at my back. The need to get as much space between me and whoever had jumped after me outweighed everything else.

The ground sank beneath my feet, mossy. Every step was torture, taking more energy than walking should have. Somehow, I'd managed to keep my shoes. A lot of good ballet flats did when I sank in the earth an inch or two with every step, but at least I wasn't barefoot. I breathed through the pain in my ankle, knowing I didn't have the luxury to stop. Gossamer webs brushed my face and arms, clinging. Some bug bit my thigh and I swatted at it.

I'd never felt so useless as I did right now. If I could shift, I would be able to see better in the dark. The thought of shifting sent another spike through my brain. Gasping, my hands flew to the collar. I needed to get it off. But Sabrina had told me not to touch it. After everything, I had to trust her. My chest ached with the truth. She'd sacrificed herself to free me.

It wasn't any warmer on the ground than it had been in the air. Freezing, I rubbed my fingers together, blew on them, and kept moving. Damp earth and pine—the scents mixed together in my head. I had no idea if I was traveling toward or away from help, but I knew I needed to keep going. If my sister was still a captive of whoever had taken us, I needed to find her and free her. I had to believe she was alive. There was no other option.

How the hell am I going to find her? If it hadn't been for Sabrina, I wouldn't have gotten out of that plane in the first place. I would have curled up and cried and whatever that cougar had planned for me would have happened.

My foot crunched on something and I stopped. It took me a second to understand what it was—snow, an icy sheet of it. *What the?* The last time I checked it was May, Spring. There shouldn't be any snow.

Where the fuck am I?

I kept going, careful not to step on the patches of white and slip in my gripless shoes. Each step made my ankle burn more. The terrain shifted from spongy ground cover to rock, to sand, then back to mossy. Every time I stepped on rock, it was a relief, easier to walk. I wished it was all rock. My legs were overtired and shaking. My teeth clattered in my head from the cold. What I would give for a parka and winter boots.

The light of the moon guided me forward. The trees were different here than the ones I was used to. Instead of the dogwoods, oaks, and maples in Sleepy Hollow State Park where Sabrina, our mother, and I used to camp years ago, these pines were skinnier, their trunks gnarled. They reached for the sky like aged fingers between the white trunks of birch trees.

Wet areas appeared beneath my feet before I knew I stepped in them. My shoes became soaked with sludgy water. I stumbled over a root, twisting my ankle again. The ground met my hands as hot pain shot through my leg. Grabbing on to the nearest tree for support, my hand sank into something soft—moss.

Moss grows on the north side of trees, a lesson Sabrina taught me when we'd gone camping as kids. I stood, running my hand up the side of the tree, the moss softening the rough bark. That meant I was heading east. My sister would be so proud I remembered something outdoorsy. My breath hitched. God, I hoped she was okay, that she was able to break free, too.

Knowing which way I traveled did me little good. I had no idea if heading east was a positive thing or not.

A nearby scurrying noise made me jump. The animal hadn't

sounded big but my heart raced anyway, my fingers digging into the moss growing on the tree I braced against. I stood in the middle of nowhere. Who knew what other kinds of creatures lived here? There could be deadly ones. Would any be worse than who had jumped out of the plane after me?

Swallowing, I trekked onward, breathing through the pain in my ankle with each step. Stopping only made me colder and I was already freezing. My teeth chattered nonstop. My shoes were total shit, meant for a night of light dancing and that was it. They pinched my pinkie toes and rubbed against my Achilles tendon. Each new step made it worse. The way my feet sank into the earth amplified the pain. If I took off my shoes, my feet would probably look like hamburger.

I walked and walked, telling myself to keep going, to put one foot in front of the other. My frantic breaths filled my head, a counter-balance to the buzz of insects that surrounded me in a low hum. I wiped cobwebs from my face and scratched another bite on my arm. Some of the tree branches were so heavy with moss it looked like they dripped with it.

The night sky lightened, turning a deep indigo. Hunger and nausea twisted my stomach. If I could shift, then I could hunt for my dinner, but as a human, I was useless. I didn't know how to set a trap like Sabrina. I didn't know how to make a fire out of nothing like her. She was the one who went on week-long wilderness hikes with nothing but a backpack. I was the one who waited in the hot tub of an upscale lodge with my martini in one hand and my phone in the other.

My phone. I hadn't thought of it until just now. The kidnappers must have taken it because it had been in my back pocket along with my ID, bankcard, and a bit of cash. If I had my cell, I could call for help. I looked up at the lightening sky. Would I get a signal out here? Where was here?

A defeated sob ripped from my chest. My legs gave out, and I fell to my knees. They stung. I knew I'd ripped some skin off and didn't care. *So tired.* Giving up, I laid down and curled into a ball. All the tears I'd been trying to hold back came loose. I couldn't do this anymore. Every part of me hurt. Every part of me was cold. My skin felt tight. My head pounded. My stomach clenched, empty and painful. I wanted to sleep and wake up in my cozy, warm bed.

Get up.

My instincts were telling me to keep moving, that whoever had jumped out of the plane after me followed. I didn't understand who could have grabbed us. We were always so careful since we lived on our own, not in one of the rare shifter communities. There were two dominate species in this world: us and them. Our instincts made sure we kept our animals sides secret from humans. But that guy had been a cougar. Why would he want to hurt us?

Whoever had jumped out of the plane, they were probably better at survival stuff than me, considering the plane and guns. And most outdoorsy types traveled faster than I could ever hope to out here. I touched the collar encircling my neck. Did it have some sort of tracking device on it?

The thought made me struggle to my feet again. Groaning in pain, I kept pushing forward. The sky continued to lighten, now a deep shade of ultramarine.

Something bright reflected in front of me and I paused, wary. When I couldn't hear anything, I moved forward, but cautiously. The same thing flashed again. My heart sped up. Picking up my pace, I broke through the tree line, then stopped.

A lake lay just ahead, the setting moon reflecting off its surface.

I'd never been so happy to see a lake in my entire life. A sudden thirst erupted along my tongue and the back of my throat. I couldn't remember ever being so parched. I stumbled toward the water. Rocks edged the shoreline instead of a beach. I made my way along it, looking for a place to reach down to the water where I wouldn't fall in. I'd freeze to death in this cold if I did.

Finally, I found a spot where a flat rock stretched toward the water line. I walked almost to the edge, then got down on my hands and knees to crawl the rest of the way. My torn skin stung. When the water was inches away from my face, I cupped both hands and scooped some up.

It was so cold my fingers went numb. I took a sip. It tasted fresh. I drank some more, did it again and again until my stomach told me stop. The sudden urge to retch made me slap a hand over my mouth. Was the water bad or was my stomach too empty?

I breathed through my nose, trying to will my insides to settle. Taking slow breaths, I stared at the water, then dropped my hand when my stomach calmed. A light wind created ripples across the surface. I tensed when I realized something else reflected in the lake besides the moon, a different kind of light. I lifted my head, and blinked.

A cabin. On the other side of the lake, light shone through someone's cabin windows. Relief poured through me. I could get help. I could use their phone. They could give me a ride to the nearest town. *I'm saved.*

It didn't look far if I could go straight to it. But I wouldn't swim across a freezing lake. I glanced right then left, trying to figure out which way would be shorter. They both seemed equally challenging.

I limped my way across the mossy-covered rocks to the left, keeping the cabin in my sight at all times. If I looked away, I feared it might disappear.

Stumbling from tree to tree, using the trunks to keep me upright, it took me longer to circle the lake than I would have thought. By the time I could make out each brown log and the four-paned windows, the sky had turned a lighter shade of blue, the underside of thin clouds painted pink.

My legs shook as I stumbled my way across an open area to

the rustic porch. The angled awning kept one wicker-style chair safe from the elements. Light leaked from the windows, welcoming and warm. Teeth chattering in my skull, my arms wrapped around my ribs, I stepped up onto the landing and knocked.

"Hello?" My voice croaked out of me. No answer came and no one moved around inside that I could hear. It was early. Maybe they were asleep, but the lights were on. I knocked again, then tried the doorknob.

It turned easily and I pushed it open.

"Hello?" This time I said it louder. "Is anyone here?"

Smells wrapped around me, familiar scents that made me gasp in relief. Lemon cleaner, the hint of a meal recently cooked, wood, and something else I knew I should recognize.

I stepped farther inside the warmth. It was a kitchen, living room, and bedroom altogether. The walls were the same on the inside as they looked on the outside, stacked logs. A black potbelly stove took up the space between the kitchen and a stone fireplace which was flanked by two windows shrouded with thin, white curtains. The bed was large, the quilt thrown back like someone had just gotten up. At its foot, a desk was wedged in between a wardrobe and a window. Sitting on it was a computer monitor next to some sort of workstation, small pieces of metal inside a low, wooden box.

I scanned back toward the kitchen. A plate with three apples sat in the middle of the small dining table lined up parallel to the one row of kitchen cupboards. *Food.* My empty stomach clenched in pain. I stumbled toward the table, overturning a chair in my haste to reach an apple. I bit into it, ravenous, barely swallowing before I took the next bite. My legs gave way under me. Pain shot through my ankle as I crumpled to the floor, exhausted. I devoured the fruit while leaning against the table leg for support.

My limbs wouldn't stop shaking. After everything, the heat inside the house made me shiver and tremble. I swallowed, my stomach unhappy with how fast I'd eaten. I pressed a hand to my abdomen. *Please stay down.* I didn't want to throw up again.

Thud. I froze, my eyes flying to the door I'd left open. The hair on the back of my neck stood on end. My heart raced. *They found me.* The thought trigged my shifting instinct, and a slice of pain cut through to my stomach before I could stop it. My eyes went to the swing-bar lock on the door but there was no way I'd make it there in time. Frantic, I struggled to my feet, searching the room for a weapon.

The countertops were bare. I dashed to the closest drawer and opened it. Cutlery. I grabbed a butter knife and held it in front of me.

A white man with a full, scruffy beard stepped through the door, a big guy with sun-bronzed skin, wearing jeans and a red flannel jacket. He held a shotgun casually over his shoulder, and even though he looked rough around the edges, his features were striking, making me aware in a surprising way.

Not one of the kidnappers. Relief made my knees weak and I clutched at the counter to stay upright.

He blinked at me, shaking his head slightly. A distinct scent wafted toward me, making every fine hair on my body stand on alert. I realized what I should have known as soon as I'd stepped into the cabin. My numb brain hadn't been able to place the familiar scent. He was a shifter. His scent was everywhere. And I'd crossed into his territory.

My instincts told me to shift, to fight or flee. As soon as I had the thought, pain spiked through my head to my stomach. I screamed. The apple I'd devoured came right back up.

The knife slipped from my fingers. I clutched at the collar around my neck, then collapsed.

3

KANE

"Help me." The words whispered through her lips a second before she passed out on the floor.

I blinked, trying to comprehend the scene in front of me. There was a woman in my cabin. She'd just puked and fainted. The need to help her tugged at my chest.

But where the hell did she come from?

About an hour ago, my perimeter alarms signaled something had crossed onto my land. I thought it might be a black bear even though they'd stayed well away from me since I'd moved here five years ago. I'd been prepared to scare it off with a warning shot.

Not in a million years would I have guessed I'd find a woman.

She looked so fragile, broken, there on my floor. I took a step forward, then stopped. Her scent wove its way through the cabin, putting me on alert. *A shifter.* I hadn't met another since living here, and for a moment, the unlikeliness of it paralyzed me. A feline fragrance filled my nostrils. She was a cat of some sort, mildly familiar, intoxicating, but also different than anything I'd scented before.

And what was that around her neck? An icy sensation spread through my chest. I placed the shotgun in the rack between the door and the whiteboard I used for my grocery lists and moved closer.

Crouching beside her, I brushed long, blonde hair out of the way to have a better look. She appeared to be in her mid-twenties. The scratches on her arms, smeared makeup, and dark circles under her eyes did nothing to distract from her beauty. Attractive as she was, none of that drew my attention like the collar around her neck. The design was so shockingly familiar I could only stare. The width of it was different, the digital locking system was different, the frequency gauge, a red light moving up and down on the side, was different. But from the way she lay, I could see how it attached to her neck at the bottom of her skull, two spikes into the base of her brain—that's exactly how I'd designed it.

If I could have sworn out loud, I would have.

Her features were now relaxed into the easy expression of sleep, but when she'd fallen, she'd been in pain. It was like the collar had shocked her unconsciousness. Someone had been hurt because of one of my designs. Queasy tension squeezed my stomach.

My eyes slid to the bottom drawer of my desk where I'd stashed a very similar collar, then back to the woman in front of me.

Landon betrayed me.

Anger washed through me, coloring the edges of my vision red. If my cousin stood in front of me right now, I would strangle him with my bare hands.

The anger felt comforting and familiar, seductive. I wanted to give into it. I wanted to tear something apart, to roar and bash the table with my fist. But as my vision tunneled, and every muscle bunched with the need to lash out, the unconscious woman on the floor commanded my focus. She was a mess, like she'd had a rough night at a bar. The closest one was more than four hundred kilometers to the south through muskeg, lakes, and hard terrain. There was no way she could have walked that.

To battle the red haze threatening to take over, I kept breathing, focusing on her face. My fingers relaxed; my fists loosened. I had lived all these years alone without incident. I refused to have one now.

Slowly, the haze lifted. I wanted to rip that collar right off her neck, but the active frequency gauge on the side made me hesitate. It was armed. It looked like a remote might be the only way to turn it off. There were enough similarities to see the connection to my design but enough differences that kept me wary of messing with it. If I tried to force it, I might end up hurting her even more. I couldn't risk it.

The angry red scratches that scored her bare arms and legs drew my attention. Her jean skirt was dotted with vomit. Chunky bile lay beside her face along with an apple core. I glanced at the table. Yep. She'd eaten an apple from there.

A fresh wave of sympathy made my chest ache. She probably ate too fast. There wasn't anywhere close to get food. No matter where she'd come from, it had to have been a long way off. How many days of walking had it taken her to get here?

I touched her bare arm and gave her a shake. The sequins of her top picked up the overhead light and glinted at me. Her head lolled back and forth, but her eyes remained closed.

Not wanting to leave her on the hard floor, I carefully rolled her onto her back and slid one arm beneath her knees, the other under her shoulders. I stood, hitching her up on my chest to support her neck. Protective instinct flared through me. She was small in my grasp, as light as dandelion fluff. Her skirt rode up. Bare skin pressed against my forearm like she wore nothing underneath. I wouldn't look to double check.

I took her to my bed and gently laid her down. Outside, the sunrise broke over the horizon, bathing the cabin in a soft, yellow glow. Five in the morning.

Blood smeared on the bright white sheet beneath her feet. I leaned forward to take a closer look. Broken skin covered the backs of her ankles, rubbed raw from her shoes. That wasn't all, either. Scrapes reddened her knees, the skin missing in places, and a swelling bruise blossomed around one ankle.

A scratchy growl emerged from my chest, surprising me. Her shifter fragrance must be getting to me. Turning away from her slight form, I crossed to the kitchen where a first-aid kit lived in the cabinet above the sink. White box in hand, I returned to the bed. She hadn't moved. Sitting beside her feet, I carefully slipped off her shoes, trying not to cause her pain. She winced in her sleep.

Setting the impractical shoes on the floor, I examined her injuries. Not only were the backs of her ankles raw, so were most of her toes. I reached for the tube of ointment in the kit. Cold skin met my fingers as I rubbed salve over the open wounds on her feet and knees, then covered the larger cuts with Band-Aids. A tensor bandage came next. I wrapped her bruised ankle with careful movements, making sure not to hurt her further, securing the end with two metal clips.

Kneeling beside the bed, I dug out a pair of socks from the bottom drawer of my dresser. Her toes were freezing, and I wanted to warm them up. Because the sock was so big, I was able to slide it up and over the tensor. The other one remained loose and baggy on her good foot. I pulled it up her calf as far as it would go.

With that done, I covered her with my blankets and stepped back. Her distinct feline scent filled the room, heavy, overtaking everything I'd once found familiar. I shook my head to clear it, then backed away slowly like she held a loaded gun. Her expression didn't change.

Yesterday, my life was as normal and monotonous as it had been for the past five years. Now I had an unknown woman in my bed. I'd grown up in a town of both shifters and humans, the shifters keeping themselves separate and secret. The older I got, it became more and more apparent that I wasn't in control of the beast inside me enough to live with either species. It was why I'd left despite Landon and Walker's protests.

I'd bought this piece of land in the boreal forest from a trapper six years ago with the promise to never develop anything beyond the one cabin. It was literally in the middle of nowhere, everything self-contained. No one bothered me here, and I needed it that way. For everyone's safety.

I rubbed a hand over my face, hoping my world would return to normal. But everything remained the same: the knocked-over chair, the missing apple, the splat of chunky puke on the floor. The weight of the situation made me feel older than my thirty-one years.

I glanced at the bed. How had she ended up here? And why was she wearing the collar I'd helped design? She'd been scared, like she thought I might hurt her. Had others already done so?

Another growl emerged from my chest, and I stopped it with a shake of my head. Standing in the middle of the room looking like a fool wasn't getting me any answers. I forced myself to move.

The chair came first. I righted it and tucked it in its place at the table. Then I retrieved a rag to clean up the mess on the floor. With the rag rinsed and the apple core in the compost bin underneath the sink next to the water filter system, I headed for my shotgun beside the door.

After a last look at the woman in the bed, I left the cabin. I needed to figure out where the hell she came from and if there were more people out there.

4

BROOKE

EVERYTHING HURT.

My toes, my ankles, my legs, my arms, my stomach, my face and scalp—everything. I didn't remember ever being so sore. It was like a truck had rammed into me, backed up, ran over me again, and left me for dead. I didn't want to move. I didn't want to breathe. I just wanted to stay wrapped up in this warm cocoon that smelled like lemon and shifter, safe and protected.

Shifter. My eyes flew open, my body tingling.

It all came crashing back to me. I remembered the airplane and the cougar. I remembered falling from the sky. I remembered stumbling to the cabin and eating the apple, then seeing the big man with the gun. Panic shot through me. I needed to get away. I needed safety. There were people after me. Most importantly, I needed to find my sister.

My hand inched its way to my throat. I still wore the collar, the metal cool against my fingers. Panic ripped through me, making my breaths come out in little bursts. Stars dotted in front of my eyes.

Throwing the covers off, I sat up and winced, my head spinning and stomach clenching. I curled into myself, needing it all to stop. Breathing properly became a difficult task. I inhaled deep through my nose, like how I was taught in those yoga classes I took a year ago then bailed on.

Slowly, the world around me stabilized. My insides calmed but my skin felt like it belonged to someone else, itchy, tight, and sore.

Lifting my head, I scanned the cabin. I was alone. The bed was snugged up against the wall. A series of bookshelves hung above me. They were packed with books of all sizes, and on the far end of one sat a small stereo and some CDs. One dresser blocked out a portion of the window to the left of me, a lamp with a white shade on top. Everything was made of wood, nothing modern about the place in the least.

A rustic couch sat in front of the fireplace. It had the same look as that chair out on the porch but was covered in blue cushions. The kitchen was a row of cupboards against the far wall with a window overlooking a sink in the middle. There weren't any other doors except the one at the front, the one I'd come in.

In the middle of the small dining table sat two apples. My stomach squeezed in remembrance of throwing up the other. I wasn't sure if I was hungry or sick. I felt a little bit of both, but mostly just empty.

Swinging my feet to the floor, I realized the man put socks on me. Band-Aids covered my knees. Underneath the one sock, a tensor around my ankle made the sock bulge. My foot throbbed, a steady low bass of a beat in sync with my heart. A medicinal fragrance, an ointment, wafted up to me.

My ballet flats lay next to the bed, and I winced at the sight of them. There was no way I could put those on again. My toes ached with the memory of being squished and rubbed raw, my skin being torn off.

I stood, my legs shaky. As soon as I put weight on my bad foot, pain shot up my shin and calf. I gasped, reaching out to steady myself on the dresser, and shifted my weight so I was mostly using my good leg.

My jean skirt had ridden up, and I tugged it back down to cover my ass and thighs. As soon as gravity kicked in, I needed to go to the bathroom so bad my eyeballs burned. I glanced around, searching for the elusive door that would point me in the right direction. There was none.

No bathroom.

Boot steps echoed on the porch outside. I stilled, my whole body going on alert. The fine hairs on my arms stood on end. The person moved toward the door. My heart pounded. Unable to move, I gripped the edge of the dresser so tight my fingers ached.

The door opened, soundlessly swinging inward. The same man who'd found me earlier strode inside, the shotgun in his hand. His scruffy good looks made me inhale once, quickly, then I held my breath. He froze when he saw me, his eyes assessing and slightly wary— wariness that made me exhale slowly between my teeth. He wouldn't be wary if he was going to hurt me.

With his focus entirely on me, my nerve endings hummed. He turned and put the gun in the rack by the door. Beside it hung a whiteboard with a few words written down: bread, potatoes, turnips.

My gaze flicked back to the man. I hadn't noticed earlier, but scars textured the skin of his throat where his beard tapered off. The sight of a scar on a shifter made me tense. I'd never heard of it. Shifting took away injuries, healing them as the muscle and tissue morphed from one form to another. The regeneration was the reason we could live so long. The scar took up most of the space on his neck, disguised in part by his beard.

I tensed when I thought he would shut the door, trapping us together, but he left it open. Cool air swirled and mixed with the heat of the cabin. The visible escape route made the tension in my shoulders ease a bit. He turned to me but stayed put. We stared at each other, him with curiosity on his face, me full of caution. I didn't know if I could trust him. After everything that had happened last night, the big shifter made me nervous.

There were questions in his eyes, but he didn't speak them. The silence between us stretched. The fact that he didn't have an agenda, that he wasn't pressuring me for anything, made me relax a fraction more. I loosened my death grip on the dresser.

When I could take the silence no longer, I cleared my throat. "Hi," I managed to say, my throat scratchy. Introductions were probably in order, but I needed to use the toilet so bad I couldn't see straight. "Where's the bathroom?"

He continued to stare at me, but after a moment, he stepped to the side and gestured to the great wide world beyond the front door.

"You can't be serious." I was supposed to find a tree?

A fleeting smile quirked the corner of his mouth so fast I would have missed it if I hadn't been watching him.

He was laughing at me? Fine. I could find a tree. I'd been wilderness camping before. Straightening my spine, I took a small step forward and winced when I put weight on my bad foot. The pain shooting up my calf snatched my breath. It would take a while before I could make it to a tree, and the pressure in my bladder intensified with each passing second.

How was I supposed to do this? A strange sort of embarrassed panic overtook me. I'd already thrown up on his floor, I didn't want to pee on it too.

Bracing myself, I took another measured step.

A strangled sound came from the man by the door. In the next instant, he moved toward me. Every muscle in my body bunched to run. A very large predator was headed straight for me, and my instincts told me to flee.

The three steps it took him to cross the distance between us gave me no time to react. Then I was up in his arms, thick muscles supporting my legs and back. My arm became squished between his chest and my ribs, the other hanging free. I had no time to protest before he strode out the door.

The cool air slapped at me as birds chirped happy tunes in the distance. The bare skin of my legs prickled with goosebumps, but wherever his body pressed against mine, his heat warmed me. I'd never felt as small as I did right then. With his muscles surrounding me and the soft fabric of his flannel jacket pressing against my cheek, the sudden sensation of safety I felt surprised me.

He walked a steady pace up a slope and along a worn path through the trees. About twenty yards away, a little brown shack hid nestled among a circle of pines. *An outhouse.* Embarrassment burned my cheeks, my fingers flexing involuntarily where they rested against my ribs.

The wind picked up around us, rustling my hair as he set me on my feet in front of the door. I couldn't stop my shiver at being separated from his warmth. After a moment of hesitation, he took off his flannel jacket and settled it over my shoulders, then turned and left me there.

I stared after him. More tension eased from my body. He was helping me, not hurting me. His distinctive scent wafted off the jacket, filling my head. I tipped my nose down and inhaled deep. It held notes of earth and spice and shifter and man. When he disappeared from sight, I felt strangely bereft but turned and opened the door of the outhouse.

The tiny building had only a few things inside, and it smelled like...outhouse. A bench with a white plastic toilet seat in the middle took up the biggest part. A roll of toilet paper hung on the wall beside a bottle of hand sanitizer. There were two red coffee cans, one upside down and one holding three magazines. I lifted the other revealing an extra roll of toilet paper hiding inside.

When I closed the door, only a slice of light came through the mesh windows running along the top of the shack. Without further delay, I took care of business. The magazines turned out to be *Afar*, *Maclean's*, and *Men's Health*, all the dates on them from months ago. After a few minutes, I finished up with the hand sanitizer and gingerly stepped outside, keeping my weight off my bad foot as much as possible.

With mother nature taken care of, my mind went to more important things. Like, where the hell was I? Was my sister okay? My mom? How could I get this collar off my neck? Who had come out off the plane after me? Sabrina or someone else? The guy with the cowboy hat?

The thought put me on alert. He could be out there right now. I glanced around, looking through the trees for movement. The contented sounds of the birds made me believe I was safe for now. But I hadn't told the big guy I was in danger. I hadn't told him anything. With my mind racing, the wilderness pressed against me, overwhelming, and made me feel so very alone. I didn't want to be alone.

On a pathetic whimper, I started down the path. The cold air made my legs tremble. My hands began to shake and wouldn't stop. I limped one step at a time, careful to avoid the roots and rocks in the ground. Pain shot up my leg every time I used it.

He found me that way, hobbling, hurting, and scared. I stopped and stared as he walked up the path. The rapid staccato of my breaths slowed as he neared. Sunlight highlighted his features better than the light in the cabin had. His hair was almost red; not ginger, more auburn. Jeans hugged muscular thighs, his black T-shirt clung to wide shoulders and thick arms. He didn't seem to feel the cold like I did. Even with his jacket, I kept shivering.

The daylight made the scars on his neck more pronounced. I stared at them a moment when he stopped in front of me. How had it happened? My eyes flicked up to his. They were an arresting shade of brown, cognac, but like they glowed from within. And when they were focused on me like this, my breath caught in my throat.

"I need help," I said when he continued to stare.

With a nod, he stepped forward and swept me up into his arms without ceremony.

I'd been talking about the bigger picture, about needing to get to a town, but I couldn't fault him his logic. A shot of embarrassment went through me before I relaxed into his embrace, his warmth chasing the chill away. My one arm curled around his back to hold on tight, the other laying useless against my chest. Muscles bunched and moved beneath my hand through the thin material of his T-shirt. Since he wasn't wearing his jacket this time, my cheek rested against the firmness of his pectoral muscle.

It took no time at all for him to carry me to the cabin. He set me on my feet beside the table, shut the door, then crossed to the kitchen area without saying anything. Bracing my hand on the back of the chair, I watched as he ran water from the tap into a kettle.

Feeling awkward and unsure, I wrapped my free hand around my middle. "I need to find my sister," I said when he plugged the kettle into the wall. He paused and turned his head. "I need to make a few phone calls," I went on. "I'll need to rent a car or something, but I have no money. I'll pay you back for everything as soon as I can. Will you help me?"

He faced me, his full attention on me now. My fingers tightened on the back of the chair as I waited for a response. Then he shook his head. *No.*

I swallowed. He wasn't going to help me? A nauseous ball climbed through my stomach and into my chest. What was I supposed to do if he wouldn't help me? With a frantic feeling threatening to claim me, I glanced around the cabin. There was a computer in the corner, but I couldn't see a phone. Who could I email for help? He had to have a cell phone. Why wouldn't he help me?

Another, more disturbing thought made me stiffen. I was trapped here with a stranger. He was refusing to help. There was no one else around. He was bigger than me, stronger, and I had a fucked-up foot. All I'd been thinking about was getting away from whoever came out of that plane after me, but what if this guy was worse?

He'd gone back to puttering in the kitchen, and I backed away toward the door while keeping my eyes on him. My ankle screamed at me, telling me to rest and put it up for a while, to ice it, but I ignored the shooting, throbbing pain. Survival had become more important.

I had no qualms about stealing a car from a psychopath. I even knew how to hot-wire one thanks to running with a shady crowd in high school for a while. I'd take his vehicle and run, follow the road until I found a town. There had to be a town somewhere.

He didn't turn around as I grabbed the doorknob. Holding my breath, I yanked it open and escaped.

5

KANE

I HEARD THE DOOR OPEN, HEARD THE SQUEAK OF WOOD PLANKS AS she walked across the porch, then silence. Turning, I blinked at the exposed slice of wilderness. Where the hell did she think she was going? She could barely walk.

Leaning over the sink, I peered out the window. After three heartbeats, her head came into view, bobbing up and down as she hobbled around the side of the cabin. Even in her disheveled state, her beauty shone brighter than the morning sun. Her elfin features and wide eyes made her look vulnerable, but also ethereal in this rugged terrain. It was hard to take my gaze off her. I didn't understand why she insisted on walking around on her injured foot, but I wasn't going to stop her either.

I lost sight of her as she rounded the back. Shaking my head, I poured hot water over the coffee grounds in the French press, the aromatic scent wafting up in a steamy swirl. When I leaned back on my heel to look out the window, she'd stopped by the flat rock where I chopped wood. Her arms lifted in a "what the fuck?" manner. Was she muttering to herself? I couldn't hear from inside, but it looked like she was.

Abruptly, she spun around, then hobbled and winced her

way farther along, toward the other side of the cabin. She disappeared beyond the windowless wall.

Setting the lid on the French press, I waited until her limping form crossed my line of sight at the door, then grabbed two coffee mugs from the cupboard.

Oh, she is definitely muttering to herself. Since the door was still open, I could hear her now. She'd stopped on the bottom of the path toward the outhouse. I stepped to the side to see her better. She lifted her arms and dropped them in that same hopeless manner. My shoulders tensed. The animal in me didn't like her feeling hopeless. Hell, neither did the man.

She turned and limped out of sight, toward the lake. When she passed by the window, I pushed down the plunger of the coffee press. The fragrant scent wafted up to me, stronger than before. Her head didn't bob up and down outside the kitchen window this time. I poured the brew into the two mugs, took the powdered creamer and sugar out of the cupboard, then went to see what the hell she was up to.

I found her near the dock, staring at my canoe and aluminum fishing boat. Both were upside down. I hadn't gone fishing since last fall. The ice on the lake had only fully melted last week.

Her shoulders slumped forward. I walked closer, wanting to help. The socks I'd given her were covered in dirt and pine needles. She spun around when she heard me coming. Fear shone in her wide eyes. I stopped. They were tawny in color, luminescent. *Stunning.* If it wasn't for her shifter scent, I would have known she was a cat by her eyes alone.

A long silence passed between us with me not wanting to scare her, and her looking like she was about to lose it.

Finally, she threw her hands in the air. "Where the hell is your car?" she shouted to the sky.

I shook my head. I didn't have a car.

"Where the fuck am I?" She whispered this time, but I heard her.

There were bigger questions going through my head than that one. I stuck out my hand in a gesture for her to wait, then turned around and strode to the cabin. In one of the drawers under the kitchen counter I found the pad of paper and pencil I always kept there. I wrote three sentences: *Hello, my name is Kane Baird. I'm not going to hurt you. What is your name and how did you get here?*

I tore the top sheet off the pad, folded it, and slid it into my back pocket along with the pencil. Then I fixed one coffee with creamer and sugar and left the other black.

When I stepped outside, both coffees in hand, my eyes went right to her. She'd walked to the end of the dock and sat on the edge, her knees pulled into her chest, her arms wrapped around her shins—a protective posture. She still wore my jacket, and it made her look like a ball of red flannel topped with a halo of blonde. The serene scene—calm water with loons swimming along the lake's edge behind this strange, beautiful woman—was postcard perfect.

Hesitating, I almost went back inside. It looked like she wanted to be alone. But the helplessness, the desperation on her face when she'd yelled at the sky, kept my feet firmly planted. I stared at the two coffees, the steam wisping white in the chilly air. Hot coffee was always better than cold coffee. If she told me to fuck off, I'd leave. Decision made, I walked toward her.

As soon as I stepped onto the dock, her shoulders stiffened; her spine straightened. My weight made the wood creak loudly in the quiet of the morning. She didn't lift her gaze until I stopped beside her. Tears wet her cheeks. She glanced away, swiping furiously at her eyes with the too-long sleeves of the jacket.

When she looked at me again, her tawny eyes focused on the coffees in my hands. Her lips parted. After a second, she scooted over to make room for me. I'd thought she was going to tell me to bugger off, and the sharp relief I felt because she hadn't surprised me. I sank down beside her, crossing my legs, and held out both coffees to her.

Staring at the mugs a long moment, she finally took the one with cream and sugar. "Thank you," she murmured, then stared across the water, clutching the mug like a lifeline.

The water drew my eyes too. There wasn't a lot of wind, and the surface was smooth, only rippling once in a while. Black flies danced along the edge of the dock, then flew closer for a sniff. Since it was spring, they weren't bad. But later in the summer, they could get so thick it would be hard to breathe without inhaling one.

"I don't know where I am," she said, breaking the silence, her mug cradled tight. "None of this looks or feels familiar." She shook her head. "I mean, the trees, the terrain."

The husky quality of her voice made me shiver. I ignored the sensation and reached into my back pocket to pull out the paper, then passed it to her.

She stared a moment before taking it. After reading, her gaze bounced to the scars on my neck, then back to my eyes. "You can't talk?"

I shook my head and sipped my coffee. I'd tried over the years to make sounds, but my vocal cords had been so damaged as a teen that all that came out were strangled, inhuman noises. The results made me stop trying. I'd learned ASL, but most people didn't know it. And out here, I'd been alone, not needing it. With most of my vocal cords ripped out, all that was left was my growl.

Breaking my gaze, she looked back at the water. "My name is Brooke. I'm from Detroit. That's where I was last night, Detroit. And now I'm..." She flicked one hand towards the lake. "Here. Wherever here is," she said quietly, almost to herself.

Detroit? That was so far away but explained her slight accent. Why the hell would someone from Detroit end up here? If my cousin was involved like her collar suggested, then I assumed she would have come from Vancouver. Had she been on her way there instead?

When I extended my hand for the paper, she gave it to me. I took the pencil out of my back pocket and wrote another sentence under the first using the hard surface of the dock. *You're in northern Saskatchewan, Canada. Tell me how you got here.*

Brooke read the words, then looked away. "I've never been to Canada before," she murmured.

The expression on her face told me she was figuring out how much to trust me. I waited, allowing her to sort through her thoughts. It took a while, the sounds of the trees rustling in the wind and a duck making its presence known farther along the lake. Peaceful, but now changed. Besides John and the occasional trapper, no one else visited here.

After taking a slow sip of her coffee, she said, "My sister and I were abducted. She called them hunters." Her voice came out strained, her knuckles on the mug turning white from her tight grip. "I woke up on a plane. They'd put these collars on us." Her fingers lifted to touch the metal around her neck.

A growl rumbled in my chest, threatening to emerge. Hunters? People who were after shifters, specifically? As far as I knew, we hadn't been hunted for a long, long, time. Our secrecy protected us. And Landon wouldn't have anything to do with hunting.

But I knew my cousin owned a private jet. I gripped my mug until the handle was in danger of breaking. He could have picked up the pair of them in Detroit to fly them back to Vancouver, but flying over northern Saskatchewan was going far out of the way. It made no sense.

I closed my eyes, trying to picture a flight path that would connect Detroit with where we now were. They could have been heading to a bunch of different places: Alberta, BC, Yukon, or even Alaska. Any of them could have been her intended destination. But Vancouver? Not likely.

My eyes went to her collar. It didn't matter. Even if Vancouver wasn't her end destination, Landon was involved somehow. The urge to physically harm him for selling me out made the red haze dance around my peripheral vision. But there was nothing I could do about it now, no reason to get worked up when I couldn't follow through. Trusting my cousin was a mistake. One I wouldn't repeat.

"We weren't alone on the plane," she said quietly, her gaze fixed in the distance. "There were other animals, regular ones, like a monkey and a wolf. And a bunch of crates."

Other animals? I rubbed the growing ache between my brows. Then she hadn't been flying on my cousin's private jet. That was a passenger plane, not a cargo plane. And Landon didn't have anything to do with animals. His company was dedicated to technology, mostly hardware, but some software, as well. Why would he be keeping animals and shifters in cages? None of this made any sense.

"My sister and I managed to get out of the cages," she went on, oblivious to my rage-laced confusion, "and Sabrina got me into a parachute, but then we were attacked. I was the only one to get free." Her voice broke and she looked at me. "I need your help, but you said you wouldn't." Her tawny eyes pleaded with me.

I shook my head. I hadn't said I wouldn't help. Bracing the paper against the dock, I wrote some more. *There is no car here. No phone. No Internet. No towns close by.*

She stared at those words, her cheeks flushing red. Turning away slightly, she swiped at the moisture in the corner of her eye. "Someone else came out of that plane after me. It was either my sister or one of the people who abducted us, maybe a cougar shifter."

I was on my feet before she finished speaking, the pencil snapping between my fingers. She startled back at the movement, but I didn't pay attention to her as I scanned the area around the cabin and across the lake. If it was her sister, then I needed to find her.

If it was a cougar shifter...

The red haze colored the edges of my vision as I walked up the dock toward the cabin. I didn't remember getting rid of my mug or grabbing the shotgun, but when the haze in my vision began to clear, I was well away from the cabin, gun in hand, all my senses alert, searching for an intruder.

When I'd patrolled the perimeter where she'd crossed onto my land last night, there'd been nothing except her tracks and scent. But I hadn't been looking for anyone else.

I stopped where my motion sensors ran the edge of my property. Attached to some of the larger trees, they were solar powered and connected wirelessly to my computer back at the cabin. They also weren't foolproof. Gaps existed, but animals wouldn't notice them or try to get around the obvious pathways. Shifters might.

Crouching, I examined one small footprint set in perfect relief in the sand between two rocks. Brooke's footprint. Because of the terrain, there wouldn't be many, but there'd be some, like this one. Her scent had been stronger earlier and would eventually disappear except for where she touched trees and rocks. There wasn't much I could do about it, but I could remove other traces of her.

Methodically, I erased her tracks, following along out of my land for a while. I made sure to leave my own. If there was a cougar shifter out there, I wanted him to damn well know he was crossing into some else's territory.

If it had been her sister who had jumped out of the plane, would she have traveled in the same direction as Brooke? I was the only person for kilometers, the only cabin. If she'd gone another way, she'd be walking for a long time before she found anyone else. If she'd gone straight north...there was nothing. If south, then she'd get to civilization eventually, after days and days of walking. How long would the sister be able to survive on her own?

I could try to find her. Walk in the direction Brooke had come from and try to catch her scent. It would take a while. But with Brooke's injured feet, she wouldn't be able to come with me. I'd need to leave her at the cabin.

The thought of Brooke being on her own made my heart pump hard in my chest. I'd left her alone right now. A cougar shifter could have circled the lake in the other direction, and I wouldn't have scented it.

I stopped and spun around, intent on returning to the cabin. The sudden urge to get back to her and make sure she was okay outweighed everything else. I stomped through the underbrush the way I'd come, leaving my scent and prints wherever I could, masking Brooke's trail.

When I broke through the tree line near the cabin, my eyes went to the dock. She wasn't there. My heart lurched into my throat, and I ran the rest of the way to the cabin. In my haste, the door swung open with a bang.

Brooke jumped and spun where she stood by the sink, one hand against her chest, the other holding a mug. Startled, wide eyes stared at me. Her chest rose and fell in gulping breaths.

I'd scared her for no reason. She was here. She was safe. And I was an ass. Turning away, I put the shotgun in the rack by the door, then ran a hand over my head. Until that moment, I hadn't realized how long I'd let my hair grow. My hand stroked my beard. I hadn't trimmed it in months.

When I turned around, Brooke still watched me, trapped in her wide-eyed stare. I didn't know how to make the tension I'd created disappear. I didn't want her to be scared of me. The thought made my stomach turn and brought about the memory of another set of eyes, those ones brown, staring at me in fear.

Maybe I should leave. The second I had the thought, I pushed it aside. I'd returned out of fear for her safety. Leaving would start the cycle all over again.

Carefully, so as not to startle her, I closed the door, needing to keep the ambient heat inside the cabin. The nights still became cold this time of year. As it was, I'd need to light the wood-burning stove for a while to replace what had already been lost. Brooke was a slight thing and probably couldn't do the cold like me, especially in her meager outfit.

We stood that way, watching each other until she lifted the mug and gestured to the sink. "How do I get hot water?"

6

BROOKE

HE SHOOK HIS HEAD AT ME.

My stomach did a little flip in my belly, and I pressed my lips together. I was starting to get tired of the head shaking. Whenever I asked a question, Kane would say no.

What did that "no" mean? There was no hot water? I wasn't allowed hot water? All I'd wanted to do was wash the dirty mugs, but no matter which tap I turned, only freezing water came out.

But I was glad he was back. He'd been gone so long I'd begun to worry. I couldn't stop my mind from racing with scenarios. What if he'd encountered one of the men from the plane? What if it was the cougar shifter, and the cougar attacked and won? What would I have done if a cougar had burst through the door instead of Kane?

I swallowed my fear. None of those things had happened. "Did you find anything?"

Another shake of his head as he strode toward me. I couldn't stop myself from tensing further. He was so big compared to me, bigger than either of those guys on the plane. To keep the weight off my injured foot, I leaned against the counter, but slid away when he drew near. My ankle twinged, and I bit my lip to keep from wincing. He didn't look at me as he filled the kettle, then set in its base. A flick of the switch on its side turned it on.

"That's it?" I asked, looking up at him, a bit of panic rising in me. "That's the only way you get hot water here?" This close to him, it was hard not to stare at the ridged scars hidden beneath his beard. How did he get them? Why hadn't they healed when he shifted?

In answer to my question, his lips twitched, and he shook his head slightly. After a hesitation, he walked away from me, opened the door, and strode outside with purpose.

Staring at the closed door, I gripped the countertop. I was starting to worry about the amenities of this place. If there wasn't any hot water, that meant no hot showers. I wouldn't consider myself high maintenance, but I had standards.

At least the cabin was wired for electricity. I'd noticed three outlets already, one here, one near the desk, and one by the dresser where the lamp was plugged in. There were also two overhead lights, one above the bed area and one between the kitchen counters and the dining table. When I'd taken my trip around the cabin, I'd noticed there weren't any power lines. But when I'd hobbled up the dock, I'd taken note of the solar panels on the roof. Was that the only source of power here? Did he store the power in batteries somewhere? I didn't know much about solar power.

I stared after Kane, the dirty coffee mug clutched in my hands, and remained that way until I heard him on the other side of the cabin. Shuffling to the side, I watched him out of the window beside the fireplace.

I'd noticed two other small buildings on my tour outside. One looked like a shed, and I assumed it held tools and the like. The other was set in the ground, its door at a forty-five-degree angle like a storm shelter. Both were padlocked. I'd had visions of dead bodies in that underground room. Now I thought it probably held food. There was no fridge in the cabin.

Two large, flat rocks, slightly mossy, took up a wide portion of the view out the window. Together those two rocks probably made up the same square footage as my apartment. Kane stood near the one where an ax stuck out of a big stump. A small pile of newly chopped wood sat beside it. A larger rack of wood leaned against the cabin. I couldn't see it now but had noticed it on my short tour, the logs neatly stacked.

As I watched, Kane bent down and picked up a few of the smaller logs beside the stump. His T-shirt stretched over his back. His jeans hugged his butt and thighs. Both the feminine and feline sides of me liked what I saw. The man was built, thick everywhere.

I guess that's what chopping wood does to a person.

When he straightened, I stepped out of sight, not wanting him to catch me staring. Footsteps thumped on the landing before he opened the door, the logs nestled in the crook of his arm. He strode to the potbelly stove and dropped his load in the wood box beside it.

The front of the stove opened and he placed kindling from the wood box in the bottom, then stacked some of the smaller pieces in a triangular shape around it. I didn't move while he lit the kindling, blew on the newly made flame, then tended it until the larger logs caught before closing the front of the stove.

I knew an expertly made fire when I saw one. Sabrina had done the same thing when we'd gone camping with Mom. My heart lurched in my chest at the thought of my family. My stomach sank to my toes. God, I hoped they were okay.

Chest aching, I tried to swallow my fear for them as I watched Kane retrieve a big silver pot from the cupboard next to the sink, fill it with water, and set it with its lid on top of the stove.

When he turned to me, he swept his hand toward the set up he'd just created.

Trying to smother my rising panic, I blinked up at him. "That's the only *other* way to get hot water?"

A nod. Finally, a nod instead of a shake of the head.

I would never take freely flowing hot water for granted again. That thought led to another. I gripped the countertop tighter, my fingers aching. "You don't have a shower, do you?" The kettle bubbled behind me, clicking off because it was done heating.

With another fleeting quirk of his lips, he gestured toward the lake.

Right. Just jump into the lake to get clean with only a mild case of hypothermia as a result. *Sounds like fun.* Even with his bulky jacket over my shoulders, I was cold. There was no way I was going to take dip in that freezing lake.

My gaze scanned the cabin, searching for something to make me feel like this situation was less dire. The two apples on the table drew my attention, and my cheeks became hot. He'd cleaned up my vomit. I'd only drank a little of the coffee he brought me, and now it settled like acid in the bottom of my stomach. I needed to eat something or I'd retch again.

Cheeks burning now, I looked up at him. "I haven't eaten anything in a while."

After a moment's hesitation, he stepped beside me and reached in the cupboard above my head. The scent of pine and spice wafted over me along with a wave of body heat. I shivered. The man was his own personal furnace, and he wasn't even wearing a jacket.

Straightening, he set a red box on the counter. Soda crackers. The same thing my mom would give me after I'd been sick. *Perfect.* Setting the dirty mug to the side, I grabbed the box and cradled it to my chest. "Thank you."

He nodded and stepped away, taking the heat of his body with him. I hobbled to the table and sat in one of the chairs, relieved to not be standing anymore. My legs were tired from the trek through the forest, then my jaunt around the cabin earlier. My throbbing ankle needed ice.

One of the packages in the box was already opened, secured

by a rubber band, and I rolled it off. I ate two crackers quickly then stopped, waiting to see how much my stomach could handle —what I should have done with the apple when I'd arrived. Again, my cheeks heated at the memory of retching on his floor.

It wasn't only the apple that had made me vomit, though. I touched my collar. My body had wanted to shift when I'd been threatened by another shifter. Except, I hadn't been threatened, I'd just been scared. But the pain had certainly been real enough.

Kane moved around in the space behind me as I ate another cracker. I heard him put a plug in the sink then run water. A cupboard opened and closed. The tap turned off, then there was a splashing sound as he added the kettle water to the sink. The fire in the stove crackled behind me, warming my back. Besides waking in his bed, it was the first time I'd felt warm since I'd woken on that airplane.

Gripping the package of crackers so tight some of them broke, I bent my head. God, I hoped Sabrina was okay. Guilt wracked through me. I'd abandoned her. She was alone and who knew what was happening to her. My mind went to a dark place. If Sabrina remained on that plane, I had no doubt she was back in that cage. These collars kept us helpless, at the mercy of others.

The crackers I'd eaten threatened to make a reappearance. My head bent, I closed my eyes and willed myself to keep it down. I wouldn't puke. Not again.

When I lifted my head, Kane sat across from me at the table, a mug in his hands, his expression concerned.

I swiped at the tears on my face, angry that I let myself cry again. There was no point. "It's been a lot," I said as way of explanation.

He nodded once, but the concern in his eyes remained.

I touched the collar at my neck. "Could you maybe help me get this off?"

He shook his head.

A shot of anger made my hands tighten on the package of

crackers, the crinkling plastic mimicking the fire crackling behind me. He was refusing to help? He'd keep me like this? For what purpose?

No, he hadn't refused to help me earlier. The shake of his head meant he didn't have a phone or a car, not that he'd been unwilling to help. Maybe he didn't mean "no" right now but something else.

I swallowed around the emotions clogging my throat, and asked, "Why not?"

A pad of paper lay next to him, beside it, the broken pencil I'd place there when I'd returned to the cabin. He didn't write anything immediately, just stared at me, then the paper, then me, like he was figuring out what to say.

When he finally scrawled words across the page, he stared at it long and hard before passing me the pad. I almost didn't want to look, but I spun it toward me and read. *It's armed. I don't want your head to explode.*

"What?" I shot to my feet, adrenaline masking the pain in my foot and obliterating the fatigue in my legs. My hands flew to the collar, wanting to rip it off. Panic swam up through my chest. The crackers became a lead weight in my stomach.

After everything, finding out my head could explode was too much. My fingers paused as soon as they made contact with the cold metal. *Don't touch it.* That's what my sister had told me. Like she'd known something bad could happen to me if I tried to get it off. They could make Sabrina's head explode?

A sob shuddered through me. The urge to escape overwhelmed everything else. I searched the tiny cabin, looking for a way out of this mess. A collar kept me captive, my injured foot kept me captive, the wilderness kept me captive.

A whimper escaped my lips and I pressed them together, embarrassed by the sound. I didn't want to lose my shit, but after the night I'd had, my emotions felt like a pot ready to boil over.

The urge to scream overwhelmed me. I wanted to punch something.

None of this was fair.

When I'd gotten ready to go out to the bar the evening before, the only problem I'd had on my mind was which guy I'd pick for a night or two of fun. Now I had no money, no clothes, no phone, and no way to get home. On top of that, I needed to worry about my head exploding? About my sister's exploding? But that cowboy had shouted to keep us alive. If it hadn't been for that, I might believe she was already dead.

I pressed a hand to my chest. It hurt. Everything hurt. I was crawling out of my skin with worry and had no way to stop it. I wanted to slink into the bed behind me, hide under the covers, and wish every problem away like none of it had happened.

Closing my eyes, I took a deep breath and tried to regain control of my thoughts. There were always solutions to every problem. I wasn't going to be stuck here for the rest of my life.

When I opened my eyes again, Kane was in the same place with the same concerned expression on his face. I cleared my throat and leveled him a stare. "You have apples. You've got to get your supplies from somewhere." I gestured to the whiteboard with its short grocery list.

He nodded once, then stood, moving to a calendar on the wall beside the kitchen cupboards. I limped toward him. It showed May, and he pointed at Friday the 27th, circled in pencil.

I lifted my eyes to his. "That's when you go for supplies?"

He shook his head and pointed out to the lake.

"I don't understand." Defeat made my voice come out weak.

With a frustrated breath, he took the two steps to the table and picked up the pad and pencil. After he wrote a few words, he passed it to me. Ignoring the sentence he'd previously written because it made my hands shake, I read: *Airplane drops off supplies every month or so.*

"And there's no way to contact the pilot to get them to come earlier?"

He shook his head.

"But I could get a ride back with them when they come?"

He nodded once.

I let out a long breath. Two weeks. That's all I had to wait before I could get back to civilization.

Two weeks.

It seemed like a lifetime. Would my sister be okay on her own for that long? I didn't know where that airplane we'd been on had been headed, so how would I be able to help? If I could somehow be magically transported home right now, who would I call? Who would I ask for help? My mom could already be taken. If she wasn't, then asking her for help might put her in danger, but not warning her could do the same thing.

Since I lived on my own, there was no one to call into missing persons when I didn't come home. My best friend Corey wouldn't have any clue as to how to help. She didn't know I was a shifter, but I guess that wouldn't matter if she thought I was in trouble. But she'd never been great in a crisis. Her last big drama involved wearing the same dress as someone else at the bar. She hadn't handled it well.

I could call the police and report our abduction. But I couldn't tell them the people who'd abducted us were shifters, or that we were, and I had no idea where they'd been taking us. Whether we were shifters or not, people had kidnapped us. It was still a crime. I just didn't know if telling the human police would result in our discovery as a race. The threat was there. My instincts told me to fix this problem among my own kind. Maybe our kidnappers counted on that.

I thought of my colleagues at work, the dermatologists' clinic where I was an esthetician. The clinic was renowned for its services, and I'd beat out fifty other applicants for that job. *I'm going to get fired.* I'd worked so hard to get there. They wouldn't hesitate to cut me loose if I didn't show up. I was already walking a fine line with them because I'd come to work hungover one Monday. Even if I asked any of them for help, they would tell me to call the police.

Swallowing, I rubbed at my forehead, trying to think. I'd need to call Sabrina's work, the forest rangers at Sleeping Bear Dunes National Park. They might know something. And there was Sabrina's friend, Frank, our old neighbor who'd gotten her interested in becoming a forest ranger in the first place. He wasn't a shifter, and didn't know we were bobcats, but he always seemed resourceful. Maybe he would have connections to help us. It was dangerous to ask humans for help with this in case our race was discovered, but it didn't look like I had many options.

The idea gave me a sense of purpose but there wasn't anything I could do about it now. Stuck here at this cabin, what were my other options? I didn't have any.

Defeated, I set the pad of paper on the kitchen counter and turned away from Kane's worried expression. Him wanting to help but not able to do anything significant was messing with my emotions. Two weeks here, then I could figure everything out. Two weeks of no clothes, no phone, no anything.

Breathing deep, I hobbled to the front door and outside, needing to be alone. I sank into the wooden chair and wrapped my arms around my knees. Staring out into the forest, I cried.

7

KANE

I stood frozen by the calendar, staring after Brooke, and didn't know what to do.

That last look on her face tore through me. She'd seemed so lost, adrift in her circumstance, and the urge to make all her problems go away made me clench my fists. I wanted to be a superhero for her, to fly her to wherever she needed to go, to find her sister, to beat the shit out of the people who put her in a collar, let them heal, then beat the shit out of them some more.

What sort of person would put a collar around a young woman's neck? She'd said her sister had called them hunters, but who and what were they? Anger coursed through me, accompanied by the seductive red haze edging the periphery of my vision. I wanted to give in to the feeling, to lose myself in it, but there was no one here to take the brunt except Brooke.

And putting her in any more danger was out of the question.

Gripping the countertop behind me, I used the breathing techniques I'd taught myself over the past few years to cool my emotions. In through my nose, out through my mouth. I took deep, long breaths all the way to bottom of my belly. The haze of red slowly receded, but the need to do something for Brooke remained.

John would be here with supplies in two weeks. There was enough food for Brooke and me until then. We might need to eat a bit more canned soup than usual, but that wasn't a big deal.

She'd said someone came out of the plane after her, and it made me edgy. I hadn't seen or smelled any sign of anyone else out there. Could she be wrong? Assuming so would be a mistake. I needed to stay vigilant.

I strode over to my computer station and shook my mouse to wake it up. The perimeter alarms were connected to a program I kept running in the background. It would let me know if someone tripped a sensor. I clicked onto the icon for the program. Nothing indicated a breach.

Straightening, I ran an agitated hand through my hair. Who had put that collar around her neck? It couldn't have been Landon. My cousin might have sold my design for profit, but he wouldn't resort to abducting women. I knew him at least that much, didn't I? But selling the *one* design I'd made with shifters in mind... My stomach rolled at his betrayal.

It had been the three of us all the time—me, Landon, and Walker—inseparable until everything had gone to shit when I was twenty. Until that day when I ran from Goldenlach Ridge, looking over my shoulder the whole time, waiting for the authorities to pick me up. I'd tried to do it their way, to settle in a small city and mind my own business, but the anger inside me won. Just like Walker had once accused me of, I gave up—on society and myself.

After that, I left BC and didn't look back. My actions broke up our trio like it hadn't meant anything. Maybe if I'd stayed, I'd be working with Landon right now at his company and could have stopped what happened to Brooke. Maybe if I'd stayed, I would know where the hell Walker was right now instead of not knowing if his time overseas in the army had killed him.

That made me shake my head. If that was the case, Landon would have told me.

I missed them. Being out here on my own was its own kind of peace, but it wasn't a substitute for our friendship. The stab of regret and guilt got me right in the chest.

None of that explained Landon's betrayal. I'd received guarantees from my cousin. We'd signed contracts about the design. Why would Landon breach that? Were all the designs he said he would work on at Urick Enterprises in jeopardy of being sold off to the highest bidder? If the collar around Brooke's neck was any indication, then the answer was yes.

I needed to get it off her as soon as possible. With my cousin's resources, I could find a way. I also needed to find out why Landon had fucked me over. Whether he was behind Brooke's abduction or not, he had to be behind the bastardization of my design. There were too many similarities to ignore. Even if that plane's intended target hadn't been Vancouver, my cousin had to be connected somehow.

When John arrived in two weeks, not only would Brooke step on his plane, but I would too.

The thought made fingers of dread tickle down my spine. I'd been gone from civilization for so long. It held no appeal for me, nothing but foreboding. What if I wasn't able to keep it together? Being alone all these years made it certain I wouldn't hurt anyone ever again. Now I had a woman in close proximity to me, I and was planning on returning with her. Funny how things could change so fast.

I wasn't laughing.

Glancing at the clock above the kitchen cupboard, I noted that it was getting on to the noon hour. I would make some lunch and change the bedding. It wasn't laundry day, but with a new person in my cabin, in my bed, I wanted things to be clean. There was water already heating, after all.

In my bed. The thought twinged something deep inside me,

and I shook it off. I had no business thinking those kinds of thoughts.

But first, lunch. Since she kept the crackers down, she might be able to eat something more substantial. I grabbed the bread, peanut butter, and honey out of the cupboard—the items for my favorite sandwich—and hoped she wasn't allergic to anything.

A strange sensation crept up the back of my neck as I made two sandwiches instead of one and set them onto plates. I'd been alone for so long, doing things for another person felt foreign. I hadn't taken care of another person since I'd been a teenager—and look how that had turned out. My sister might be happily settled down with kids of her own now, but the last time I'd seen Emily, before I'd moved west for good, she'd still looked at me with wariness.

When I realized I touched the scar at my neck, I dropped my hand, angry at myself. It did no good to think about that day.

Picking up one of the plates, I headed to the porch. I found Brooke in my chair, her arms wrapped around her knees, her vacant eyes fixed on the forest. I took a step toward her, and she lifted her gaze to mine. My breath caught in my throat. Even though she'd had it rough over the past day, her features were stunning. High cheekbones, arched eyebrows, and her tawny eyes made her look like she belonged on a runway. My hand tightened on the plate.

It took her long seconds before she focused on me. She'd been far away.

I extended the plate to her.

"Thank you," she said, taking it. After staring at the sandwich for a moment, she picked it up and took a small bite.

The socks I'd put on her that morning poked out from beneath the flannel jacket and were covered in dirt and pine needles from her walk. Frowning, I went back inside and found the first aid kit above the sink. I would need to add some medical supplies to my next order.

With the kit tucked under my arm, I found some fresh socks in my dresser and strode back outside, closing the door behind me. When she peered up at me, I gestured to her feet.

Brooke swallowed her bite of sandwich. "You need your socks back?"

The question amused me, but I tried not to show it. Shaking my head, I squatted in front of her, needing to make sure her wounds were clean so nothing became infected. When I gestured to her feet this time, she changed her position, stretching her legs out in front of her. I hadn't been sure she'd allow me to take another look. She could tell me to fuck off if she wanted.

Carefully, I peeled the socks off her feet and set them aside. The toes of her one foot were turning purple. Being as gentle as possible, I unhooked the tensor and unwrapped it. When she sucked in a quick breath, I slowed my movements. Once free of the bandage, the bruise at the side of her ankle looked worse than it had a few hours ago. It had spread the length of her foot to her pinkie toe.

"I don't suppose you have ice?" she murmured. A frown pinched her brow as she stared at her foot.

Actually, I did have ice. I stood. I retrieved the key to the cold room from where it hung on a hook beside the kitchen cupboards before heading to the side of the cabin.

The permafrost here had allowed me to build the in-ground cellar, one of the reasons I'd picked this section of land for my cabin. I kept most of my food there. Ironically, I needed to keep it locked because of bears. If their berry crops ended up being poor this year, the black bears would migrate into my territory to look for other sources of food. In the winter, the cold room was more of a deep freeze, and I used the corner cupboard in the kitchen as a fridge instead. But right now, the temperature was perfect for keeping everything fresh.

When I walked down the few steps, frigid air surrounded me, hovering around zero degrees Celsius. A box for ice ran along the length of one side. Before the big thaw of the season, I'd put enough ice in there to last me the entire summer. I broke up some smaller chucks with the ice pick beside the box, then took one of the clean socks out of my back pocket and filled it halfway.

Before returning to Brooke, I grabbed a sturdy stump from near the wood pile and hefted it over my shoulder. I found her in the same position I'd left her, her plate empty. I took it, set it aside, and crouched in front of her again. I slid the stump beneath her foot. It wasn't entirely flat, but it would do. I tied off the end of the ice sock then repositioned the chunk inside so it would cradle most of her injury.

She hissed when it made contact. I was about to snatch it away when she said, "It's okay," staying my hand.

I waited for her to settle against the back of the chair, then satisfied the makeshift icepack would stay put for a while, I turned my attention to her other foot. Carefully, I pulled the Band Aids away from her skin to take a look. Everything seemed to be healing okay. I refreshed the ointment and bandages then turned to her knees. They still looked pretty bad. I squeezed out a small bit of ointment on a piece of gauze and added more where the skin might scab.

She hissed another breath.

An apology rumbled through my throat. I was trying to say sorry for hurting her further, but it came out a growl.

Her whole body became rigid.

Not wanting to make her uncomfortable or scare her, I finished up as quickly as I could. The other clean sock went over the new bandages.

"Thank you," she murmured when I was done, then pulled her free leg up to her chest.

Skin flashed beneath the borrowed jacket, making my breath stall in my throat. Her skirt was short, and I still wasn't sure she wore anything beneath it. I blinked and stood, so she wasn't in my line of sight anymore.

I'd been away from women, especially beautiful ones, for way too long. Of course, my body reacted, but that didn't mean I wanted to act on it. She'd been through something traumatic and wore a possibly explosive collar around her neck. I'd be an ass and a half to even think about doing more than helping her.

Keeping my gaze away from her bare legs, I left the tensor bandage there for later, but picked up the first aid kit, her empty plate, and the dirty socks, and opened the door to go inside.

Busy work. That's what I needed in order to keep my mind off the woman outside. I'd no sooner had the thought, then I realized she was probably cold out there. I grabbed a blanket from the wardrobe at the end of the bed.

She lifted her head when I stepped outside. Without lingering, I settled the blanket over her lap, draping it over her leg and making sure her toes were covered, then went back inside.

The big pot of water wasn't boiling yet, but it would be soon. I didn't really need it to super hot for laundry, but wanted it to stay warm for as long as possible. I checked on the fire in the stove, satisfied it would burn itself out. The cabin was warm enough now that I didn't need to keep it going.

With the remaining water in the sink, I made short work of the dishes, put the sandwich stuff away, and scrubbed the already clean counters. Next, I stripped the bed, finding the sheets smeared with the blood that had come from her wounds. There were a few dirty clothes items in the laundry hamper, so I grabbed those too, along with the socks I'd lent Brooke.

She'd asked about a shower. I didn't have one, but it wasn't often I used the lake as a bathtub. Sometimes, but when it was hotter out. I grabbed the big rubber laundry tubs out from their place in a bottom kitchen cupboard, along with a smaller tub I set on the dining table. A quick trip to the wardrobe let me find some other things for Brooke: a face cloth, hand towel, new bar of soap, and a toothbrush in its package. She'd have to share my toothpaste. Everything went beside the tub on the table.

After a moment's hesitation, I wrote another note and tucked it in my pocket. I set out a pair of my drawstring sweatpants and one of my T-shirts on the stripped bed. The sheets and my clothes went into the laundry tubs beside the biodegradable detergent already there, then I took everything outside.

A puddle formed on the stump where the ice from the sock had melted. Brooke shivered beneath the blanket. I lifted the corner, took the soggy sock out from beneath it, and threw it into the tub with the rest of the laundry. Setting everything aside, I crouched in front of her and used the edge of the blanket to dry her foot.

Before I started re-wrapping the tensor around her ankle, I passed her my latest note. *If you change into something else, I can wash your clothes.* She'd been through a lot in those clothes and would probably appreciate changing into something clean.

She lifted her head. "I don't have anything else to wear."

Finished with the tensor, I gestured to the cabin.

A frown pinched her brow. She stood and hobbled her way inside. When she saw the clothing I'd laid out for her, she closed the door. While she changed, I took the bins to the spot where I usually did laundry and set up everything the way I liked it, grabbing the washboard from where it hung on the outside wall. When I returned to the front of the cabin, the door was closed. I waited.

Five minutes later, Brooke opened the door wearing my sweatpants and T-shirt, everything way too big on her. She shoved a small bundle of clothes at me, her cheeks bright red.

Was she embarrassed about wearing my things? It didn't bother me.

"Thank you for the toiletries. I'll pay you back."

I shook my head. I didn't need her money.

A second later, she closed the door in my face. She was definitely embarrassed about something. I knocked.

The door opened. Her cheeks were a brighter red now. I

gestured inside, and she stepped out of the way to let me in. It
wasn't lost on me that I was acting like a guest in my own home
because a woman had invaded it.

Tucking her bundle of clothes under my arm, I grabbed an
oven mitt to pick up the water off the stove. Before heading
outside, I poured some of it in the tub on the table. When I
returned to my laundry set up, I tossed her clothes in the bin with
mine. The hot water came next. I drenched everything until it
was all mostly covered. There was about a quarter of the water
left in the pot and I straightened, staring at it. If I returned to the
cabin and put it on the stove, then it would stay warm. But I also
wanted to give Brooke space if she needed it.

Debating with myself for a moment, I took the pot back to the
cabin. When I opened the door, Brooke had her hair over the tub
on the table, splashing water everywhere as she tried to wash it.

I stopped and stared, considering the set up. I'd never thought
about how to wash long hair before now. Something better
should be figured out for her. Setting the pot on the stove, I
retreated, closing the door quietly behind me.

The water in the laundry tub steamed in the cool air. Rolling
up my sleeves as far as they would go, I got to work, adding a spot
of detergent, then grabbing my first shirt. I scrubbed it against the
washboard for a few minutes, dunked it in the water, rung it out,
and tossed it in the empty bin. Next came Brooke's black
sequined shirt, then her skirt.

Something fuchsia pink floated in the water. I blinked. It
looked like a piece of string. I picked it up with the crook of my
finger. A G-string dangled and dripped.

I glanced at the cabin. A flash of movement came and went at
the window. This was what she'd been wearing underneath her
skirt? She might as well have been wearing dental floss for all it
protected. The triangle of fabric connecting the string wasn't big
enough to cover half my palm.

An image of her wearing the thong and nothing else took

over my mind. A pure fantasy since I didn't know what she looked like naked, but my brain was doing its best to imagine it.

A growl began low in my chest. I smothered it a second later. I had no business thinking about anyone being naked, especially a woman who'd been through a lot over the past day. Shaking my head, I sloshed the bit of fabric against the washboard, wrung it out, and tossed it in the bin with the other clothes.

With a renewed sort of energy coursing through me, I made short work of the rest of the laundry. The sheets were always the hardest, and I left them for last. Once everything was done, I dumped the dirty water in the bushes, then scooped up rinse water from the lake. Everything got doused, then wrung out before I repeated the whole process. One at a time, I secured the items to the clothesline that crossed the yard from the cabin to the nearest big tree. Like my solar panels, the line was positioned to get the most out of the southern light.

I paused when I got to the G-string. It really was a bit of nothing. I had no clue how it could be comfortable to wear. That led my mind down the path I'd veered from earlier. Snuffing out the images before my thoughts could derail me, I clipped her underwear to the line between her shirt and her skirt, then moved on to the next item. With the last of the laundry hanging on the line, I dumped the remaining water, hung the washboard on its hook, and headed to the cabin.

Brooke froze when I entered. Her scent slammed into me, making me stop. I'd been around a lot of shifters up until I was twenty, but none of their scents had done what Brooke's scent was doing to me now. Something I hadn't felt in a long time curled in my stomach, an urge for contact, a need that I didn't want to acknowledge.

Underneath her towel-wrapped hair, Brooke's freshly washed face flamed bright red. "I'm sorry," she said, her voice high and tight. "I wouldn't have given you my underwear if I'd known you were washing everything by hand. I could have done it. I thought you had a machine hiding somewhere." She muttered something else under her breath that I didn't quite catch, but I thought I heard something about her being stupid.

I grunted and set the laundry bins beside the door. I had to go. Her scent was getting to me, and since she'd cleaned herself, it was everywhere. I needed to leave before *I* started doing something stupid.

Searching for the person who might be coming after her sounded like the perfect distraction. Without looking at her again, I grabbed my shotgun and closed the door behind me.

8

BROOKE

THWACK.

The sharp sound made me flinch under the covers. I burrowed down, wanting to stay asleep and warm forever, but the cold metal pressing against my throat brought me back to reality. My hand inched its way to my collar. *Still there.* I'd hoped it had all been a bad dream.

Thwack.

This time, I uncovered my head and opened my eyes at the sound. I was in Kane's cabin, in his bed. He'd changed the sheets yesterday evening, and his scent didn't overwhelm me the way it had the morning before. It was there, just not as strong. Even then, it created a tingling sensation in my stomach.

Thwack.

I lifted my head. Morning light filtered in through all the windows. Dropping back on the pillow, I blinked the sleep from my eyes and stared at the log beams above me. What time was it?

Thwack.

Yesterday evening, Kane insisted I take the bed. Guilt stabbed me again, the same as when I'd crawled into bed. Where had he slept? I had no clue. His couch wasn't the sleeping sort. It was the same construction as the chair outside, mostly made of narrow branches. I'd been so exhausted, I hadn't moved until now, hadn't heard him leave or return or anything. Being clean, fed, and safe, everything had caught up to me. As soon as the sun set, my eyelids had felt like a million pounds and wouldn't stay open.

Thwack.

But Kane had gestured at the bed in his silent way, then backed off to make sure I understood. I'd been too tired to make a fuss. After everything, having the big guy on my side was a comfort I never expected.

I don't think my reluctant savior knew his appeal. Yesterday, when he'd been tending my wounds, I'd held my breath. Every touch of his rough fingers against my skin had created shivers over my body and I'd tried not react—and failed. Even his growl was a turn-on. I hoped he hadn't noticed.

Just thinking about it now made the tingle in my stomach intensify.

Thwack.

I threw off the covers and swung my legs over the side of the bed. I wore Kane's sweatpants and T-shirt. My ankle throbbed, but I wouldn't be able to see how much worse it was today unless I took off the tensor bandage. All my scrapes and cuts were feeling better thanks to that ointment Kane used.

A stack of clothes on the top of the dresser caught my eye. He'd taken them off the line and folded them, even attempting to fold my underwear. It lay on top.

My face heated. When I'd realized he was going to wash everything by hand, I'd almost run out there to stop him. The look on his face when he'd picked up my G-string...blank confusion followed by dawning understanding. It was hard to see from the distance and through his beard, but I was pretty sure he'd blushed.

Thwack.

Carefully balancing my weight on my good foot, I stood and

hobbled to the window. His back to me, Kane stood on the flat rock with the chopping stump. His flannel shirt stretched across the muscles of his back. The fabric of his jeans hugged his butt and thighs. My breath caught in my throat at his strength, the quiver in my stomach spreading to other areas of my body. He grabbed a thick log with one hand and set it on the larger stump. Then he stepped back, took aim, and lifted the ax above his head.

Thwack.

The log split, the halves flying off in two different directions. My body jerked, the shiver inside me turning warm and spreading to my inner thighs. Kane yanked the ax out of the stump, then grabbed another log. From the amount of wood halves around him, he'd been doing it a while.

I couldn't tear my eyes away. Watching him made a sudden flush climb through my body, so hot it felt like my nerves were on fire.

Oh shit.

I turned away from the sight and grabbed the bedpost to remain upright.

Thwack.

The sound on its own made a vision of his muscled body flash in my head.

This was bad.

The hot sensation in my body wouldn't stop, and it settled heavy between my thighs. My breaths became short. Tingles traveled up the backs of my legs and ass. My skin became tight. I wasn't just getting turned on, no. I was going into heat.

Thwack.

This time, I flinched at the sound and closed my eyes. This was so bad. The reason I'd been so focused on searching for a guy was because it was always better to stave off the heat by getting on top of it as soon as possible. Leaving it too long was always bad news. I would have gone home with the tattooed guy, fucked him for a few days, then left.

It was a familiar pattern. One I'd never had a problem with. It felt natural.

Thwack.

I twitched, then swallowed around the need building inside my throat. Ever since I'd become sexually active, my mother had been spouting safe sex rules. Sabrina and I had both gotten IUDs in our teens because Mom said, "I don't need a litter of kittens underfoot."

When it came to going into heat, Sabrina never seemed to have as much of a problem as I did. While I was always on the lookout for the next strong male to satisfy me, Sabrina went about her business like nothing was the matter. Month after month of going into heat, and Sabrina never outwardly showed discomfort. I'd never admitted it before, but her control made me jealous.

I was more like our mother in that regard. Natalie Covin was a party girl through and through.

My hand tightened on the bedpost, my skin moving from the tight stage to itchy. Sometimes I couldn't find a suitable partner, and I had to make do with a vibrating dildo for the week. It wasn't as satisfactory, but it was acceptable.

The chances of finding a dildo in this cabin were nonexistent.

And this was only the start. If I didn't get relief soon, my need would increase so bad I'd end up rolling on the floor in pain with a fever and possible delirium.

Quiet surrounded the cabin. The sounds of chopping wood had stopped. I turned back to the window to see Kane had stacked most of the logs along the edge of the rock, a solid pyramid shape. There were only a few stray logs left.

I couldn't tear my eyes away from his body, the fluid way he moved. I licked my lips. My tongue became thick in my mouth. He was strong, stronger than the tattooed guy. In fact, he was a better prospect than the tattooed guy in a lot of ways. Kane took care of himself. He'd been taking care of me.

The heat inside me roused these thoughts, my instincts telling me to weigh my options. My basic biology was the loudest voice right now, and it wanted the closest available male to quench my need. And Kane was looking like a very, very good option. My only option.

The man in question gathered an armload of wood and headed away from the pile.

I froze. *Shit.* He would come back inside. I squeezed my thighs together. He was a shifter with heightened senses like mine.

Shit. Shit. Shit. Frantically, I looked for a place to hide. There wasn't any. After a day in this cabin, I knew that.

His feet thumped on the landing outside. I gritted my teeth. The door opened, and I curled my fingernails into my palms to stop myself from going over there and jumping him.

Kane took one step inside, then stopped. My pupils dilated at the sight of him. His nostrils flared, his shoulders tensed, and his eyes zeroed in on me like I was the exact person he was looking for.

He could smell my heat.

My heart pounded in my chest. What would he do? I'd never been around a male shifter while in heat before, never searched one out either. I stuck to humans because it was less complicated. Mom always said that if we had sex with a shifter, there'd be strings attached. I also didn't want to be on the receiving end of a shifter's sexual aggression, no matter how appealing that might be. Humans were simpler.

Tearing his gaze away from me, Kane strode to the potbelly stove. He crouched, piling the newly chopped logs in the wood box with precise movements.

I wrapped my arms around my middle. Should I say something? What would I say? That I was going into heat? He could tell. There wasn't much else to talk about unless he became a willing partner. And from the way he seemed bent on ignoring me, it looked like that wasn't going to happen.

His arms empty, he stood and walked to the kitchen counter. I watched as he moved around, grabbing bread to pop in the toaster, heating water in the kettle. The more he ignored me, the more the tension in my body released. From the way my mom had talked, it had sounded like as soon as a shifter smelled heat, they'd pounce.

Kane didn't seem to have a problem resisting me. A part of me became annoyed. If he pursued me, then at least some of this ache would ease. Instead, it would keep building, to peak painfully in the third or fourth day. The thought made me swallow.

The toaster popped, the kettle bubbled, and the scent of toast wafted toward me. Kane set plates on the table along with peanut butter, jam, and honey, gesturing for me to sit. A thrum of satisfaction rippled through my stomach. I liked that he was taking care of me no matter how simple the fare.

A soft purr began in my throat. *Stop it.* I needed to remain in control of my baser instincts. It was the only way I'd be able to survive the next few days with my sanity intact.

While I limped to the table and sat, Kane made coffee, pouring hot water into a French-style coffee press. It was the kind my mom liked to use, and seeing it here sent a wave of homesickness through me. Maybe it had something to do with going into heat too. My mom might be flighty most of the time, but she would have advice for how to deal with this.

But my mom wasn't here. I was on my own with this big man who couldn't speak but knew how to live totally cut off from the world, independent. Taking a breath, I picked up the peanut butter jar and opened the lid.

He set a coffee mug in front of me along with powdered creamer and sugar.

"Thank you," I murmured around a tongue that felt too big for my mouth.

Sitting in the chair opposite me, he nodded once and picked

up the peanut butter jar I'd set down. I watched as he spread a thin layer on his toast then went for the honey. A large glop was dolloped onto the thin layer, way more than a normal person would use. The man liked it sweet.

We ate our toast and drank our coffee in silence. I kept wanting to bring up the heat thing, to lie and tell him it wasn't going to be an issue. But every time I opened my mouth, the words stalled in my throat. What was I supposed to say? There was no stopping biology. By tomorrow, we'd both be extremely uncomfortable.

I finished my toast, drank most of my coffee, and stood. When I hobbled toward the sink, intent on doing the dishes, he waved me away, taking my coffee cup to refill it. If he'd let me do the dishes, then at least I'd have something to think about other than the need building inside my body.

Letting out a breath, I fixed my coffee. I hobbled out the front door then sank into the wooden chair, trying not to spill the brew on myself. The fresh air was crisp, but I liked the feel of it. It cooled my hot cheeks and cleansed my head. A bird sang a two-note song followed by a longer trill. For a moment, I wished I could have my mom's bird book in front of me so I could figure out its name.

My ankle ached from the short trip to the porch. The tree stump sat there from the day before, and I set my foot on it. Having it elevated eased the throbbing some. It felt like I had a second heart in my foot, beating away.

I'd almost finished my second cup of coffee when Kane joined me. He gestured to the path that went to the outhouse.

"Yes, please," I said, scrambling to my feet. A shot of pain went through my calf. I winced. *Moved too fast.*

Strong arms swept me up a second later. I gasped. Not from the pain, but from how good it felt to be cradled. My body craved the connection, *needed* it. My heart rate accelerated, and my hands moved around his neck like they had a mind of their own.

The heat between my legs intensified. The sudden urge to press my face against his throat and inhale his scent deeper into my lungs made me shiver. Maybe I would take a nip at his flesh.

The voracity of the primal thought had me leaning away from him in shock. This was going to get so bad if I didn't find relief soon.

He set me on my feet. I'd been so caught up in the sensation of being held, I'd missed the whole trip.

"Thank you," I murmured, opening the door, but I wasn't sure if he'd heard me. He was already halfway down the path.

Taking a fortifying breath, I took care of business and found Kane waiting a few feet away when I opened the door again. This time when he picked me up, I held my breath, trying not to get any of his scent in my nostrils. If I could keep myself apart, then maybe it wouldn't be so bad.

I'd almost convinced myself everything would be fine when he settled me into the chair on the landing. Instead of leaving, he crouched in front of me. While I'd been using the outhouse, he'd found more ice and some clean socks. They were laid out next to the stump.

Without looking at my face, he took my calf in his hand and lifted my injured foot carefully onto the stump. Shivers spread across my scalp in awareness. He kept his focus on my leg as he rolled up the fabric of the sweatpants and began to unwind the tensor. I watched, mesmerized. His fingers were strong, a light dusting of hair on his knuckles and the backs of his hands. My breath caught in my throat when his thumb brushed the skin of my calf.

He paused, then continued to remove the tensor around and around. Underneath, my ankle had turned into a horrifying mix of several shades of purple. My skin was raised in lines from the tensor. God, it was ugly. The sight didn't seem to bother him as he cradled the uninjured part of my foot in his hand, adjusting it on the stump so he could put the ice on my ankle.

For a big man, he was exceedingly gentle. I wondered if it would be the same if we had sex, or if he was one of those guys who took charge in the bedroom. The thought created a rush of heat between my thighs.

Kane froze, his thumb on the bare arch of my foot. I sucked in a breath. It felt so good to be touched right now. My entire body shouted for me to lean into him, to take more of it.

Instead, I held incredibly still, my nerves humming. When his thumb brushed the tender flesh of my arch, need flooded me. I didn't want him to just stroke my foot, I wanted him to stroke me everywhere, to soothe the ache building inside me with each passing second.

His gaze focused on my foot, he moved his thumb again, slowly, back to where it started. My lips parted. Tension formed between us, thick and pulsating. I didn't know if I'd experienced anything like it before.

I shivered.

Kane stood abruptly, reentering the house and coming back with a thick blanket a minute later. He settled it over my shoulders and adjusted the ice on my ankle before striding away.

I let out a slow breath. He might have left, but the tension remained. The desperate aching of my body didn't abate.

Leaning back in the chair, I closed my eyes. What was I supposed to do? This was an impossible situation. As the ice did its magic on my swollen ankle, I weighed my options. I couldn't pick out a random guy this time around. There wasn't a club nearby, so I could leave Kane alone like he plainly wanted.

The forest around me buzzed with life, but I couldn't hear anything from Kane. I didn't know where he'd gone. For a moment, I felt mildly abandoned and slightly rejected. *It's not his fault.* He hadn't asked me to come for a visit. The man obviously liked his solitude and I'd disturbed it.

What was he doing out here all on his own anyway?

It was a long while later when footsteps alerted me to his

presence right before he rounded the side of the cabin. He'd left me alone so long, the ice sock had half melted, a puddle forming under my foot. Without meeting my gaze, he crouched in front of me, removing the ice and picking up the tensor. This time he didn't hesitate while he wrapped my foot, and he didn't take his time. Before I could blink, he was done, the new socks back on, and he headed inside.

"Thank you," I said. It seemed I'd done a lot of "thanking" since I'd arrived. He might have nodded in acknowledgment, I wasn't sure.

A minute later, he stepped onto the landing but didn't look at me as he went around to the other side of the cabin again. I rubbed my temples, a headache forming. How were we supposed to deal with this in a one-room cabin?

Tired of sitting, I shrugged out of the blanket and stood, careful to keep my balance on my good foot. My head spun from the movement, and I waited until the world slowed down. Hobbling, I opened the door and entered the cabin. Everything was as neat and tidy as it had been when I arrived. He'd made the bed. My cheeks grew warm. I could have done that.

I needed distractions from my too-thick tongue, my itchy skin, and my sensitive nipples abrasively rubbing against the material of my shirt. Curiosity made me limp toward the desk at the foot of the bed. His computer was an older style, beige, with the tower on the floor with two disk drives. The monitor didn't have a flat screen. How long had the guy been up here on his own? Being a shifter, he could be way older than the late twenties, early thirties that he looked.

My skin tingled, the sensation climbing up the back of my scalp as I jiggled the mouse. The computer woke up and a screen full of square file folder icons appeared. Among dozens, one said, "Security," one said, "Old Files," another, "Ongoing." He'd said there was no Internet. The X in the WiFi symbol at the bottom corner of the screen confirmed it. I was tempted to click on one of the file folders but then let the mouse go. He didn't deserve me snooping when he'd been so nice to me.

My eyes were drawn to the little workstation beside the monitor. It held tiny pieces of things: wires, circuits, gears, all sorts of bits of metal. Everything neat in its own way beside what I thought might be a soldering iron. I flicked a few of the stray pieces with my fingernail. He must make things for a living. Or fun. Or whatever. Maybe just to keep busy since he was alone up here.

When I stepped away from the desk, movement outside caught my eye. I moved the thin, white curtain aside. Kane was on one of the flat rocks doing some sort of slow, controlled movement, like a martial art. But I didn't know much about any of them except that my sister was a black belt in karate.

Even though the sight of him brought a rush of warmth between my thighs, my chest tightened at the thought of Sabrina. Was she okay? What about Mom? Would those same shifters abduct her too? Was someone after bobcat shifters for a specific reason? Experimentation? Something even worse?

Every shifter had heard of the times when we were hunted for sport and glory. It was why we were so secretive now, why our instincts *demanded* that we stay hidden from humans. But those people on the airplane...at least one of them had been a shifter too.

Swallowing around the tightness in my throat, I forced my mind to loosen its hold on morbid thoughts and stared at Kane. He was graceful for such a large man. His hands moved and flowed in interesting patterns, always coming back to the center of his body. He shifted his weight from one foot to the other, never losing balance, his focus entirely on himself and nothing else.

I became mesmerized by the fluid athleticism of it all. When I realized I was panting, I turned away from the sight. I *would not* go out there and rub my body against him like my instincts were telling me to do.

Taking care not to lean on my ankle too much, I moved away from the window and climbed on the bed to take a closer look at his bookshelf. Quite the assortment. The man had eclectic tastes. As I read the spines, I realized I scratched at my arms and forced myself to stop. There were cookbooks, math textbooks, sci-fi and fantasy novels, horrors and mysteries, even a selection of romance novels. A horticulture manual leaned against a random assortment of magazines. A physics textbook was shelved next to a few on mechanical engineering. There was a selection of books on eastern religions, tai chi, and yoga, and one dedicated to breathing exercises.

I glanced at the stereo and the few CDs beside it. Most were classics like The Beatles, U2, The Rolling Stones, and Velvet Underground. But there was also something called Lemon Jelly and Ninja Tunes.

Grabbing two magazines, one called *Canadian Geographic* and the other *Dwell*, I sat on the bed and leaned against the head-board, scratching my scalp and face. I got in a few minutes of reading before another flush of my heat distracted me, my breasts becoming heavy. The temperature in the cabin rose. Kane wouldn't need to light the fire today with the way I was giving off heat.

Thwack.

Alert energy made my body still. He was cutting wood again. My stomach twinged.

Thwack.

Dammit. All I wanted to do now was watch, and that would gear me up, not down. Even as I told myself to stay put, I pushed my way to the edge of the bed and stood. When I was next to the window, I moved the curtain aside.

He wasn't wearing a shirt this time, and the muscles of his back rippled with movement. The tingle in my stomach spread outward, wrapping around my middle to shoot down between my legs. My mouth dried. He had so many muscles it was like his muscles had muscles.

Holding an ax in one hand, he positioned a log on the stump with the other. Once balanced, he stepped back, aimed, and brought the ax down in one sure movement.

Thwack.

The sound hit me right between the legs, making me jerk. His jeans rode low on his hips, his biceps bulged and shifted with every movement. I couldn't pull my eyes away from his ass, his thighs, imagining how strong he'd be if he took me.

Thwack.

We could do it right there on the rock. He could bend me over the stump and press into me, and it would ease the ache that pulsed between my thighs.

Oh, God. My need was so bad already. What would happen when it peaked?

As I watched him pick up another log, my hand slid inside my sweatpants. I needed relief, even if it was for a moment. My fingers encountered the slick wetness between my lips. I rubbed my clit, gently, because it was already so swollen.

Keeping my eyes on the moving muscles in Kane's back, I rotated pleasing circles. Already being so primed, it didn't take me long to climax.

My orgasm rocked through me, and I closed my eyes, pressing my forehead against the window frame. Some of the itch on my skin abated, and the swelling of my tongue went down. God, that was good but short-lived. It might have taken some of the edge off, but now I ached deeper inside. I needed a man or a dildo to ease the throbbing hurt. I needed to be fucked. Bad.

I opened my eyes, then stiffened when I realized Kane was no longer on the rock. Where had he gone? Footsteps on the landing made me spin away from the window, yanking my hand out of my pants.

Oh shit. The whole cabin smelled like my orgasm, and I had nowhere to hide.

The door opened. Kane took two steps into the cabin, then stopped like he hit a brick wall. The logs in his arms crashed to the ground. His nostrils flared.

A whimper escaped me. Everything inside me was telling me to go to him, to ease the pressure and pain building in my body. My skin crawled with need. "Can you help me?"

He slashed a hand through the air, negating my request.

Desperation made me tremble. "You don't want me?"

A tortured expression crossed his face, a nod turning into a shake of his head.

"You *won't* help me." I knew my voice contained defeat and mortification, but I couldn't stop either from coming through.

He made another movement with his hands, then turned to the whiteboard, writing *I can't* beneath his shopping list. With one last apologetic grimace thrown at me over his shoulder, he left.

9

KANE

Holy hell, I needed to get out of there. If I'd thought her scent intoxicating before, now it cracked over my skull like a sledgehammer. It was everywhere, infused with the need to breed. The edges of my vision hazed with color.

I couldn't focus where I was going, just stumbled away from the cabin, away from the desire to take her. I wanted to, God how I wanted to. My erection was painful, but I couldn't let the beast inside me take over, couldn't put her in danger like that. I *wouldn't* allow the animal to take control.

The red haze continued to climb over my vision, and I tried to suppress it. Even away from her, the scent of her heat clawed through my body. The desperate expression on her face wouldn't leave my mind.

The farther away I traveled from her, the more insistent the need to return and take her pumped through my veins. I forced one foot in front of the other, increasing the distance between us. Safe. I needed to keep her safe from me.

I'd been away from people, from women, so long that my biological need to mate buzzed through me like an angry swarm.

I couldn't shake it. The only thing I could do was stay far, far away. I couldn't go back there, not like this.

I had to keep it together. I couldn't put Brooke's life in danger.

When I shifted, I lost myself to the animal. There was no *Kane* left. And every time I'd let emotions rule me in the past, it had spelled disaster for someone else. It was why I was out here alone. It was why I'd designed those collars, for people like me. For shifters like my father. My grandfather had been the same, and the town we'd lived in had eventually banded together to put him down. My dad... He gave into his animal completely and now lived fully as a grizzly in the mountains. We hadn't seen him since I was a kid.

Some shifters weren't able to control their baser instincts. Rabid was what they called us, though it had nothing to do with the infectious disease that sometimes affected regular animals and had everything to do with a shifter's mental state after shifting. I'd separated myself from society so I wouldn't end up like my grandfather, held down so they could put a bullet between his eyes. Or like my dad, who no longer possessed a sense of his human self.

And now Brooke's condition was making me forget all the calming techniques I'd taught myself while out here. The yoga, the Tai Chi, the meditation... It was like I'd made zero progress as soon as I scented a feline shifter in heat. All I wanted to do was turn around, go back to her, and mate.

I wouldn't do that. I kept my feet moving. I wouldn't take advantage of her. She was stuck here, in a state she had no control over, and I wouldn't use that against her. I wasn't my animal. I could rationalize. Staying away meant she'd be safe from me. Even if she was uncomfortable, even if she needed help, I had to stay away. If I returned, then I was putting her in danger.

The forest became still around me. I stopped. My skin tightened, expectant.

A low, beating pulse echoed the air. I lifted my head,

searching for the sound. It was coming from the direction of the cabin. *Whop, whop, whop, whop.* I'd traveled far in my attempt to get away from her scent and was now off my property. But I could hear it. A helicopter.

Brooke.

I ran back the way I'd come, ignoring the bushes and trees grabbing at my clothing and scraping my body. I'd left her vulnerable. She'd told me someone was after her, and I'd left her alone. I ran faster, my arms and legs pumping.

The thought of someone hurting Brooke made a savage growl erupt from my chest. I jumped over a fallen tree, then a patch of bushes, startling a squirrel. I had to get back. She was in danger.

The red haze moved in on my peripheral vision. I couldn't stop it. I didn't want to stop it. My instincts took over. The landscape around me blurred as I ran faster and faster. Then, for the first time in a decade, I shifted.

10

BROOKE

I STARED AT THOSE WORDS ON THE WHITEBOARD, DEFEAT AND dread spiraling through me. How would I survive these next few days without his help? What kept him from helping me? Was I that undesirable to him? I dove under the covers, mortified at the rejection but confused because I'd seen the bulge in jeans. He *did* want me.

The heat climbed through me like a sickness. It made my skin hot and tight, my hair follicles itchy, my throat close and my tongue heavy. Every nerve ending in my body demanded release. The pressure inside my stomach built and built.

My hand moved down my stomach and into my sweatpants. There was no point in pretending that wasn't what I'd been doing or deny that he'd understood. At least I was pretty sure he wouldn't be back for a while. If he did come back, it would be because he'd changed his mind and was willing to put me out of my misery. But he'd told me he couldn't help me. If he couldn't, then I'd have to take care of myself as best as possible.

God, I was so wet, drenched with my need. I never let it get this bad, always looking for a guy a couple days before to prevent the phase from going too far. Visions of Kane chopping wood filled my head. Sweat, muscles, skin. It took less than a minute for me to climax.

I lay back and exhaled. The heat wasn't gone, but it didn't hurt so much. I stared up at the beams in the ceiling. How was I supposed to get through the next week without losing it? I'd probably have to touch myself every fifteen minutes to keep my sanity. Not wanting to dwell on that depressing thought, I allowed myself to doze, to drift in my post-orgasmic bliss.

Boots thumped on the landing. My eyes flew open. Kane was back. My face flamed again, and like a coward, I pulled the covers over my head.

The door opened. "Where's the little kitty hiding?"

The sound of a man's Texas accent made me freeze. An icy sensation ran through my veins. *Not Kane.* My heart beat hard in my throat.

I stayed still and quiet under the covers, willing myself to become invisible. The distant sound of a helicopter cut through the silence, making my pulse race. They'd come for me.

A sudden shot of pain from my collar made me scream. Kicking the covers off, I tried to get away from the burning sensation that spiked from my brain into my stomach. I thrashed, then fell off the bed, *splat.* The pain wouldn't quit, and tears rolled out of my eyes.

Finally, it subsided. I clutched at the collar on my neck, needing to tear it off. Cowboy boots stopped in my line of sight. I turned my head to look up.

"There you are." The man from the airplane popped the brim of his cowboy hat farther back on his head and waved a silver remote at me. "You're going to be a good kitty now, aren't you?"

Fear and residual pain made it hard to breathe. The sound of the helicopter kept getting louder and louder.

As he stared at me, his nostrils flared, and he inhaled deep. "Well, the little kitty's got herself a problem doesn't she?" He smacked his lips. "Don't worry, we can fix that once we get where we're going." I shrank away from him, but he grabbed my upper arm and started hauling me to my feet.

Despite my struggles, he dragged me outside. The wood Kane had dropped still lay everywhere. I grabbed a log and swung it with all my strength. It hit him in his side. He grunted and let go of my arm. I scrambled away on my hands and knees then struggled to my feet, my ankle shrieking at me to stop.

I'd almost made it to the door when a spike of pain stabbed me through my brain and into my stomach more painful than any I'd experienced before. A scream tore from my chest, my legs collapsing beneath me. My fingers clutched at the collar, the metal hot and vibrating as I tried to rip it off.

The pain went on and on until it felt like my brain melted. Lightning bolts of agony extended through my arms and legs, making it impossible to move. Sweat broke out all over my body. I curled into a ball and shook.

Finally, it stopped. I lay lifeless on the floor, my breaths coming out in short pants, my head pounding, my stomach wanting to let loose the food I'd eaten today.

This time when he hauled me to my feet, he brought me face-to-face with him. Stubble covered his jaw, and his eyes were a cold yellow. "You've been a lot of trouble for nothing, you know that?"

My teeth chattering in my skull, and I forced words from my lips. "Where's my sister?"

A cruel smile flashed. "You'll be joining her shortly."

The helicopter was so loud now the sound overtook everything else. I saw a flash of the rotors through the window as it landed between the cabin and the lake, one of the few open spots around.

His hand tight on my arm, he dragged me through the door. The rough handling made my injured ankle burn. A small, black helicopter hovered two feet from the ground, lowering closer to the rocks. Two men in tactical gear jumped out as soon as it settled. They wore black helmets, goggles propped on top, and held machine guns.

The cowboy yanked me along. I couldn't get in that helicopter. My sister had sacrificed her freedom for me to escape. I wasn't going to throw that away now. I needed to break free.

With all my might, I struggled against the grip on my arm, trying to get away. The cowboy jerked me in front of him and gave me a long-suffering stare.

"You really want to get shocked again, don't you?" he yelled over the noise of the rotor blades.

I spit in his face.

He blinked, then wiped the spittle off his nose. When he looked at me again, his eyes held deadly promise.

I swallowed, my stomach rolling. Another yank and we were halfway there. He kept dragging me along, and I kept struggling. His hold was tight, my skin bruising beneath his fingers. The tactical guys stood at the ready beside the open door of the helicopter, their guns angled toward the ground. I was close enough to scent shifter on them, but not the pilot inside.

I *could not* get on that helicopter, but no matter how hard I yanked, the cowboy's grip wouldn't loosen. My ankle burned, telling me to rest. My stomach reminded me what it felt like to get shocked. The pressure of the rotor blades slapped at me, making me duck my head. This was happening. I was about to be shoved on the helicopter. I couldn't stop it. A defeated shriek erupted from my lips as I struggled with renewed force.

A roar made us all stop. The cowboy and the two tactical guys, even the helicopter pilot, turned toward the sound.

In the next instant, the pair lifted their machine guns. A distinct *ratatat* punched through the beating of the rotor blades. I flinched and ducked.

The cowboy let me go. I scrambled away, toward the cabin, tripped on the baggy hem of my sweatpants, then turned in time to see a bear charge out of the bushes.

It wasn't just a bear— it was a massive mountain of enraged fur. I didn't know bears could get that big. Its fur had a reddish tinge to it, sticking straight up along the hump at its neck. A grizzly bear. I'd never seen one before.

It moved fast, faster than I would have expected a bear to move. A distinct and familiar scent wafted toward me as it charged the three men.

"Kane," I breathed.

Whatever the tactical guys were shooting at him didn't seem to do any damage. He kept charging until he was on top of them. One swipe and the guy on the right went flying, another swipe and the other went down, their machine guns clattering to the rocks.

Kane pounced on the one, his jaws closing around his neck. A scream ripped through the air as he bit then shook the body like a rag doll. I cringed, covering my head with my arms.

The cowboy veered to the side, away from the bear and toward me. I tried to scramble backward as fast as possible.

Behind him, the other tactical guy tried to crawl to his gun again. Kane was on him in the next instant, going for a kill bite at his neck. Another tortured scream shouted above the sound of the helicopter.

The cowboy yanked me to my feet. Turning, he held me in front of him like a shield.

Like the pilot didn't want to be close to a rampaging bear. The helicopter lifted from the ground, away from the struggle. Kane noticed and launched himself at the landing skid. He caught, and the helicopter tipped, the one side of the rotors angled toward the rocks. One blade hit, crumpling, then another. A screeching metal sound replaced the rhythm of the rotors that had hovered over everything. I covered my ears. The rotors folded into themselves like origami. The bear spun, throwing the helicopter away from him. It hit the rocks that lined the lake. Glass smashed. A fire caught in the engine, then was put out a second later when the bulk of the helicopter hit the water with a splash. If the pilot wasn't already dead, they became trapped as it sank into the lake.

The grizzly turned toward us. My heart leaped into my throat. I'd never seen anyone with such a feral look in their eyes.

The cold metal of a handgun pressed against my temple. "Stay right there or she's dead," the cowboy shouted at him.

Either Kane didn't understand the demand, or he didn't care to obey. Walking on all fours, blood on his jaws, he stalked toward us. My heart pounded so loud I could barely hear anything else.

"I said stop," the cowboy shouted again, his shrill voice rattling in my head.

Kane didn't stop.

The cowboy pulled the gun away from my temple and aimed at the grizzly. *Bang, bang, bang.* Three shots made me jerk, but they didn't seem to do anything except make Kane move faster. He broke into a run. Another three shots and Kane kept coming.

The cowboy emptied the gun, then shoved me away from him. I fell on my injured knees, crying out. My body wanted to shift, but the collar kept stopping me. Pain spiked into my stomach.

Another roar split the air.

The cowboy braced, then jumped, the sound of tearing clothes snapping a second later. He shifted into a cougar. They collided. The eerie sound of a cougar's screech mixed with Kane's roar.

I scrambled backwards away from the fight. The pair crashed toward me, and I rolled over, struggling to my feet. The cougar screeched again, and I turned in time to see Kane bite his hind leg. He held on, then swung the cougar away from him. The feline flew, then landed on his side and skidded across the rocks.

Before the cougar could regain his feet, Kane was on top of him. Another screech reverberated, this one ending in a gurgle.

Then nothing. Silence. No helicopter, no roaring, no sounds

at all except my own breathing, a rapid and panicked rhythm, loud in my ears.

The cougar lay dead and bloody. The two tactical guys hadn't moved. One of the helicopter's rotor blades stuck out from the water. No one had come out. Everyone was dead. The scent of fresh blood hung over everything. My stomach rolled.

The grizzly huffed a breath and turned away from the dead cougar. My limbs froze in shock. I didn't move as he ambled away from the body. I couldn't look away. I waited for him to change back into Kane, to become human again. I didn't trust this killer. I wanted Kane back.

But he didn't immediately return to human form. The bear ambled to the water's edge, slowly, and took a deep drink. Water splashed, washing the blood from his jaws and neck.

I couldn't breathe for the fear coursing through me. I'd watched him kill four people and he didn't change back into a human. He should change back. That's what normal shifters did. This wasn't normal.

Finished with his drink, he turned on me, his eyes filled with purpose.

"Oh, God." The bottom of my stomach dropped into my toes.

None of the blood lust was gone from his eyes, the intensity instead morphing into something more predatory. And it was entirely focused on me. My body twitched with the need to flee.

I knew better. In my bobcat form, I was a predator too. I knew what it was like. If I saw a squirrel run, I wanted to chase after that squirrel. If a rabbit bounded across my path, I chased that rabbit. I knew I should stay put. But seeing Kane's bear form look at me like that, my human self-preservation instincts took over.

I knew better.

But still, I turned and ran.

11

BROOKE

TREES AND BUSHES SCRAPED AT ME. I RAN BLINDLY, MY ANKLE screaming in pain, but I wouldn't stop.

I didn't know what would happen if I stopped.

At first, the quiet around me made me think he wasn't following. The birds weren't chirping, the wind was calm. My heart pounded in my throat.

Crash. Branches broke behind me. It sounded like a whole tree shattered. He was following, and fast.

I pushed onward, the need to get away overwhelming every other thought. A grizzly bear chased me, and I was alone. Pine needles poked through my socks like tiny little knives. My ankle hurt so bad tears leaked from my eyes with each step.

Stupid, stupid. I should have run into the cabin and locked myself in. I should have thought this through. At least there was a shotgun there. Right now, I was defenseless, and I was having a hard time keeping the bulky sweatpants up around my waist. I was seconds away from running bare-assed through a forest.

Thud. A tree root tripped me. I went down on my knees and cried out. *Get up. Get up. Get up.* He was getting closer. Each branch he broke went off like a firecracker in my head.

I struggled to my feet and kept moving. He sounded so close, I was sure he could have pounced on me, but no matter how fast I ran, he kept pace.

He's stalking me.

The rational part of my brain acknowledged this and tried to analyze it. If he'd wanted to attack me, he would have by now. I'd seen him take down three guys and a helicopter. He could overtake me right now if he wanted. Was he toying with me?

The thought gave me a shot of adrenaline. Instead of using the burst of energy to run faster, I slowed. I couldn't outrun him. This was pointless and stupid, and my ankle burned like I'd stepped in lava. I stopped, gasping for breath, my heart pounding so hard it hurt.

Crack. A twig broke behind me. I cringed and held my ground. I didn't turn around, not wanting to look aggressive.

Heavy footfalls padded across the mossy rocks. Wrapping my arms around my middle, I squeezed my eyes shut, wanting everything to go away. A huff of breath left him, almost like a sneeze. I flinched. He crept closer and closer, each footstep louder than the last.

My legs shook with fatigue and fear. He was right beside me now. I could feel the heat of his body and hear each of his exhales. Swallowing around the dry lump in my throat, I opened my eyes.

God, he was big. On all fours, his shoulders were at the same level as mine. I didn't turn my head and look at him directly but kept him in my peripheral vision. His fur was a mix of red, brown, and in some areas, black. His long snout angled toward me, inhaling my scent. His paws were three times as wide as my feet. Long claws stretched outward, streaked with blood.

My arms tightened around my middle. Why wouldn't he shift back to his human form? I could reason with a human, but right now, it seemed as if all of his humanity had left him.

He circled in front of me, blocking my path, then stopped. *So big.* I'd never been in the company of a bear shifter before and had only seen black bears once at a zoo. I hated zoos. They were cages for animals, no matter the zoo's good intentions. But those bears had been half the size of the grizzly in front of me now. Were all of them this big?

Dropping his head, he sniffed the ground in front of me.

"Kane?" His name came out like a croak.

He met my eyes briefly, and his nostrils flared. I was still in heat, but with all the adrenaline pumping through my body, it had become a secondary thing. He'd be able to smell it, especially in animal form. And with his head in line with my pelvis, he'd be getting a front-row seat to my breeding fragrance. The realization made my stomach tighten. I clenched my teeth.

A loud breath huffed out of him, then he circled me. I stood perfectly still, not wanting to make him angry. He lumbered behind me, then to my right. It was a deliberate movement. When he completed a full circle, he looked at me, then did it again.

Every fine hair on my body stood on end. What was this? What was he doing? When I tried to swallow, my throat clicked with dryness.

The grizzly stopped behind me, and my whole body tingled in awareness. My hands moved of their own accord. Like I lived in slow-motion, I took the bulk of my hair and swept it over to the side, exposing my neck. I didn't understand what I was doing. I wasn't a submissive person. I liked being in charge, but my instincts told me this was important. My fingers brushed the metal of my collar before I tugged my T-shirt down my shoulder, revealing as much skin as possible.

His big body settled behind me. My heart thudded hard in my chest. He was so close now I felt his breath on my neck. I stiffened. Even though a big part of me shouted for me to run, my instincts told me to hold still.

His snout nudged me, and I held my ground. I turned my

head enough to see his face, then held my breath when he opened his jaws.

Massive teeth closed on my flesh. I gasped from the pain of it. He had the bulk of my shoulder in his jaws. After piercing the skin, he held still and unmoving. My shoulder pulsed. A bit of blood trickled across my collar bone. It hurt, but a primitive satisfaction ignited in my stomach from the act. Whether I wanted to acknowledge it or not, my body craved this.

After holding motionless for long moments, he released me. His tongue swept out, cleaning the trickle of blood from the wound. Then he moved away, circling me again. This time the circle was tighter, the sides of his furry body brushing up against mine.

He's marking me.

While my shoulder throbbed, my body shook from mixed emotions, confusion warring with a strange sort of satisfaction. I stood immobile and waited for what he would do next. When he completed his circles, he stopped in front of me.

I wasn't sure what I was supposed to do now.

His forehead against my hip, he nudged me in the direction of the cabin.

"Okay, okay," I muttered, turning. I limped forward. Adrenaline coursed through my veins, but I felt all my wounds at once: my ankle, the pine needles in my feet, the new wound on my neck—everything twinged. I wanted to rest. I wanted to find a nice flat, mossy rock to lay on and have a quick nap. I wanted some ice for my ankle. I wanted for this day to be over.

My legs like jelly, I concentrated on putting one foot in front of the other. Anytime I stumbled, he nudged me.

Finally, the cabin came into view, along with it, the bodies of the cougar and the two tactical guys. Nothing had changed since we'd been gone except it looked like the helicopter had sunk farther into the lake.

I averted my gaze from the bodies and focused on the door of the cabin. It remained open from when the cowboy had snatched me. What if Kane didn't return to human form? What if he was stuck this way forever? If he could change back, why hadn't he? Something was wrong with him.

Despite the burning in my ankle, I picked up my pace and tried to put some distance between us. The bear jogged to keep up. My ankle howled, but I ignored it. As soon as I was through the door, I slammed it. It smacked into his face and bounced at me.

He roared. The force of it pushed me back. I stumbled, falling on my ass. "Oh, God."

The bear stopped. His shoulders got stuck in the doorway. He was too big. He couldn't come inside.

As soon as I had the thought, his form rippled and shifted. The fur disappeared, his features flattened, his limbs lost their bulk and turned into muscled strength. It only took a few seconds for him to transform, then Kane stood in front of me, naked, his thick cock bobbing between his legs.

He was a man again. Relief made my limbs shake. He'd be reasonable. We'd be able to talk this out. Or I'd talk and he'd listen, and we'd be able to figure out what was happening here.

He growled low in his chest, and I stiffened. The cognac eyes that stared back at me didn't contain the man I'd gotten to know over the past two days. His eyes held the same predatory look they'd held since he'd shifted.

No, the bear was still in charge of this very human, very sexually aroused body.

12

BROOKE

He advanced toward me, his face a mask of pure possessiveness.

I tore my gaze away from the sizable erection bobbing between his legs and scrambled to my feet as quickly as I could with my ankle so sore. Nervous energy shot through my chest, my breaths leaving me short and fast. I stumbled around the couch, putting it between us. He followed.

"Kane?"

Every step I took away from him, he matched. The real Kane had to be in there somewhere. The bear couldn't take complete control of him, could it? I'd heard of shifters going rabid, that their animal side took over and they'd need to be put down, but I'd never known one personally or seen it in action. How far gone was he?

He stalked me, undeterred. My body hummed at the ownership in his eyes. My instincts liked his strength and dominance. I wanted to submit, but my feet moved me away from him.

You're only making it worse. By running, I was inciting his more basic instincts.

Kane never broke his gaze from me. He had one objective and

I was it. Earlier, I'd practically begged him to fuck me, but this animal side of him made me nervous.

No matter what had happened since the cowboy found me, my body needed sex. My skin itched and tingled. My tongue still lay thick in my mouth. A sexual ache built inside me. I was in heat with only one option for release. I'd spent the whole day fantasizing about him, watching him work, obsessing. Now Kane was here in front of me and wanted it too.

Except, he'd told me he couldn't be with me. In the state he was in, did he really understand what he was doing? I didn't know his reasons for refusing me earlier, but from the way he was acting, he didn't seem to have them on his mind either.

Indecision rippled through me, but I stopped myself before I could run for the door. After everything, I wouldn't get far if I tried to escape. My ankle was swollen, my feet hurt, and my body was at war with itself. So much of me wanted this. My animal, my biology, and...me.

The distance between us shortened as Kane closed the gap. The width of his bare chest filled my vision, the thatch of curls at its center a shade darker than his head of hair.

My instincts shouted at me to submit. This was so different than what usually happened with a guy, and I felt like I was drowning. I didn't know how to handle this situation. I didn't know how to stay in control.

Maybe there wasn't a way.

Swallowing, I bowed my head and pulled my hair to one side, exposing the stinging marks he'd bitten in my neck. A growl rolled through his chest. I closed my eyes when he moved behind me. The heat of him spread across my spine. His breath warmed the skin of my shoulder. When his lips skimmed the exposed flesh, the scruffy hair of his beard tickled my skin.

His tongue darted out and caressed one of the puncture marks. I gasped. Liquid heat spiraled down my spine and thighs, making my core clench. His teeth scraped along my skin. Tension oozed out of my limbs, my body softening.

When he paused with his lips over the bite he'd given me, I opened my eyes and turned my head. He watched me with that same predatory look.

With his focus entirely on my eyes, his hand inched across my stomach. Shivers cascaded down my legs. Spanning my abdomen, he pulled me against him. My breath caught in my throat. His cock pulsed hot against the base of my spine.

With purpose, he stepped forward, taking me with him until my body was caught between him and the wall. My hands splayed flat over it, my cheek pressed against the rough wood of the log.

His lips on my jaw, one of his hands covered mine, holding me in place. His other roved over my body like he owned it. Along my hip, under my borrowed T-shirt, his fingers brushing the undersides of my breasts, then back down into the loose elastic of the sweatpants.

My chest rose and fell in an excited rhythm. Everywhere he touched, my body burned. Seductive sensations bombarded my brain one after the other. When the blade of his hand skimmed down the crack of my ass, I groaned. My body gave him no resistance as he slid his hand lower until his knuckle touched my wet core. I moaned. My pussy was so wet and ready. I rocked back into him, needing friction.

The scent of my heat and sex rose around us. A growl rumbled through his chest, making all of my nerve endings come alive. He rubbed me over and over again. The movement made my sweatpants fall lower and lower until they were around my ankles. The wood of the cabin walls scraped against my palms.

I was too hot. An inferno built inside me and wouldn't let go. His cock pressed against the side of my hip as his hand ground against me. I was so empty. I needed to be filled. The fever of my body now consumed my mind. I couldn't think anymore, just feel.

"Please." The word came out a groan. "I need you."

Pressing against the wall, I angled my ass toward his cock. He growled and grabbed my hips. With ease, he lifted me up, then settled me on his cock in the next heartbeat.

There was no resistance. I was wet and swollen, and he slid right in. Another growl mixed with my moan of pure pleasure. After a whole day of burning up inside, this was exactly what my body needed. The way he braced me between him and the wall, my feet barely touched the floor.

He pulled back and thrust. Sparks burst behind my eyes. He hit my spot perfectly. A frenzy overcame me. I needed release. I pressed back against him again and again. Faster and faster. My body demanded the pace and Kane didn't slow me down. It turned into a primal, uncontrollable thing. The sound of flesh smacking flesh, the scent of sex, my moans and his growls—it reached a fevered pitch.

I'd never been fucked so hard or deep in my life.

My climax built inside me until I couldn't stop it. Every thrust of his cock touched the exact place I needed him to be. Fireworks exploded in my brain, a rainbow of color and light. My fingernails tried to dig into the logs of the wall to keep my balance. My feet lifted off the floor as he adjusted our position. He had me entirely in his grasp and pounded into me as my brain slowly floated down to earth.

One last growl and he strained, his entire body taut. His arms squeezed me to him, tight, as he came inside me. I gasped, a warm sensation spreading through my body. I'd never felt anything like it. It was beyond an orgasm. This was like being wrapped in contentment then dipped in satisfaction. The sensation traveled to every part of me, all the way to the tips of my fingers, to the ends of my toes. It was hot and tingly and delicious in an addictive way. For a long moment, I forgot to breathe.

Slowly, my mind came back into myself. What the fuck was that? I felt owned. I'd never had sex with another shifter before. *Was this what always happened?* My skin eased from its near-constant itch; the swelling of my tongue lessened.

Kane set me on my feet and stepped back. The loss of him inside me made me groan. My body wanted more.

I turned, searching his face for the man I knew him to be, but only found the bear—a disoriented and dazed bear inside the man's eyes.

He stumbled to the side. It looked like everything about him was shutting down, all energy spent. I stepped out of the sweatpants bunched on the floor and into his path. If he hit the floor, I wouldn't be able to get him back up.

"Kane?"

His brow furrowed like he was trying to figure out who I was. I took his hand, closed the front door, and limped my way to bed with him in tow. "This way," I murmured. He stumbled after me.

And when he fell into bed, weak, I crawled in after him wearing only his shirt.

13

KANE

Morning light stabbed through the window, high on the horizon. I didn't usually sleep this late.

I stretched my arms over my head, then paused. Something was different. Something had happened. I rolled to my side, then froze. I wasn't alone in bed. There was a warm woman beside me. Brooke. She was snuggled against me, her delicious bare bottom pressed against my hip. The T-shirt she wore slid down her shoulder, exposing bite marks. A bear bite. *My* bite. Remorse punched me in the stomach. I'd hurt her.

Fuck.

The events of yesterday came back to me in a disjointed blur. There was a helicopter. I'd shifted. Men had tried to take Brooke. A cougar shifter. I'd attacked them. My body shuddered in realization.

I'd killed them all.

But that wasn't the only thing that had happened. I'd... We'd...

All of me was bare, naked. I'd shredded my clothes when I shifted. My gaze went to the door where the sweatpants I'd given Brooke lay in a heap by the wall. Turning, I examined her peaceful face, her cheeks stained pink in a flush, and her lips parted. My scent clung all over her body.

I'd been inside her.

Please. I remembered her desperate voice, remembered the way she felt, how amazing it was to fuck her. *I need you.* I shook my head to clear it, not sure if I was remembering correctly, everything so disjointed that I couldn't trust my memories.

I hadn't impregnated her. *Thank fuck.* She was still in heat; I could smell it. If I'd gotten her pregnant, then her heat would be over. Instead, her intoxicating scent overwhelmed the space beneath the blankets. *Lucky.* I didn't have condoms. Who the hell would I have used them with before now?

The urge to gather her in my arms and inhale the scent of her throat made me sit up and swing my legs over the bed. Her warm hand touched my bare back. I stiffened. The hand dropped away.

"Kane?"

I got up and moved away from her hesitant voice. She'd seen me at my worst. I'd lost control of my animal. She'd witnessed the bear taking over. Had I been too rough? Too crude? I couldn't look at her as I opened my top drawer and took out a shirt, putting it on without seeing it. Next came a pair of jeans.

The mattress shifted, the springs squeaking as she moved to the edge of the bed. I needed to get out of here before I grabbed her and fucked her again. *Her scent.* It was too much, and it was everywhere in the cabin, smothering me. A flash of a fleeting image made every part of me throb, the memory of taking her against the wall, of how she felt inside… I'd never experienced anything so good in my life. The bear in me demanded I take her again so she wouldn't forget who she belonged to.

Dammit. Even now, the bear was trying to gain control. I'd claimed a mate and needed to exert my dominance. This was so very dangerous, and I needed to escape before I did something more stupid. *How much further can I go?*

I stalked toward the door.

"Kane." This time her voice was firm, making me pause at the door. I turned my head but didn't look at her fully. She appeared small and lost beneath my shirt, her hair a wild mess of golden curls around her head. I fisted my hands.

"You were gentle. You were perfect."

A savage growl erupted from my chest. I strode through the door, slamming it behind me.

Taking a deep breath of fresh air, I stopped on the porch. I didn't need her to lie about what happened. I remembered fucking into her hard and fast like an animal, and thinking about it made me want to turn around and do it all over again.

I was so screwed.

The scent of blood carried over to me on the breeze. I turned, seeing the cougar shifter's body. The man had died a cougar and stayed a cougar.

Cougars were such assholes. I'd only known one good one, Walker Hayles. My hometown, Goldenlach Ridge, had been divided that way, the asshole cougars on one side, the grizzlies on the other. Walker was the only one to cross that divide, to make friends with Landon and me. And that was because he thought all cougars were assholes too.

My chest twinged with regret. I hadn't seen or talked to Walker in a decade. Those last angry words we had with each other were a permanent brand in my mind. It wasn't like I hadn't thought of reaching out, to see how he was doing, to see if he was still in the army. Every time I thought of it, I dismissed the idea. I could only believe he would deny any attempt at reconciliation between us.

I blinked away the memories, focusing on the two bodies beyond the cougar, clad in all-black tactical gear. They'd fired their weapons and I'd ripped out their throats. I remembered being shot, the bullets going right through me. The wounds healed when I'd shifted back to human, any bullets remaining pushed out of skin and muscle.

The helicopter sank into the lake, only a couple feet of rotor sticking out. There'd be another body there too. I'd killed four people and felt no remorse. I'd been protecting my mate.

Dammit. I needed to stop thinking that way but couldn't. I'd claimed her. Rubbing a hand over my face, I tried to get a hold of the possessiveness rolling through me. I hadn't given her a choice. I didn't walk up to her and say, "Hey, would you like to mate with me? I know it's a long-term decision, but I'd really like a bite and fuck." *Bad, bad, bad.* If I could talk, it probably would have come out worse.

Another memory hit me, making me freeze in place. We stood together in a copse of pines and Brooke pulled her hair over her shoulder, offering me her neck. I remember feeling triumphant. Then she'd bent her head, submissive, an invitation. I'd bit her, hard enough to leave a mating mark.

Why had she offered me her neck?

Her scent was all over me, wafting through my sinuses, making me growl with possessive instinct. No matter what my brain shouted, the bear inside claimed ownership and would not be quieted.

I stared at the dead on the ground, telling the bear to fuck the hell off. Right now, the need to get rid of the bodies outweighed everything else. The helicopter was my biggest problem. It was practically on my front doorstep. More assholes could come looking for it. It might be underwater, but the lake was clear. A person would be able to see it if they flew over. The only bright side was that my lake was one in a literal million in one of Canada's boreal forests.

I couldn't do anything about it now, but I could take care of the easy stuff. Striding toward the bodies, I slowed when I neared the cougar. A piece of metal glinted on the back of his neck. Crouching, I took a closer look. A green light shone dully in the bright sun. A tracking device? Something else? The metal and the smooth cleverness of the design were similar to Brooke's collar. If it was a tracking device, I needed to destroy it.

With a firm hand, I grabbed hold and ripped it free. Some sort of shock wave traveled from the piece of metal to the cougar, making his dead body shake. My fingers tingled. I was pretty sure if I'd done that when the cougar was alive, it would have killed him.

I glanced at the cabin. There was no doubt in my mind that the same things would happen to Brooke if I tried to remove her collar. The thought made my stomach clench with rage, the red haze climbing up my peripheral vision. I wanted to get that thing off her so bad pressure built in my temples.

Taking a deep breath, I pushed my emotions aside, pocketed the bit of metal, and picked up the cougar's limp and massive body beneath his armpits. I dragged him toward my boats, breathing heavy with exertion. The motherfucker was big. His paws were as wide as my face. This would all be easier if I shifted into my bear form, but I didn't trust what would happen to Brooke if I did so. There was no way I could resist claiming her again if I let the bear take over.

Once I dropped the cougar beside my boat, the two tactical dickheads followed. They were shifters too, but not cougars, something avian instead, and they had the same bits of metal in the back of their necks. Once I tore the pieces out of their skin and pocketed them, I piled their bodies, one on top of the other like the pieces of shit they were. When I thought of how the one had yanked Brooke around, the other two with their guns out... I remembered her screaming in pain.

Red hazed my vision. If I could kill these guys again, I'd happily do it.

Tearing my gaze away, I focused on overturning the fishing boat and sliding it into the water. As soon as it was in far enough, I tied it to the dock.

I contemplated the tactical fuckers. After a moment's hesitation, I began to remove their clothes. The bodies would decompose faster bare. If someone came looking for them, I wanted to make it impossible for them to be found. The one overriding instinct above all others right now was to protect Brooke. Wherever these guys came from, whatever they wanted with her, it wasn't going to happen.

She was my mate. I'd shield her from harm or die trying.

Every time I moved, Brooke's scent wafted up to me. It clung to my fingers and body. I swallowed, battling the urge to return to the cabin and get some more of her scent all over me.

Once the men were naked, I searched their pockets for identification. I didn't find any, but there were knives, spare bullets, and a multi-tool I set aside on the dock along with the three neck chips from my pocket. One guy had a high-end walkie-talkie. I held it in my hand and stared. It wouldn't work for calling John here early. Still too far. I set it with the rest of the gear.

I piled the clothes, helmets, boots, and goggles in a heap by the shoreline. I'd take care of those after I got rid of the bodies. Standing, I scanned the shoreline for the cougar's clothes—torn jeans and shirt, a cowboy hat and boots, another walkie-talkie too. That was probably how the helicopter found us. If they'd known where Brooke had jumped from the plane, then all the cougar had to do was wait for his buddies to arrive before he made his move.

Growling, I tossed the cougar's shit with all the other stuff. A shadow shifted in the window of the cabin. Brooke was watching me. Knowing that made me step toward her. I stopped myself, shook my head to clear it, and focused on the task at hand. There was one more body in the helicopter.

Grabbing one of the tactical knives, I strode to the end of the dock, stripped, and dove into the ice cold water. The first shock of it stole my breath. These northern lakes weren't warm even in the middle of summer, but right now, a couple weeks after thaw, the water was only a little above freezing.

I surfaced, took gulping, gasping breaths, then swam the rest of the way to the helicopter. As soon as I was close enough, I dove down. The side of the helicopter was open, allowing me to swim inside.

The pilot's body was trapped in the seatbelt. I cut it with the knife, then resurfaced for another breath. My fingers were almost entirely numb from the cold. I gave myself a shake, then dove back under, making sure I could pull the pilot free before abandoning the knife.

It took a while to get him to the shoreline. If I hadn't been so cold, I might have been able to heave him onto the dock, but as it was, I could only get him partially up on the rocks. Once I was satisfied the body wouldn't drop back into the water, I climbed out.

At first, I just lay back and spread my arms wide, allowing the sun to warm me a bit. The light breeze didn't help my body temperature and I shivered. I either needed to get dry and warm or move to stave off hypothermia. I could grab a towel from the cabin. The thought made me look for her.

Again, the shadows shifted in the window. The swim hadn't helped get her scent out of my head. It clung to me, or had become a permanent fixture in my brain. Either way, I couldn't escape it.

Going inside the cabin right now was a bad idea.

I stood, shook the water off, and dragged the last body along the shoreline toward the boat. Using the other tactical knife, I cut his clothes off since they were plastered to him. No ID on this guy either, only a water-logged cell that was totally dead. I tossed it with the other shit, then checked his neck. He didn't have one of those clips. Probably because he was human. I was pretty sure those things were meant to control shifters, some modification of the collar.

One by one, I hefted the bodies over the bow of the boat, balancing two on either side. I didn't want their blood to drip in the bottom, to be reminded of their stench every time I went out on the lake.

I redressed, untied the boat, and climbed inside. I grabbed a paddle from underneath the seat and backed away from the dock until I was in deeper water. Two yanks of the motor's cord, and it roared to life. I turned the tiller and angled the boat away from the cabin.

One last glance over my shoulder, and I saw Brooke standing on the porch. I looked away, hating myself for the past twenty-four hours. What I wouldn't give for a do-over right now. But do-overs were for kids, and I'd long used up any of them I'd had.

A strange sensation tugged at my chest, instructing me to turn around, a thin strand of *something* that told me Brooke continued to watch. I focused on the water in front of me.

Muskeg, the northern swamp, was unpredictable. It could look like it was a foot deep but be six instead. I'd had an incident due to that a couple years ago. About five kilometers from my cabin, there was a section full of reeds. I'd thought it a couple feet deep, but when I'd jumped out of my boat, I'd gone in over my head. I navigated my way there now.

My lake ran into another, and I slowed the boat for the reeds that separated them, needing to use my paddle when they got too thick. Not a good idea to get the motor all tangled up. Once through, I kept going, angling north to the next lake, sticking near the shoreline so I wouldn't bottom the boat out on the rocks that often hid just below the surface.

A few minutes later, I entered another section of reeds. This one didn't lead to a lake but transitioned into muskeg. I killed the motor and tilted it partially out of the water so it would stay clear of the reeds. Quiet surrounded me. Bugs buzzed, a few birds chirped, but otherwise, it was peaceful. I took out the paddle and rowed. When I arrived close to the spot I'd been to before, I set the paddle on the bottom of the boat.

Rubbing my face, I glanced around. The other part of this

place that worked for this particular situation were the rocks. There were a lot of loose, big ones on the shoreline.

I pushed the cougar's body into the water with my foot. It slid in with a quiet splash. Taking off my clothes again, I jumped over the side of the boat and into the frigid water. Since it was shallow, it wasn't quite as cold as my lake, but it was murky. Already I'd lost sight of the cougar beneath the waterline. But I couldn't afford to assume the body would stay under.

Zoning in on a rock that looked about twenty or thirty pounds, I swam to the shoreline, then waded when it got shallow. With effort, I wiggled the rock out of its sludgy home in the mud and moss, then carried it back toward my boat. When the sandy lakebed gave way to deeper waters, I hefted it, throwing it as close to where the cougar's body submerged as I could.

Then I dove underwater, slaloming through the reeds to find both the rock and the body. My hand touched fur. I surfaced, took another breath, then pushed the body down as far as it would go. It took me a minute to find the rock. I rolled it toward the cougar, then lifted it onto its center mass. Satisfied that it wouldn't budge, I surfaced for gulping breaths of air.

Close to an hour after I'd left the cabin, I'd done the same thing with the three other bodies. No one came out here. No one would find them. And now no one flying over would see anything suspicious. Fish would have a fine feast in this peaceful resting place. It was more than these fuckers deserved.

I clambered into the boat dripping wet, shivering, limbs numb from the prolonged exposure to cold water. Leaning back against the bow, I once again spread my arms wide and let the sun warm me.

When I was dry enough, I got dressed and rowed, easier going now without the added weight of the bodies. As soon as I was out of the reeds, I lowered the motor and started it.

A nagging sort of urgency crawled inside my stomach. I'd been away from my mate too long. She could need me or want something. Or she could be in danger. I hadn't made sure she had eaten. I needed to take care of her—

Fuck. My instincts were getting annoyingly insistent. The desire to make the world right for her in every way possible overrode all other thoughts. I was driven to take care of her, a sensation that burned in my chest so hard my breastbone ached. *This is insane.*

As soon as the cabin came into sight, I slowed. I shouldn't go back inside. I was liable to jump Brooke as soon as I caught whiff of her scent again. But I also needed to make sure she was okay. How could I do both?

I pulled up to the dock, secured the boat's rope to the post, then jumped out a moment later. The dead fuckers' pile of clothes was where I left it. I would burn it all later and make sure to bury what didn't turn to ash.

Something glinted in the sunlight close to the cabin, making me pause. I walked toward it, then stooped down. A remote. It was active, a frequency gauge bleeping red. This was for Brooke's collar.

I thought of my initial design, the one I'd given Landon to develop properly, to save those who'd gone rabid instead of putting them down. My cousin wouldn't have employed the fuckers I'd buried, would he? He might have turned into a rich asshole, but he wouldn't use an asshat swat team to abduct someone. I stared down at the remote. My design had never included a remote. There was something else going on here, and I'd need to talk to Landon to figure out what it was.

But now that I had this remote, I could free Brooke.

My heart thumped hard in my chest and my feet moved toward the door of the cabin. I barged in, startling her where she stood by the sink. She spun around, clothed in my T-shirt and sweats. Her fingers gripped the counter behind her. Her eyes were wide, her breathing rapid.

Her scent slammed into me, hot and heavy, intoxicating. I

wanted to bury myself in that scent and never leave. Instead, I made myself stand perfectly still, not advancing toward her like I needed. Not bending her over the counter so I could take her again like I wanted.

I opened my palm and stretched the remote toward her.

When she saw what I held, her hand flew to her collar. "You can get it off?" There was so much hope on her face, it almost hurt to look at her.

I gave her one nod and gestured to the table, trying to breathe through my mouth so her scent wouldn't turn me back into the beast.

She hesitated a second, then pulled out a chair to sit. The closer I moved to her, the more the mouth breathing thing wasn't working. Her scent had overtaken my cabin, and now it was overtaking me.

Once settled in the chair, she pulled her hair over to one side, exposing the collar completely. The action froze me in my tracks. It was like she was offering herself to me again. The bear inside me reared up, demanding I take her.

That's not what this is. She was just making it easier for me to access the collar.

The bear wasn't listening. A growl emerged from my chest.

She stiffened, her head turning to look at me. "Kane?" Worry pinched her brow. "Is everything okay?"

Nothing was okay, and I was so fucked up I shouldn't come within shouting distance of her.

I swallowed and stepped forward, carefully, making sure I wasn't going to lose control. I moved behind her chair, keeping my eyes on the collar. *Concentrate.* This was important. I focused on the instinct to help her. This was something my mate needed and wanted. I grabbed hold of that thought and didn't let go.

The frequency of the remote and the collar matched. I pressed the disarm button. All the lights went off on the collar.

"Is it working?" she asked over her shoulder.

The skin of her neck was tantalizingly close. I could see the puncture marks I'd given her. A possessive growl emerged from my chest. *Stop it.* The bear might like the claim, but I'd hurt her.

She stiffened at the sound, her shoulders hunched forward in a protective posture. "Is it working, Kane?" Her voice came out stronger than her bearing showed.

I forced myself to focus on the remote in my hand and pressed the button marked "release."

The collar clicked, separating at the back. Brooke gasped as the prongs retracted from the base of her skull. In the next instant, her hands grabbed at it, frantic. It dropped with a heavy *thunk* on the table.

She stood, her movements frenzied, her breathing fast. I didn't know how it would feel to be free after all that time in the collar, but from her actions, it had to be euphoric.

She stumbled toward the door. The borrowed T-shirt went flying in one direction, the sweatpants shimmied down her legs. Golden, bare flesh blazed in the sunlight coming through the windows.

I took a step toward her, my breaths trapped in my throat, then stopped. I grabbed onto the back of the chair to keep myself from reaching for her.

Naked, she turned to me. "I need some...time," she whispered, a plea in her tone.

She shifted in front of me, smooth skin sprouting fur, her form becoming a diminutive version of her human body. A bobcat appeared before me, silver-gray fur, striped on her face and spotted down her body. Black ear tufts pointed to the ceiling, and long white whiskers twitched. Her tawny yellow eyes stared at me a moment, blinked, then she leaped away in one graceful stride. *Beautiful.*

As soon as she flew through the door, I tightened my hand hold on the chair. Every part of me shouted to give chase, to not let her escape.

What if she didn't come back? What if she kept running south until she found civilization? It would take days, but as a bobcat, she could survive.

The back of the chair cracked beneath my grasp.

My mate was leaving me, and it felt like my heart had been torn from my chest, a ragged hole in its place. My legs collapsed. Sinking to the floor, I held my head in my hands.

14

BROOKE

A SHIFT HAD NEVER FELT SO GOOD.

It was like coming home after a long time away. Like settling into a warm bath after a hard day. Like a piece of chocolate lava cake all to myself. Like the satisfied tail end of an orgasm where everything was right in the world.

Each one of my senses became alive, heightening. Every scrape and pain disappeared, including my swollen ankle and the prong marks at the back of my neck. Invigorated, I bounded through the bushes. The particles in the air glinted and sparkled. Every insect and critter became their own sight and sound, each of their movements as loud as a thunderclap. The threatening unknown as a human became a playground for my bobcat. There was nothing for me to fear.

I ran as fast as I could, didn't think about where I was headed, just ran. The mossy ground bounced beneath each stride. The terrain I'd been cursing on my journey to the cabin now acted as a springboard, giving lift to my every jump. My paws hit sand, then rock, then moss. I leaped over one fallen log, then used the next like a ramp. I jumped off the end and kept running, my tongue lolling out of my mouth in pure joy.

The air was fragrant and sweet. Pine needles, moss, water, leaves, dirt—everything combined to create an aromatic cocktail. I hadn't taken note of how beautiful it was before, but now it filled my head, beguiling, the forest's seductive perfume.

The wind whistled through my whiskers. Another scent almost had me veering off my course—a rabbit. My instincts told me to hunt it down and feast. My feet told me to keep running. Other animal scents crossed my path: a squirrel, a wolverine, a ptarmigan. Each had its own distinct flavor, something I couldn't identify in my human form.

I could keep running for hours and part of me wanted to. After being jailed in that collar, my freedom became a heady sensation. I could run live as a bobcat for days, living off the land and trusting my instincts.

But something stopped me from following through. An unfamiliar emotional tug in my chest made my pace slow.

When a larger pine tree, its trunk a good foot wide where it sank into the earth, appeared in my direct line of site, I headed straight to it. There weren't a lot of branches on the bottom. I adjusted my pace enough to scramble up its jagged bark. My claws dug in, tearing chunks out of the trunk. I climbed as high as I could before the branches were too small to hold my weight.

One paw in front of the other, I balanced my way to the end of a branch. It bobbed under my movements until I stretched out, using my claws to keep me secure.

I could see everything from here. Not the cabin, I'd run too far, but my view in every direction was unobstructed. I didn't know where I was. *No matter.* I could follow my scent back to the cabin. I'd headed east, but otherwise, the land was unfamiliar to me. Clouds spread across the sky like dollops of whipped cream, the sun breaking through to warm my fur. Flies buzzed around my head, and I twitched my ears to keep them away.

The forest spread out in all directions. I thought of how it looked when I'd been falling in the parachute, scary and overwhelming. Now it was a blanket of life, teaming with opportunity. As a bobcat, I could live here and be happy.

As a human, everything I wanted and needed in my life was out of reach, hundreds of miles away back in Detroit. *Is Sabrina okay?* My claws curled into the tree branch. If one of those guys had survived Kane's attack, then maybe we could have made him talk, forced him to tell us where my sister was. It had to be somewhere northern. Maybe somewhere not too far away since they'd used a helicopter.

The thought made my heart rate accelerate. Maybe my sister wasn't that far away after all. It gave me hope.

The sun climbed higher along the horizon, carving an arched path across the sky through the vanilla clouds. As time ticked by, the strange sensation in my chest tugged more and more. It told me to return where I'd come from, back to the cabin. Back to Kane.

This was new.

I'd never been physically drawn to returning to a guy before. When I was in heat, I'd have fun with someone, then move on. A few more nights of hot sex with Kane would hopefully cure me of this foreign sensation.

If he was willing.

Thinking about our first encounter together created a purr in my throat. It rumbled through my body.

But he hadn't felt that way, had he? My purr stopped abruptly. When he left the cabin this morning, I'd panicked. I wanted to have another round of sex and he kept resisting, couldn't get away from me fast enough.

Practically speaking, even though he'd left the cabin instead of satisfying my burning need for sex, he'd taken care of me. I'd watched him dispassionately dispose of the bodies, relieved he handled it. Allowing him to figure it out calmed me. But when he'd left in the boat, the panic overwhelmed me all over again. It had felt like hours before he'd returned.

And now I was here, on my own, enjoying nature, but not feeling...exactly right. There was something missing, I felt empty inside—and none of that made sense. On the upside, now that I'd shifted, my wounds were healed: my swollen ankle, cuts, and bruises.

I must have dozed, because when an owl hooted from a nearby tree and I lifted my head, the sun had already started its downward arc toward the horizon. That strange, tugging sensation in my chest had grown, telling me to return where I'd come from.

Standing, I stretched, arching my spine but keeping my paws balanced on the branch. With precision, I jumped to a lower branch, then another, until I was able to descend down the trunk headfirst.

As soon as my paws hit the ground, I took off in a run. The wind whipped by me; rodents scurried out of my way. When I caught sight of a ptarmigan, I veered toward the speckle-feathered bird. It didn't get far. I snapped its neck quickly, then settled down to feast. Bones crunched in my jaws, blood squished out onto my jowls. After my run and my nap, I was starving.

Tastes like chicken.

I made short work of the meal, then ambled farther along, my old scent leading me. Between the tugging at my chest and the heat in my belly, my skin itched again, uncomfortably. It might be a relief to have finally shifted, but I didn't feel like my old self.

The sound of a creek made me veer in the other direction. It was strange. I could hear it, but I couldn't see it. When the noise was the loudest, I dug down through the moss. There it was, hidden beneath the roots and overgrowth. I balanced and leaned forward to drink. The water was crisp and clean. I pressed my whole face inside, cleaning the remains of the ptarmigan from my whiskers.

The tug in my chest increased. I needed to get back to the cabin. It had become imperative for some reason. I loped my way through the bushes and trees, ignoring the smaller rodents that would have been fun to chase another time. I didn't run as fast as I had when I first shifted but kept my pace quick and consistent, a marathon instead of a sprint.

The closer I drew to the cabin, the more the pressure in my chest eased. A curl of smoke lifted into the sky, leading me. The scent of something delicious hit me in the face. Even though I'd just eaten, my body told me I could use more.

I paused at the tree line that encircled the cabin. Besides the rotor of the helicopter in the lake and the lingering scent of dried blood, it looked as it did when I first arrived. Light blazed from the windows, welcoming. Kane was inside. I could feel it. The incessant tug inside my chest turned into something else— contentment at knowing he was near.

So weird.

My eyes fell on the chair by the door. A stack of folded clothes lay on the seat—a white T-shirt, my jean skirt, another pair of sweatpants. I inched my way toward it. When I stepped up onto the landing, I shifted.

It felt as satisfying, as heady, as it had earlier, the relief of a yawning stretch. The sensation was brief, and the cool evening air bit at my bare skin. I dressed quickly in the T-shirt and sweats, wanting to wear comfortable clothes rather than my jean skirt.

Taking a deep breath, I placed my hand on the doorknob and pushed inside. Warmth enveloped me. The cabin smelled like dinner and burning pine. Kane stood near the potbelly stove, stirring a large pot of something. He'd changed into a different shirt and jeans and looked delicious as hell. His hair was less unruly as well, like he'd given himself a haircut, and his beard a trim.

My instincts told me to jump him immediately and ease the ache between my legs, an ache that doubled in its intensity as soon as my eyes landed on him. The itch across my skin intensified. The clothes I wore became a burden.

He lifted his head, his hand stopping mid-stir. His nostrils flared. His hand tightened on the wooden spoon so much his knuckles turned white.

And I saw something in his eyes I wasn't expecting: relief. Had he been worried about my safety? Or had he thought I was going to leave for good? Spending days and days traveling in the woods as a bobcat held no appeal for me. Not when a plane was coming next week. I didn't know how to get to Detroit from here. I didn't know where my sister was. I needed to be smart about this if I was going to help Sabrina, not run off blindly into the night.

Plus, the thought of leaving right now made that same, new non-heat related pressure resume in my chest.

"Hi," I said, suddenly nervous. I'd never shifted in front of someone other than family, and wondered what he thought. "It smells fantastic in here."

I closed the door behind me and walked toward him. He'd done something with my collar. The table was clear. If I never saw it again, it would be too soon. His death grip on the spoon didn't ease. The byproducts of what he'd put in the pot lay on the kitchen counter: an onion skin, potato and yam peels, and an empty package that could have held meat. All was stacked in a neat pile beside a cutting board along with a chef's knife.

When I stopped on the other side of the stove to peek inside the pot, Kane still hadn't moved, a deer caught in headlights. *Or a bear.*

Thinking about his animal form made me shiver. I'd never encountered such a large beast before. I'd grown up around bobcats, my mom and sister, the cousins I saw occasionally. We hadn't intermingled with other species a lot. I'd heard of larger communities of shifters, but we preferred to stay on our own. One of my mom's old friends was a wolf, but I'd only met him a couple times and he'd never shifted in front of me.

Feeling awkward, I stared at Kane's chest. The top three buttons of his plaid shirt were undone, revealing tanned flesh and a dusting of hair. I licked my lips. Our first encounter had been quick but satisfying. I wanted to get to know him better the next time. I wanted to find out what his skin tasted like. Could I convince him to a pre-dinner interlude? Because this close to him, the pulse between my legs increased in intensity with each passing second. My lips parted.

I lifted my eyes. His were shut, his jaw clenched. He leaned his weight back, like he was about to bolt.

He had to smell my heat. My shifting and run may have helped the craving a little, but he had to understand I was uncomfortable and needed release. But he seemed bent on ignoring me. Would I have to crawl onto his lap naked in order to get his attention? The thought had a cascade of fantasies rushing through my head. Ones where he fucked me in every position in every spot in the cabin.

I took a step back. I wasn't going to throw myself at him. I had too much self-respect for that. But it wasn't like I could hop on over to the next cabin to find someone more willing. Another truth followed close behind that one, startling me. I didn't *want* to find someone else. I wanted Kane. No one else would do.

Crossing my arms over my chest, I backed away. I could leave. I could go for another run. I turned around, intent on at least doing *something* to take the edge off, when I heard him move.

I glanced over my shoulder. He puttered around in the kitchen, taking bowls out of the cupboard, spoons out of the drawer, filling two glasses of water. A moment later, he was back at the pot, ladling out a healthy portion into each of the bowls. He set one in front of each chair at the table along with a glass, then sat.

He dug into his meal without looking at me.

Fine. If he could act like everything was normal, then dammit, so could I.

15

KANE

I RELEASED A SLOW BREATH THROUGH MY TEETH THE MOMENT Brooke decided to stay instead of go. As much as I needed to keep away from her, I didn't want her to leave.

Her movements were stiff as she stepped up to the table, pulled out the chair, and sat.

I took another bite, not tasting the sausage and vegetable soup I'd been simmering for hours as I tried to breathe through my mouth as much as possible. As soon as she'd stepped inside the cabin, all the work I'd done to air it out went right out the window. The scent of her heat was too strong. When she'd moved closer, I'd been seconds away from taking her by the shoulders and bending her over the end of the bed.

"Did you have a good day?" Her words were garbled like she had trouble speaking. And she didn't look at me when she asked the question, instead stirring the contents of her soup around and around.

What was she on about? My day had been torture. I'd gone after her a half dozen times, turning around again as soon as I realized what I was doing. The farther she traveled, the more insistent the pull became in my chest, the one that told me to find her and bring her back. But no matter how far she went, I was aware of her, that thin strand, a connection that kept spooling out but never breaking.

If she'd gone south, then maybe I would have panicked more, thinking she was headed home. Instead, I'd been an emotional mess, needing to follow but wanting to give her space—a tug-of-war inside my chest.

Only focusing on manageable tasks had kept me occupied. First it was building a fire outdoors, burning all those fuckers' belongings and burying what didn't turn to ash. I'd made sure none of their electronics were traceable, taking out batteries and using a hammer to destroy anything that might send a signal, including those metal bits from their necks, only keeping pieces for my tinkering station that were untraceable.

After that, I'd done some grooming I'd been putting off for months. Even as I trimmed my hair and beard, I'd told myself I wasn't doing it for Brooke, that it was just time. Not much of me believed that lie.

The only other task that kept me occupied enough to not go after Brooke was to make this elaborate soup. Even then, as soon as she'd walked through the door, nearly all my control evaporated in a puff of steam. It was all I could do not to press her up against the wall and fuck her again.

To answer her question, I gave her one, short nod.

A brief, breathtaking smile, then it was gone as she concentrated on her soup. The space underneath my breastbone warmed. I wanted more of those smiles.

"I thought the forest was scary when I arrived," she said after taking a bite. "But now I find it calming. Are there many predators in the area?"

I shook my head.

Another smile, and my heart rate accelerated. "They probably stay away from you."

One nod.

Underneath the table, she adjusted her position, her legs rubbing together, making the scent of her heat waft toward me.

I blinked, gave myself a shake, and concentrated on eating.

"If you're worried about pregnancy, I have an IUD. It's never failed me."

A potato lodged in my throat. I coughed and slapped my hand flat down on the table at the same time, trying to expel the obstruction. It took two big coughs and a lot of water to free it. When I was relatively certain I'd be fine, I stared at the woman across from me.

Brooke continued to eat her soup calmly, like she hadn't announced her birth control choices out of the blue and I hadn't choked on a potato. I waited for her to say something else, but she continued to eat, took a drink of water, and otherwise carried on like we were having a normal conversation.

When she didn't say anything else, I scooped a bit of soup into my spoon.

"And I might be sexually active," she said in that same calm tone, but her words thick.

My spoon hovered between my lips and my bowl.

"But I'm always as safe as possible. I insist on the guy wearing a condom as well."

A growl emerged from my chest, unbidden.

She raised her eyebrows. "What I'm trying to say is that, as two consenting adults, I'm as safe as I can be. The rest would be on you since I arrived without my purse. I'm assuming there isn't a drug store nearby to buy that second layer of protection."

Her last words barely registered. The thought of my mate being with other guys made a hot rush of volatility whip through my body. I wanted to track them down and make them forget they'd ever touched her. I wanted to shred them all with my claws. I wanted blood.

When the red haze colored the edges of my vision, I took a deep breath—which was exactly the wrong thing to do. The scent of her heat filled my head, making my entire body tighten. My spoon clattered into the bowl, splashing broth onto the table.

She kept looking at me calmly.

I wanted nothing more than to give into my more primal urges, but I wouldn't do that to her again. I wouldn't allow myself to lose control where I had no idea what I was doing until the next day. I *couldn't* subject her to that.

Standing abruptly, I pushed my chair back with my knees. The scraping sound echoed against the walls. The only way to keep her safe was to remove myself from the equation.

I turned away from her dejected expression and strode to the door. Even though I had the urge to slam it, to put all this excess energy inside me *somewhere*, I closed it with a soft click.

Without a destination in mind, I strode into the forest. I didn't make it far. With every step I took, the more the pressure in my chest told me to return to the cabin. I stopped and ran a hand over my face and beard, staring at nothing, only aware of that insistent tug that told me I'd made the wrong decision.

The last of the snow had melted. I stared at a patch of moss, the yellow-orange of it picking up the highlights of a setting sun. As I stood there, the pressure inside me grew. It had only been a few minutes, but it felt like I'd left Brooke alone too long. I was supposed to take care of my mate. Could I be a bigger ass? I needed to make sure she was okay. I turned around and headed back.

Quiet blanketed everything as I picked up my pace. It didn't take long for the cabin to come into view, the lights shining from the windows. They reeled me in, along with the insistent tug in my chest.

Something told me Brooke was in distress. By the time I reached the door, I'd broken out into a full-blown panic. I stopped myself before I could barge in there a madman, took a breath, and slowly opened the door.

The scent of her heat slammed into me, stronger than

before. It filled the whole cabin, erasing the supper smells I'd created. She'd started the dishes, everything stacked by the sink, but she was hunched over, one hand braced against the table like she was in pain, the other down the front of her sweatpants.

When she lifted her head to meet my gaze, her wide eyes were full of desperation, her face flushed bright red. "I need you."

My entire body went taut with desire. *Dear God.* My willpower cracked and shattered. I couldn't fight it any longer. I'd been cruel to resist.

I was across the room before I could blink. The red haze emerged in my peripheral vision, threatening to take over, but I pushed it away. The bear could not win this time. I stood behind her and took her hips in my hands. The curve of her bottom swelled under my hands, lush. I squeezed.

Arching her back, she looked at me over her shoulder. "Please," she whispered, then pushed back against me.

My hands tightened in response. Desire spiked to my cock, making me so hard I ached. I skimmed my fingers up to her waistband and pulled them down over her ass.

I swallowed. Each inch the fabric traveled revealed more of her perfect flesh, lower and lower until she kicked the sweats aside. I fell forward on my knees, my face in line with her need. She was bare down here, waxed. Her pussy lips were swollen and puffy, juices dripping down her thighs. I should never have left her in this state.

Leaning forward, I licked the juices from the inside of her thighs. She tasted of sugar and musk, so sweet I growled as I lapped it up. Heat curled in my stomach, rising in my chest.

Her hand moved in front of her as she touched herself. I released one of her hips to replace her fingers with my own. She gasped, braced both of her hands on the counter, and leaned forward until her ass thrust toward the sky. God, she was gorgeous, her pussy ready for me. While my middle finger toyed with her clit, my thumb massaged the swollen entrance to her sex, her satiny skin exquisitely perfect.

Trying to take more, she thrust back into my hand over and over again. Her moans echoed off the walls, filling the cabin as much as her scent. Each of her reactions made my chest vibrate with a growl. I wanted to please my mate. I wanted to make her pant and moan all night.

Her movements became frantic, and I increased the tempo of my finger on her clit. She gasped for breath, fingernails scraping against the counter. "Fuck me, fuck me, fuck me," she murmured right before her body jerked with release.

Her orgasm gushed over my hand. *Holy shit.* Her body convulsed like she'd been shocked. I slid two fingers inside her. *Fuck.* She was tight, and wet, and so ready for my cock it was insane. Each of my exhales came out labored, like I'd just run 10K without stopping.

Holding her hips in my hands, I stood. I turned her, then lifted her to sit on the table. Her expression was dazed, her knees spreading, her pussy opening like a beautiful flower. I growled again and undid my jeans. She watched me, licked her lips, then threw her T-shirt over her head.

With her naked skin all aglow, I paused, my breath catching in my throat. Pert, little breasts pointed to the ceiling with dusty rose nipples, sweat glistened on her shoulders, chest, and stomach. My gaze drew to my bite at her neck. A growl of pride and ownership rumbled through me. The bear inside made me step close and lick it.

She gasped, then in the next moment, her fingers were pawing at my clothes, pulling at my fly. Quickly, I kicked off my boots and whipped off my jeans and underwear. She reached for me. My cock swelled in her hand as I thrust into her grip. I groaned at the sensation of her hot fingers around me. While she played, I leaned forward and nipped at her breast then squeezed, bending down to brush my lips against the peak. She tasted so fucking good. Her nipple pebbled hard under my tongue.

Hand on the base of my cock, she tugged my hips closer. "I need this."

Keeping my mouth on her breast, I let her guide me in. I shuddered at the feel of her around me. *Perfection.* Because she was so much smaller than me, it didn't go far. The angle wasn't right. Not when I was paying attention to her other perfect breast right now. I licked and laved, liking how her breath caught in her throat.

"More," she demanded, thrusting her hips forward. I only slid in a little farther. "Kane, please."

I lifted my head from her nipple and gave one hard thrust, pushing my way deep inside her. A growl ripped from my chest. *So good.* Better than good. Amazing.

She moaned in pleasure, her head thrown back in bliss. I withdrew and slid deeper the second time.

"Yes." The word came out a hiss.

I repeated the movement, and a low rumble began in her throat. Was she purring?

"Your cock feels so good." She met my stamina with her own, arching her back with every thrust. "Don't stop. Don't ever fucking stop."

She yanked at the hem of my shirt, and I helped whip it over my head, never slowing the pace we'd set. Her hands roved everywhere. My shoulders, my chest, my arms, my abdomen. My skin blazed. Her fingers tugged at the patch of hair, then toyed with my nipples. She bent her head and bit one.

Pleasure shot to my scalp. As she played with me, shivers zigzagged down my ribs.

With one last lick, she looked up at me. "Faster."

I grabbed her hips and pumped into her.

She leaned back, pulling her knees up to take me deeper. "Harder," she moaned

God, she was driving me to the edge of reason. Scooping my hands under her ass, I lifted her up, keeping us united. Her legs wrapped around my hips, her arms around my neck. I spun and pushed her up onto kitchen counter. Something crashed to the floor. I didn't care what.

I fucked her harder than before, giving her what she needed. Balanced like this, I was in complete control, and from the way she moaned, she liked it that way.

A flash of taking her against the wall yesterday aroused me to a level I'd never experienced before. Everything about her was over-the-top hot.

She wrapped her limbs around me. "More," she whispered into my ear, her cheek pressed against mine.

I couldn't stop. My orgasm built and built, but I tried to keep it at bay, needed to make sure my mate was satisfied first. Red hazed my vision as the bear tried to take over. I pushed the sensation to the side as I fucked her. Breaths released from her lips, frantic. Her fingernails dug into my shoulder blades. She was close. I adjusted our angle, then reached between us to thumb her clit. She gasped and moaned at the same time, that purring sound vibrating into me.

Then her entire body became taut. She squeezed me to her, core clenching, and threw her head back. A gush of her juices coated my cock. I couldn't hold on any longer. The red haze took over. I shut my eyes and poured everything I had into her.

When my vision cleared, I was still inside her, my hands braced against the counter. I'd trapped her against the cabinets. Her feet and arms circled me, holding tight. With her cheek rested against my shoulder, her fingers tickled up and down my spine, soothing.

I'd completely lost it. I'd blacked out. I didn't remember the last few minutes. God, I was so fucked up. But I hadn't hurt her. And from the purr rumbling through her, she was very satisfied.

My chest swelled. I'd pleased her, and that stroked something deep inside me I didn't know was there until yesterday.

I lifted my head, and she straightened away from me. "Are you okay?"

A breath huffed out of me at the same time as I nodded. That was what I should be asking her, not the other way around.

Keeping my arms under her thighs, I stepped away from the counter and lowered her to her feet. My cock slid out of her. She whimpered, reaching for me in the next instant.

I swept her up into my arms and carried her to the bed. For the brief trip, she leaned her face against my bare chest. I only set her on the floor for the second it took to throw back the covers, then tucked us both inside.

I stared down at her, my heart in my throat. I couldn't even describe what we'd just shared. Nothing compared. With her eyes closed in bliss, I had all the time in the world to stare at her, studying the way her eyebrows arched, her lashes fanned her cheeks, and how her lips parted slightly, pretty and plump.

It wasn't until the sound of Brooke's soft snore filled the cabin that I realized something.

We hadn't even kissed yet.

16

BROOKE

MY DREAMS WOKE ME. THEY WERE VIVID AND EERIE, AND SO VERY real they startled me awake. Images of a lake, a mountain range blanketed in forest, filled my head.

I sat up, pushed my hair out of my face, and glanced around. I was alone in bed, naked. The cabin looked the same but felt different. Kane had cleaned up the dishes and tidied up everything else.

The scent of sex permeated everything.

I flopped back, my arms spread wide. The flesh between my legs was tender and stretched. My nipples were sensitive from his love bites and the abrasive stroke of his beard. When I'd woken up in the middle of the night, reaching for Kane, I'd asked him to fuck me senseless, and he'd obliged. And every time I'd woken up with my body throbbing for more, he'd gone down on me until I came, then fucked me until I came again. I couldn't remember having so many orgasms in one night. He'd played with me, teased me, licked me, made me beg for more. He rode me hard, then reversed our positions so I was on top and controlled the pace. Was it possible for a clit to get tired? He'd satisfied me enough that my skin no longer itched and my tongue wasn't overly swollen. My need was still there, but manageable.

The sun had risen steadily throughout our last interlude. I'd watched his face, his expressions, as he gave what me what I needed, studied his look of bliss as he came inside me.

The way he lost himself that first time on the kitchen counter hadn't happened again. I couldn't explain it. It was like he was there one moment and gone the next. I'd said his name. I'd shook him. He'd been frozen for a time, his eyes glazed like he'd been in another place. It had been the same look he'd given me after he'd shifted. Had his animal taken over again? The thought disturbed me on a base level. I had no similar experience to relate to it. My animal and I were the same. We were *shifter*.

I hadn't known what to do except hold him and stroke his back. Only a few minutes passed, but it had scared me. I'd tried not to show it.

A scraping noise made me sit up again. Kane might not be in the cabin, but he was near. I could feel it in my chest. The noise came from the other side of the wall, like someone scratched it.

Swinging my legs over the bed, I rose to my feet. My inner thighs were sensitive, rubbed raw from his beard. After a brief hesitation, I opened the top drawer of his dresser and found a bunch of shirts folded and stacked neatly inside. I grabbed one of the plaid button-up ones and put it on. I didn't bother with anything else since it went all the way to my knees. I adjusted the collar, then paused when my finger brushed over a slight bump in my neck.

What the? I opened the shirt, trying to see my collar bone. The bite marks Kane had given me were still there, healed, but scar tissue remained. They should have disappeared when I shifted, just like the rest of the wounds on my body. Instead, they remained.

Why? What was happening? Nervous energy rolled through my stomach. I pressed my palm against the bumps, covering them. My instincts reared up, liking the marks. *What is going on?* I needed to ask Kane, to see if he knew why they hadn't disappeared.

That scratching sound again. This time it made me jump. What was he doing?

I finished buttoning up the shirt, rolled up the sleeves so I could use my hands, and opened the door.

The air outside was crisp and cool, but slightly warmer than the day before. With me being in heat, the chill felt nice, even with the goosebumps forming on my legs. I shut the door behind me and walked to the side of the cabin where I'd heard the noises.

I stopped when I caught sight of Kane. He wasn't wearing a shirt, only his jeans and work boots. A toolbox sat on the ground by his feet, surrounded by a bunch of other stuff: a bright blue tarp, some pipes, and a two-by-four. He was drawing lines on the outside wall of the cabin with a pencil and a level, hence the scratching noise.

His jeans rode low on his hips, exposing the dimples in his lower back. My heart rate accelerated. God, he was a good-looking guy. Despite the tenderness between my legs, I was ready for more. A purr started in my throat, and I tried to smother it. My core began to pulse.

He turned, caught sight of me, and smiled.

Whatever sanity I'd been trying to hold on to, whatever I'd come out here to ask him, flew right out of my head.

Had he ever smiled at me before? It had some sort of magic in it, made me walk straight to him. I ignored the rocks, and moss, and pine needles that pricked my bare feet. His expression became alert as I neared, his smile faltering.

My breaths came out short and ragged. I needed him. As soon as I was close enough, my hands were up his chest, feeling the sweat on him, then back down, fumbling with the top button of his jeans. It came free. He dropped his tools. When I nudged him backward, he didn't resist, his own breaths coming out fast now too.

His ass hit the big rock beside the wood chopping rock. Keeping his gaze, I undid his zipper and peeled down the fabric of his jeans and underwear enough for his cock to spring free. With it thick and hot in my hand, I bent forward and gave it a lick.

He hissed out a breath mixed with a growl.

Liking the sound, I did it again. His hands delved into my hair as I worked him up and down. I took him deep in my mouth. His growl grew louder. It vibrated through me, making moisture gather between my legs. His pleasure was my pleasure.

I stroked him, paying attention to his sensitive head. God, I loved the taste of him. Salt and musk. I inhaled deep, then took him as far as he'd go.

A savage growl ripped through his chest, and he jerked me away from him, his expression wild. I'd been about to make him come. Wouldn't he like that?

He tugged me upward. Heart racing, I climbed on top of him until his cock pressed against where I needed him the most. Holding him steady, I slid down onto him, groaning at how good it felt. He growled, his hands groping beneath my shirt, running up and down my spine, then moving around to fondle my sensitive breasts.

Watching the carnal expressions cross his face, I rode him slow and steady. My knees scraped against the rough surface of the rock beside his hips. His fingers dug into the flesh of my bottom, guiding me up and down on his cock. I leaned back, allowing him to hold my weight. Sparks shot off in my head.

"Right there," I murmured, my voice so rough I didn't recognize it.

He kept me in the perfect spot. The pressure built inside me at lightning speed. He hadn't even touched my clit and my release rocketed through me like liquid fire. Kane growled and picked up the pace, slamming into me over and over until his body tightened with his own orgasm.

I shook. Every little movement from him made a cascade of tremors ricochet through me. I collapsed forward and took a deep breath. Kane was doing things to me I didn't understand. Wonderful, delicious new things, but confusing, nonetheless.

My head resting on his shoulder, I finally remembered what I'd come outside to ask him.

I'm so fucked.

How was I supposed to have a conversation about these marks on my neck when I couldn't keep my hands off him? I'd had a dozen orgasms last night and was greedy for more. This had to be the worst—or the best?—heat I could remember having. I couldn't get enough of Kane.

His hands ran up and down my spine under my shirt, over my ass, and up and down my ribs. Our breathing leveled out. I lifted my head, met his gaze, and climbed off him. I did my best to straighten my shirt and hair while he pulled up his underwear and zipped up his jeans. My knees stung from being rubbed against the rock. A shift would fix that.

Kane ran a hand over his hair, making it more mussed than it already was. He looked down, his expression dazed, like he couldn't exactly remember what he'd been doing before I'd distracted him.

I cleared my throat and gestured to the pile of tools. "What are you making?"

His expression brightened. He flashed me another smile and waggled his eyebrows before striding back to the mess. *Adorable.* I could almost hear him say *it's a surprise* in my head.

My heart rate sped up again. *Double fucked.*

Whatever he was doing, it took his full attention. I watched him for a while, then took a walk to the dock to sit on its end. Deep in thought, my hand switched between touching the marks on my neck and idly chipping away at what remained of my nail polish. Water splashed on the underside of the boat and the loons called from the other side of the lake.

I wasn't the kind of person who kept a boyfriend. I wasn't the one walking in the mall hand-in-hand with my lover, or the one kissing my partner before they headed off to work. No, all my relationships were brief. I liked my solitary life. I got to do what I wanted when I wanted. I'd moved out at eighteen for that very reason, didn't want to live by anyone else's rules.

Rubbing my face, I stared at the rotor sticking out of the lake, only a foot of it visible above the water line now. A shiver rippled through me, and I hugged my arms around my knees. I'd been so close to being recaptured. If it hadn't been for Kane, I wouldn't have been able to stop it.

A small, niggling voice said that if I'd gone with those guys, then I would have been with my sister. But I understood that was my guilt talking. If I'd been taken, then we'd both be captured, and I wouldn't be able to help Sabrina escape. *A fat lot of good you're doing with that right now.* Okay, so having sex with Kane over and over again wasn't helpful, but I wouldn't be able to search for her until that plane came next week anyway.

The loons across the lake hooted, then took off in a flurry of splashes. I watched where they disappeared over the tree line until the tug in my chest told me to return to the cabin. When I rounded the back, Kane was still working on his project, lengths of pipe now fastened to the logs of the outer wall.

"Should I make some sandwiches?" It had to be past noon.

He gave me a thumbs up without looking at me.

Huffing out a breath, I went inside. I found canned salmon and bread in the cupboard along with carrots and potatoes. While I set about making sandwiches and chopping carrot sticks, Kane came inside and put a big pot of water on the stove. He built the fire, then left again.

Whatever was he up to? More laundry? I looked at the bed. The sheets were rumpled and well-used from the night before.

Of course, they should be changed. I could do the laundry this time. I'd watched how he'd done it the other day.

With a plate in each hand, I went outside. Kane wiped his forehead with his arm, a pencil gripped between his teeth.

My body twitched. *No.* I wasn't going to have sex with him again until we could have a discussion about the marks on my neck.

"Here's your sandwich." I extended the plate to him.

He stepped closer to take it with a 'thank you' nod. His distinctive scent wafted toward me right before he took a big bite. I watched how his throat moved up and down and needed to press my thighs together to stop from moving closer.

Without finishing the whole sandwich, he set the plate aside and got back to work. Staring at him a moment, I took a bite of my own. He attached another pipe to the wall, this one sticking out two feet. I liked watching him move. His muscles rippled, his arms bulged. He was strong in a bulky way, but not overly so. A mountain man without mountains. *A lake man.*

Snorting at my own thought, I pulled the one chair to the end of the porch so I could watch him while I finished my sandwich.

The mountain image wouldn't leave me. It was one of the things I'd dreamed about last night, distinct mountain ranges. A ridge with three peaks and a lake that glowed gold in the sunlight. The image was so clear in my mind, I could have sworn I knew it from memory. Except, I'd never been to a place like that.

And Kane was a grizzly bear. This place, as rugged and beautiful as it was, didn't seem like his natural habitat since there weren't any mountains. Just like this wasn't my natural habitat. I was an American Bobcat, born and raised in the States.

I finished my bite, then asked, "Did you come from the mountains?"

He stiffened, then straightened, slowly turning toward me. He raised his eyebrows in question but kept his expression blank.

"Grizzlies come from the mountains, don't they?"

He nodded once, then turned back to his task. I wasn't sure if he was admitting to coming from the mountains or if he was agreeing with me that grizzlies did indeed come from there. Either way, I took the hint. He didn't want to talk about it.

After a minute, he moved around the house, out of sight. I didn't become worried that he was going far. I could feel him.

It was so strange, this tug in my chest. No previous experience with anyone compared to it. How was it that we were so connected when we'd only known each other a short time?

When he returned, he held a ladder. It probably came from the shed at the back of the cabin. He leaned it against the wall and climbed up to secure a hook beneath the eave. Then he climbed down, grabbed a chain, climbed up and fed it through the hook.

I still didn't understand what he was up to.

He tested the chain, secured it to another hook lower down, one above a little wood platform he'd attached to one of the logs. It wasn't until he attached the chain to an empty pot that I started getting a niggling of an idea. By the time he was hanging the tarp off the pipes, I understood. My lips parted in wonder.

A shower. He was making me a shower.

My breastbone pinged pleasantly. He'd spent the morning making this for me. The idea of a shower right now made me hyper-aware of how badly I needed one. My hair was a mess. I hadn't used deodorant in days. I'd been fucked senseless all night. Yeah, I really needed a shower.

I couldn't remember receiving a better gift.

Once the tarp was hung, making a square little private box, he stepped back with a *voilà* movement.

I clapped, the sound sharp in the quiet around us. "It's fantastic!" Jumping to my feet, I moved toward him, shielding my eyes from the sun with my hand. "When do I get to try it out?" I felt all hot and sticky and gross all at once. A shower would be heaven right now.

He smiled, his eyes crinkling, and I got the distinct impression he was amused by my eagerness. It didn't bother me one bit. He could laugh at me all he wanted as long as I got to have a hot water flowing over my body soon.

When he unhooked the empty pot and nodded once, I squealed. "I'm going to find clean clothes. And that soap you gave me." He followed me inside, grabbing the pot off the stove before leaving again.

I returned outside with a clean T-shirt, a pair of sweats, soap, and a towel clutched to my chest. The steaming pot of water sat on the ground beside the tarp. He gestured to it for me to check the temperature.

"Yeah, it's okay," I said after testing it with my fingers.

He hefted it up on the shelf. A little ledge kept it in place. He looped the chain through the pot handle, then to the back of the shelf. When he pulled on the other end of the chain, the pot tipped forward allowing water to trickle out depending on how fast and hard he pulled.

"Don't waste it," I said, putting a hand on his arm. "That pot isn't that big." I was used to long showers. Now I wouldn't take them for granted ever again.

He'd set a stool beside the tarp, and I placed my bundle on it. Without hesitating, I whipped the plaid shirt over my head, threw it over the top of the stall, and stepped inside, ready to clean myself from top to bottom.

17

KANE

Bare skin, her round ass, her intoxicating scent... I froze, ready to grab Brooke and pull her to me. The bright blue of the tarp obstructed my view in the next instant. My fingers twitched, wanting to rip it aside.

The first splash of water out of the pot was followed by a satisfied moan. It hit me right in the groin. I couldn't stand there and listen to her make those sorts of noises and not join her.

Forcing myself to turn away, I walked toward the lake, stripping off my jeans before I stepped onto the dock. Next came my underwear. I dove into the ice-cold water, willing it to cool my sex drive.

I'd never been so horny or needy for a woman in my life, not even as a pimply teen with too many raging hormones. All I wanted to do was bury myself inside her and stay there all day and night. That, and make her happy. The look of joy on her face when she'd realized I'd made her a shower—I wouldn't trade the feeling for anything.

The water woke me up but didn't stymie my desire. I did a lap to the rotor blade and back, then pulled myself up onto the dock.

Lying on my back, the hard wood pressed into my spine and ass, and the sun dried me from above.

She'd asked where I'd come from. I knew it was rude to shut down her questions like that, but I didn't like thinking too much about Goldenlach Ridge. My hometown held the memories of everything I'd escaped from, each horrible event that had happened because of me. I had blood on my hands, and it kept me up most nights.

I'd moved out here to be alone, to keep others safe from me and the rabid animal that took over my body. I'd studied meditation, breathing exercises, Eastern philosophies, and yoga to contain the beast. A few days ago, I would have said I had everything under control. A few days ago, I might have even been so bold to say I could take another chance at living in civilization.

Then she landed on my doorstep and changed everything.

My control hung on by a thread. Especially when she looked at me with hungry eyes or flashed her ass at me. She'd been going around all day wearing only my shirt and nothing else. Every time she'd entered my line of sight, I'd wanted to take her or reach under that shirt and give her pleasure. The shower took longer to construct than it should have because I'd been distracted by her watchful eyes.

Thinking about it now wasn't helping any. I was becoming hard even though my limbs were chilled from the cold water. Exercise usually focused me. I'd chop some wood. Satisfied with that course of action, I hopped up, found my underwear and jeans at the top of the dock, and pulled them on.

Rounding the back of the cabin, a splash of water made me pause mid-step. She didn't moan this time, so at least that was something. I continued on to the chopping stump. Once I set a new log on the stump, I grabbed my ax.

Thwack. It split in two. I took the one piece and chopped it in half. I continued to chop wood until I created a small pile of adequate-sized logs. I placed another large log on the stump.

Thwack. Two more laid in pieces around my feet before I realized the water in the shower wasn't splashing anymore. I stiffened, a tingling awareness traveling up my spine.

A light thread of her scent curled its way to me on the breeze. I turned. Part of the tarp was open. It hadn't been like that before. Brooke was watching me, all wet and glistening. One hand was on her breast, the other between her legs. Her lips were parted, her eyes heated.

My ax clattered to the ground. I stalked toward her.

Her movements stilled. I swiped the tarp aside in a crackle of plastic. Her hair hung over one shoulder, exposing the bite I'd given her. A possessive growl tore from my chest.

She took a step back until the cabin's wall pressed against her spine and she had no other place to go. Soap suds clung to her shoulders and breasts. I grabbed her hand, the one between her legs, and lifted it to my face. It smelled like heat and her distinctive scent. With long strokes of my tongue, I licked her fingers clean.

Her breath hitched in her throat, her eyelids lowering with desire. That mesmerizing purr began low in her throat, then erupted through her body.

I'd unbuttoned my jeans to free my cock and lifted her up against cabin wall before either of us could take another breath. A combined groan emerged from our chests as I entered her. I savored the sensation of sliding deep within her warm body, dragged it out into one slow and smooth movement. Legs wrapped around my hips, she sheathed me perfectly, taking all of my length.

My arms held her close. It was like a homecoming, like sweetness and contentment entwined together. I pressed my face into her temple, inhaling deep. She smelled of soap and woman and heat.

As I moved within her, the bear inside me surfaced. Dropping my head, I licked the marks I'd already given her. Her breath caught. The pulse at her throat throbbed beneath my tongue.

I fucked her slow. She moaned, her fingernails digging into my shoulders, her teeth scraping my collarbone.

"Why do I want to bite you?" Her fingers dug into my hair on a gasp. "Why do I want you to keep biting me?"

The bear inside me took her questions as acceptance and permission. My jaw clamped on the sensitive flesh of her shoulder, inside the arched marks I'd already given her, then I increased my pace.

She turned her head enough to flick her tongue over the shell of my ear. My bite tightened.

"Oh, fuck." It was like the words were ripped from her chest. "Why does this feel so good?"

My growl echoed her sentiment. A frenzy building inside me, I slammed into her again and again. Her body clenched around me. Bracing her securely against the wall, I freed my one hand to slide between our bodies and find her clit. I needed to satisfy my mate as much as possible. The little nub was swollen and begging for my touch.

She ground into me. "Right there. Don't stop."

I didn't think I could stop to save my life.

And I couldn't let go of her neck. Not when I was pumping inside her, and she'd told me she wanted to bite me too, and little tremors of pleasure wracked through her hot little body. I recognized the feeling inside me as ownership, possessive.

Mine.

"Yes," she moaned in my ear right before she came.

The way her body tightened around me forced me over the edge. Three more frantic thrusts and I came inside her. I kept hold of her neck as my body shuddered on and on. I'd never come so hard in my life. It felt like I gave her everything. *Everything.*

Slowly, I returned to myself. I relaxed my jaw and let go of the flesh at her shoulder. The impression I'd left behind was deep, seared into her skin. It arched inside the first bite I'd given her, semicircles within semicircles.

Was she okay? Did these marks cause her pain? I pressed my tongue flat against the wounds, then kissed them. Another purr vibrated through her chest. The sound went right to my cock. She wouldn't be purring if she was angry or hurt. When I gave her one more thrust, she gasped.

If I didn't let her go, we'd be here for the remainder of the day. I stepped back from the wall. As we separated on a groan, her legs slid to the ground. Then she straightened and winced.

My entire body went on alert. I yanked up my jeans and tugged her away from the wall. A six-inch swath of red and raw skin had been scraped on her lower back by the logs.

I *had* hurt her. Angry at myself for not taking more care, I clenched my fists.

"It's okay," she said, putting a comforting hand on my arm. "It's a good kind of hurt. A shift will take care of it." To prove her point, she backed away, smoothly shifted into her bobcat form, and did a lap around the cabin. The ease with which she shifted made me envious.

Conflicted, I stood there a long moment, then blinked. It was like she'd known what I was feeling.

18

BROOKE

I couldn't decide if I was trapped in a dream or if it was real life.

My feet led me through the schoolyard. Not my school, someone else's. But I knew the school, so how did that make sense?

Kids played. Birds chirped. It was recess. Distinctive groups formed around me. Humans, cougars, bears, and other forest shifters. Everyone looked human, but I knew some weren't by their scents. They watched me. This was my first week at Goldenlach Ridge Elementary, grade seven, and I'd been labeled an outsider. We'd moved here after my grandfather was put down, to get away from the stares and speculation of those of my old town.

Wait. What? I never had a grandfather who'd been put down.

No, he had been. He'd gone full-blown rabid just like my father who now lived permanently as a bear. A genetic trait. Sometimes my mother would look at me, worry on her face before she erased it. She didn't look at Sabrina that way, only me.

No, my sister's name was Emily. Wasn't it?

Noises, someone fighting, drew my attention. A group of boys stood in a loose circle, two deep. I couldn't really see who was in the middle. A particularly loud *ooh* made me move closer. It took me a few seconds to wedge my way through the crowd far enough to see what was going on. Then I froze.

It wasn't two boys brawling, getting rid of aggression in a fair fight. It was a bigger boy, and he held down his prey by her wrists. *Her.* It was a girl, a human. Way smaller than him, maybe like ten years old. Her bright red hair frizzed out in every direction. She had blood on her face. The boy holding her down, a dickhead named Tom, another grizzly, straddled her.

My vision hazed red. I roared and pushed through the crowd, grabbed Tom by his nape and threw him. He hit three guys in the toss, landing on his ass. At first, anger colored his expression, but then he saw me. Blood covered his knuckles. Behind me, the girl whimpered. The red haze darkened. My vision narrowed down to nothing more than the sniveling face of that prick.

"She hit me first—"

He didn't get a chance to finish the sentence because my fist connected with his eye. Then I was on him, choking the life out of him, then punching. I couldn't stop. I didn't want to stop.

The things around me didn't exist, only my fists hitting his face. Only my rage existed.

There were adults there now. Some were shouting at me. The words "police" and "parents" and "expelled" were thrown around. I didn't care. All I wanted to do was finish what I started—to make sure Tom never hurt anyone again.

The world spun around me until it slowed in a blur of yellow striped wallpaper. Our kitchen smelled the same as always: the fabric softener coming through from the laundry room, bread cooking in the toaster, the peanut butter jar left open on the table. As Mom busied herself with the dishes from last night, I took a bite of the corner of my toast while Sabrina spread jam on hers.

"Do we have a dad?" I asked after I finished my bite.

Mom froze at the sink. Sabrina stared at me, her eyes bulging.

Since no one answered, I went on. "I know you said once we did, but I've never met him, so maybe you were trying to be nice. Sue called me a bastard. I don't even know what that is, but it didn't sound very good, so I pushed her and called her a liar."

My mother partially turned toward me, a plate in her hand. "You don't need a dad, you have me."

"I know that." Of course I did. She was a good mom, didn't yell like Sue's mom, didn't make us do a hundred chores on the weekend like Davy's dad. "But we have an awful lot of uncles, and we only see them once or twice before they're gone. There was Uncle Reggie and Uncle Terrence, and Uncle Peter, and Uncle—"

"That's enough." Mom's voice bit out fast and harsh, unlike her. My whole body stilled, becoming alert. Sabrina's face had gone white. Then she was moving, impossibly changing into a tree, one of many as I walked beside Landon on the well-beaten path through the forest. The entire setting had changed, as had the people with me.

"If you lose it when you shift," Landon said, his tone pointedly calm, "then just don't shift, man. I don't. It's uncivilized."

His voice cut through the quiet of the forest around us. We walked along the creek, picking up stones as we went, seeing if we could skip them to the other side. The guy wore loafers instead of runners like everyone else our age. It always made me shake my head. When we'd met the first week I'd moved to Goldenlach Ridge, I'd thought he was a preppy asshole. He'd mellowed on me since.

We slowed our pace when a boy a little older than us jumped in our path. A cougar shifter I recognized, in high school this year. He usually liked to hang out with his own kind.

He hunkered down in a defensive stance. "Get out of here. My territory."

"Says who?" I asked, tipping my head to the side. Did he think he could take on two bears by himself?

That was the weird part about this town, the divisions in it.

No one talked about it, but they were there. Cougars kept to themselves, so did bears.

A different boy ran across the rocks in the creek, splashing up a storm. We all tensed, wondering what he was doing. Would he attack? When he drew close enough, he kicked a big splash in our direction, mostly drenching the cougar shifter who sputtered, then turned and ran.

I tipped my head at this newcomer, baffled. I recognized him from school, a loner younger than us. The other cougars in town didn't seem to like him. He stood there like he knew us, his hands on his hips, then jerked his chin at where the other shifter had disappeared.

"He hates water," the boy said, spitting to the side.

I scratched my head. "Thanks for the assist, I guess."

"Once he dries off, won't he come back here and kick your ass?" Landon asked in his droll tone.

"Probably." The boy shrugged. "I'm used to it."

I raised my eyebrows at Landon, then the boy. "What's your name?"

"Walker." He spit again. "They all hate me, so it doesn't matter anyway."

"Why do they hate you?" Landon asked, genuine curiosity in his tone.

"Because I called them assholes."

The kid wasn't wrong. Cougars did tend to come with a healthy dose of asshole in them.

With a shrug, Landon and I continued the way we were headed. Walker kept following us. We didn't tell him to leave. Our pace picked up until I was running.

I ran so fast the wind whistled through my whiskers. I kept away from people and their campsites, heading directly into the forest. We always picked national parks for our camping expeditions because hunting wasn't allowed. I wasn't worried about getting shot by an overzealous hunter.

I spring-boarded off the ground in great leaps and bounds, pushing myself as fast I could go with all the trees around. I weaved in and out of the trunks. A rabbit bounced out of my way, then a squirrel. I chased it for a while, nipping at its heels until it escaped up a tree.

Passing it by, I focused on a pine with low lying branches, and bounded toward it. The next instant, I clung to the rough bark and climbed as high as I could. The crows at the top barked their displeasure. I licked my lips, letting them know what I thought about their noise. They squawked again and flew away.

It was a long while later that I slunk back toward our camp-site. I'd gone far, but my scent led me back to my family. I watched for a moment as they readied their hot dog sticks over the fire. My sister and mom looked good together, both with dark hair, unlike my blonde. They were laughing and talking. The only time my mom and I were like that was when we gabbed about shoes and boys and makeup and shopping.

The trees around me each turned into a student, large groups of them walking ahead of me from the high school to the mall. The regular, every day, lunch hour migration. Being home-schooled, I could go to the mall anytime I wanted as long as I finished my homework.

My senses went on alert when I saw Emily in one of the groups. I searched through, scrutinizing the people my sister hung out with. Not the best group. Not the worst either.

I stopped dead when she ran toward someone and jumped on them, straddling his hips. An icy sensation trickled down my spine when I realized who it was. Tom. The guy I'd beaten the shit out of five years ago. The guy that got me expelled from school when *he* was the one who'd started it—I'd just ended it. There was no way he was dating my fifteen-year-old sister for any other reason than to fuck with me. I ran toward them before I knew what I was doing.

The people around them saw me coming before either Tom

or Emily. A sudden hush fell around them. Then Tom turned, his grin changing into one of satisfaction.

Oh, yeah. He'd only dated Emily to fuck with me.

I jerked my head toward the house. "Let's go," I said under my breath. "This fucker is messing with you."

Her eyes shot to Tom then back to me, her brow pinching, wariness in her expression. I thought she was about to come with me when Tom piped up from behind her. "She likes it when I mess with her, Kane. Just ask her for some details."

I knew what he was doing. He wanted a fight. I wasn't going to give it to him this time. Keeping my sister's gaze, I jerked my head toward the house again.

When she took a step toward me, Tom lost his shit. His tackle knocked me off balance, and we tumbled.

The red haze enveloped my vision. I couldn't stop the growl that came from my throat or the way I turned toward him once I regained my feet. The back of my hand hit his jaw. A collective gasp resounded around us.

A cocky grin spread across his face as he wiped off the blood at the corner of his mouth with his thumb. "Let's do this," he growled, then lunged.

The more we fought, the deeper we went into the woods, away from human eyes. Emily kept yelling at us to stop.

Partially shifted now, Tom swiped, scratching claw marks into my back. The pain came swiftly, and I gave in to the rage. As soon as I shifted, everything turned red. Roars and movement, that was all I could remember until much later. I'd been winning, nearly ripped his arm off, when Tom's friends joined the fray. I tore into them mindlessly. I knew nothing but blood and flesh in my mouth, nothing left inside me but rage.

Through the red haze, through my tunnel vision, I saw Emily standing close by. The expression she wore stopped me. She was scared, horrified, of me, her brown eyes pleading for me to stop. I hesitated. What the hell was I doing?

That one-second hesitation almost meant my death. Bloody and enraged, Tom went for my throat. I felt his teeth rip through me before I could fend off the attack. *This is bad.* The next instant, I was down, incapacitated. If he'd wanted to go for the kill, he could have. The world stopped around me.

My body returned to human form, but my throat kept bleeding. A shift couldn't heal what didn't exist anymore. Emily was there, fear in her eyes, but this time it was *for* me, not of me. She pressed her hands against the wound, hers on top of mine. Sirens. I heard them wailing in the distance.

I tried to tell Emily it was going to be okay, but all that came out was a gurgling noise. I was so fucked. I knew it even as death crept toward me, the red haze receding to submerge me into black.

I sobbed, heartache threatening to suffocate me.

"What's wrong?" Mom asked, leading me to the couch in the living room, a comforting hand rubbing up and down my spine.

The whole story came out in between tortured sobs. Dating Troy for the last few weeks, finding him today making out with one of the cheerleaders behind the bleachers. How he'd just smiled when I'd confronted him. How I wanted to plot his murder.

"Oh, honey. Don't do that."

For a moment, I thought Mom was talking about the murder, but then she went on. "We don't let a guy hurt us like this. We don't give them our heart, because if we do, they're guaranteed to break it. We don't commit. We have a few nights of fun, then we move on. Men are bound to betray us. It's in their nature."

The words didn't comfort. My chest hurt so much, maybe my mom was right. If I hadn't thought Troy would be my boyfriend forever, then I wouldn't be suffering right now.

My mom's face changed, her hair shortening into a close-cropped style that Landon preferred. I should probably get a haircut. Emily had told me the shaggy look was "out."

Landon, Walker, and I walked along the rough shoreline of the lake, heading to higher terrain. Walker was a senior now and talked about joining the army. We told him not to, but with his family situation, he felt like it was his only choice.

We picked our way through the trees and brush. This path wasn't one of the main ones meant for humans, but it was known by shifters. The scent of shifter was everywhere, mostly bear but some deer, fox, and lynx as well. We trekked deeper into the forest. Landon had taken the last couple years off from school to work but had been accepted into the commerce program at the University of British Columbia in Vancouver. He'd be moving away soon. I tried not to feel defeated by the fact. He'd suggested I join him, but living in a big city held no appeal.

The sound of a woman's scream ripped through the forest. We all stopped, alert, and listened.

Another scream, this one cut short. We ran toward the sound. This offshoot of the trail was narrow, and the branches from the trees snatched at us.

No sounds followed that last one, and we stopped, listening. The faint sound of movement came at us from the other side of the hill. We ran upward, wading through the bushes until we broke over the crest. The sight before us had my thoughts stuttering to a stop, my mind trying to process the scene.

A woman, a human, was being dragged, unconscious, deeper into the forest by a bear shifter. I recognized him in an instant. Tom. Another human, a male, lay mauled and dead on the ground, his eyes unseeing, his throat ripped out.

"Jesus," Landon breathed, taking a step back.

Red filled my vision. There'd been reports of bear attacks in the area, hikers going missing. Reports that kept campers on alert and made the national and provincial parks put out warnings to those using tents.

Tom let go of the woman's body, snarled, then roared at me. My body shifted before I could think not to. The red haze, the beast, took over. I charged, Walker in his cougar form right beside me. I shouldered him out of the way to attack. *My kill. My kill. My kill.*

When the haze cleared, I was already back in my human form. Landon's face filled my vision, and I heard his voice. I took a step back, then another. The scent of blood filled my nostrils.

A death scene lay before me, violent and bloody. Tom was dead, but so was the woman. I wasn't sure if she'd been alive when I'd attacked Tom, but she was definitely dead now. Had our fight trampled her prone form? Regret stabbed me. I should have made sure she was out of the way before I attacked.

I wanted to ask if I'd done it. Beside Landon, Walker stared at me with a hand to his head and resentment in his eyes. I had a vague memory of pushing him into a tree to keep him out of the way. Maybe if I hadn't done that, he would have been able to help the woman. Another stab of regret.

"You need to get out of here," Landon said to me, his eyes holding the severity of the situation.

I understood. Two dead humans and a dead bear shifter. If I was found like this, the authorities wouldn't listen to reason, not with my history. Tom's dad was the fucking mayor now. The shifter side of City Council would petition to have me put down. And if that happened, there wasn't anything anyone could do about it. I'd have a death warrant hanging over my head. Anyone could take me out by any means necessary. I'd killed, and they'd have me dead as compensation.

Landon's face turned hard, harder than I'd ever seen it. "Go."

I ran. Right into the bedroom of my apartment. A different time. A different place.

"You're making a mistake."

Landon's words held no sway over me as I continued to pack, throwing every bit of clothing I owned into a suitcase and a duffel bag. Whatever didn't fit, I'd donate. I wasn't coming back here. A kid who'd just moved out of his parents' place had purchased all my furniture and would be here to pick it up tomorrow. That's it. I'd tried to live a simple life like my two friends had suggested, but I'd failed. I was done.

I hadn't even lasted a year. White Rock was a little city south of Vancouver, but it still held too many people, too many ways for me to hurt others. Every day I battled with myself. Every day some minor thing sparked the anger of the beast inside me, the red haze flaring to the surface. I needed to get out, away from everyone.

And no matter what Landon said, he wouldn't change my mind.

Movement behind my cousin made me lift my head. Walker stood there, his scowl as angry as always. His leave from the army only gave him a week off. "So you're just going to give up?" he asked, his tone bitter. "Cut everyone off? Make it so no one can find you? It's selfish, Kane."

I was doing it for them. I was leaving to keep everyone safe. Who was to say they wouldn't be the ones I hurt next? I tried to live in another town, tried city life, none of it fit. The red haze took over when I didn't want it to. I had to leave.

To get him to back off, I signed, *What do you care? You're leaving next week.*

His face became a stony mask. "That doesn't mean I'm giving up on life." He turned before I could reply. The door to my apartment slammed a few seconds later.

Gripping the edge of my dresser, I bent my head and willed the red haze to retreat. *This* is why I needed to leave. If one of my best friends could tempt the beast into revealing itself, then how was the rest of the world supposed to fair? I needed to get out of grizzly territory, to find a place where no one could find me.

I ignored Landon's watchful gaze as I packed the remainder of my belongings. The lights above me strobed blue and red to the beat of the music. I danced, throwing my hand in the air with wild abandon.

I'd maybe drank a little too much, but I didn't care. I was having fun. That's what life was about. Having fun.

A boy on the edge of the dance floor watched me with intent eyes. I faced him fully and danced closer, my eyes on him and no one else.

Then I sat at my desk, rubbing my hands over my eyes and beard. I was so close to figuring it out, but not close enough. How could I stop a shifter from shifting? Was it even possible? This could be a complete waste of time. I threw my pencil on the desk and walked away, down the dock and toward the plane that buzzed loud as it hit the water. Excitement came over me. This delivery of supplies would be different than the others.

John Clark opened the door of the float plane and jumped out onto the dock. We shook hands, and he tied off the boat before opening up the rear door. Boxes of supplies came out, but there was only one I was looking for. The parcel with my name on it and the return address from Vancouver was the last item he took out from the plane.

"This what you're wanting?"

I nodded and tried not to notice that my hands shook a little when I grabbed it. John helped me take the boxes of supplies up to the cabin, then he was off, back to town where normal people lived.

The sound of the plane taking off echoed off the trees as I tore into the package from Landon. A circlet of metal lay in a layer of foam. "Prototype" read the little sticky note attached.

I picked it up, the metal cold in my hand. My stomach dropped into my feet. *The fucker.* He'd made it too small for me to wear. *Son of a bitch.* He knew I'd try it, and he'd made it impossible. The next time I saw Landon, *if* I ever saw him again, I'd slug him for this. I opened the bottom drawer of the desk and dropped it inside.

Boom. Boom. Boom. Boom. The music beat low in my stomach.

His hands were all over me. I loved it. He was going to make me feel so good when we finally got alone.

Who the hell was I kidding? He could make me feel good right now. My skirt hitched up further on my ass as he ground against me. Too soon, my mind jumped.

Where the hell did she come from?

About an hour ago, my perimeter alarms signaled something had crossed onto my land. I thought it might be a black bear even though they'd stayed well away from me since I'd moved in five years ago. I'd been prepared to scare it off with a warning shot.

Not in a million years would I have guessed I'd find a woman.

She shifted in front of me, smooth skin sprouting fur, her form becoming a diminutive version of her human body. A bobcat appeared, silver-gray fur striped with black. *Beautiful.*

Her tawny yellow eyes stared at me a moment, blinked, then she leaped away in one graceful stride.

As soon as she flew through the door, I tightened my hand hold on the chair. Every part of me shouted to give chase, to not let her escape.

What if she didn't come back? What if she kept running south until she found civilization? It would take days, but as a bobcat, she could survive.

The back of the chair cracked beneath my grasp.

My mate was leaving me, and it felt like my heart had been torn from my chest, a ragged hole in its place. My legs collapsed. Sinking to the floor, I held my head in my hands, trying to will the red haze that colored the edges of my vision to disappear.

I could still feel her, our connection. She was heading east. She wasn't running away, she was just...running. I took a deep breath, the haze ebbing away.

When I got to my feet, my eyes landed on the collar on the table. I picked it up, feeling the weight of it in my hand, and walked to my desk. I slid the bottom drawer open and dropped it inside beside the other one. *Thunk.*

19

BROOKE

THUNK.

I woke up with a start, my heart pounding. Sitting up, I pressed a hand to my chest, taking deep breaths. Darkness bathed the cabin. I didn't know what time it was, but it had to be late. *Or early.* No sunrise glow shone through the windows.

I remembered everything I'd dreamed with startling clarity. My own memories mixed with someone else's. *Kane's.* How much of it was true? Had I dreamed about his real life?

After my shower yesterday, Kane had fed me a supper of left-over soup and bread. I'd told myself not to have sex with him again, but by the time the dishes were washed, that promise went right out the window. He lay beside me now, warm, both of us naked. His snore rumbled through his chest, making my ribs vibrate.

Instead of relaxing into the pleasant sensation, I rubbed a hand over my face. Everything I'd experienced in my dreams had been *so real*. I'd felt every emotion. My hand moved to my throat, almost believing I'd find it scarred. I'd suffered every pain, every horror. How had he survived?

There was only one way to know if it was all true. I reached over and turned on the lamp atop the dresser. Quickly, I swung my legs over the edge of the bed and moved to the desk. The sounds of Kane waking up and rolling over rustled behind me. Taking a deep breath first, I leaned over and opened the bottom drawer.

Two collars lay there, mine and one a bit smaller, both made of similar looking metal. Both with the same prongs in the back. A strange sensation raced through my body, making me dizzy, my legs weak. Everything I'd dreamed about him was true. *All of it.*

I straightened, the world around me spinning. What I'd dreamed... All of Kane's emotions engulfed me like a tsunami. Hate, fear, pain... I braced my hand against the bedpost to remain upright. I felt them all over again, a faucet on full blast. I couldn't get out from under it.

Gulping a breath, I turned. Kane sat with his legs over the side of the bed, watching me.

Swallowing around the lump in my throat, I held up the smaller of the two collars. "What is this?"

He lifted his hand then let it fall in his lap, like he was saying *I can explain.*

I dropped the collar back in the drawer. "But you don't need to explain, that's the thing." I knew my words were coming out high-pitched and panicked, but I couldn't stop them from tumbling out of my mouth. "I knew that was there," I said, sweeping my hand toward the drawer, "because I'd dreamed it. I know you made it for yourself and other shifters who can't control their shifts. It was like I was *you* in my dreams."

The more I talked, the more tension stiffened his body.

"I saw your life. I know your sister's name is Emily and she's attracted to assholes. I met your friends. I—" Squeezing my eyes shut, I pressed a hand to my chest, trying to calm my heart. "I was there when you got your throat ripped out. I *felt* it." Anger whipped through me, hot and fast, and for a second, I wasn't sure if it was mine or his. "Even though you've already killed him, I want to kill him for you all over again."

The bed creaked. When I opened my eyes, he stood in front of me, naked, tall, and muscled. I swallowed at his intense focus, like I was the most important thing in the world. "I heard your voice before you lost it." I searched his face for answers, for some reasonable explanation as to why this was happening. "You called me your mate in my head. In *your* head."

He lifted his hands and cradled my face. I squeezed his wrists tight, a lifeline. "I dreamed about your life. What is this?" My hand skimmed upward, past his fingers to the marks on my neck.

My stomach dropped out from under me in realization. *Mating marks.* The phrase came from memory, something my mom had told me long ago. My heart pumped twice as hard as usual. *No.*

I stared into his eyes, the truth settling into me like a ball of molten lava in my chest. After he'd killed those men, when I'd run from him...I'd started this. I'd exposed my neck for him to bite without realizing what I was doing.

We were going through a mating ritual.

I could have stopped this. He'd tried to stay away from me. He must have realized what was happening from the beginning. Instead of accepting the gift he'd been trying to give me, I'd begged him to fuck me. Over and over again. If I'd realized the significance of his bite, I could have put the brakes on instead of forcing our bond to strengthen. Every time we had sex, it solidified our connection.

His eyes roved over my face, his fingers flexing for a second, then relaxing, an affirmation that I *was* his mate. My heart threatened to burst from my chest. Nervous energy rolled through my stomach and spread lower. He leaned closer like he was going to kiss me, then paused.

We hadn't kissed yet. It wasn't something I was drawn to do with my partners. Just like holding hands, it wasn't an intimacy that I needed to satisfy me when I went into heat. It had always been a biological function, nothing more. Keeping kissing out of it allowed me to stay in charge.

But as I stared up into those cognac eyes, the tenderness in his expression made me want to shed my past habits. I wanted him more with each stroke of his thumb on my jaw.

I closed the gap between us on a groan. His lips were soft and strong and delicious. Tingles exploded through my body to settle between my legs. My tongue darted out, stroking his. The scruff of his beard tickled my face. He growled. His hands released my face to skim down my naked back, pulling me against him. My fingers dove into his hair.

Our kiss went on and on. The world disappeared and it was only the two of us. Hands roved, and pulled, and petted. He grabbed my bottom and squeezed, lifting me up and against him until the juncture of my thighs cradled his erection. He felt so good. His kiss, his hard body, the way he touched me, everything set me on fire.

I wrapped my legs around his hips. Feeling the head of his cock press against my heat, I wiggled until I could sink down onto him. The thick, wet, slide made me purr. I was always so ready for him. The feel of him inside me, filling me, it made the breaths in my chest stutter to a stop. We hadn't stopped kissing, and I didn't want to. Kissing Kane was the most amazing thing I'd ever experienced. His taste filled my head. He nibbled, he stroked, his tongue fucked me like his cock was doing.

My nipples rubbed against his chest hairs, making them pucker to hard points. He stepped back to the bed, then settled me beneath him. We hadn't separated our lips or our joined bodies. He kissed me and thrust slow and steady, letting the heat build between us at a tantalizing pace. His tenderness made a foreign pressure build inside my chest.

Whenever I thought he'd pick up the pace, take me fast like so many other times before, he backed off. I dug my heels into his ass, encouraging. Each slow stroke of his cock inside brought another wave of sparks that rolled through me from top to bottom. Every part of me prickled. I'd never felt this all-consuming sensation before. Need crawled over my skin. These emotions were too much. He was making me *feel* too much.

Becoming desperate for release, I broke our kiss. "Kane, please."

It came out like begging, but I didn't care. I was frantic. I couldn't take the intensity anymore.

He growled but didn't move faster, dragging out each thrust. A whimper escaped me without permission. I couldn't breathe anymore, couldn't think. My vision blurred around the edges. Grabbing on to his hair, I held on tight. His mouth claimed my lips again. His tongue stroked mine, asserting dominance. He kept me on the edge so long I couldn't see straight.

White hot heat rolled through in a wave of pleasure, an orgasm unlike any other. My ears buzzed. My body jerked, clenching him inside me. An inhuman moan tore through me. I ripped my lips away from him to latch my teeth onto his neck where it met his shoulder. I bit down hard and squeezed him to me tight.

A primal growl filled the cabin. It came from Kane. The sound of it created shivers along my nerve endings, making the fine hairs on my body stand on end. He kept his pace slow, thrusting into me over and over again, milking every tremor from my body.

His body tightened, a rumble spreading through his chest. Instinctively, I clamped my bite harder on his shoulder. I *needed* this. My canines extended in a partial shift. Kane growled, his back arching, but I couldn't stop biting him. I tasted blood. My eyes rolled in the back of my head. Another orgasm ripped through me, making my body jerk against his.

We eventually stilled. Kane's ragged breathing filled the room. My instincts told me to keep hold of his neck. With effort,

I forced myself to loosen my jaw. A gasp escaped Kane as I let go.

My fingers dug into his scalp. No, my *claws*. My teeth weren't the only things to have partially shifted. It took me two attempts to retract my claws. I didn't want to let go.

What was happening to me? I'd never lost control like that, never even been tempted to bring out my claws and teeth during sex.

Dear God, I'd given him a mating mark. A burst of possessiveness shot through me. I leaned forward and licked the residual drops of blood from his shoulder. He grunted. His taste filled my mouth, making another purr roll through me. I'd never thought blood tasted good as a human, only enjoyed it once I shifted, but whatever was going on between us was happening on every level.

I flopped back on the bed, letting him go. *Triple fucked.*

Staring past him to the beams in the ceiling, I asked, "This can't be undone, can it?" I rubbed my face with my hands, trying to scrub the truth away. Mom had told us to keep our teeth to ourselves.

If you mate, you lose your freedom.

It was something she had said often, and one of the reasons she kept kicking my father out of our house whenever he turned up. Bobcats were notoriously promiscuous. My parents never went through a proper mating ritual, but my dad still came sniffing around every few years, infrequent enough I had few memories of him as a child. Mom always said that no matter how tempting it was in the moment, she didn't want to be tied down to one man.

Kane's face filled my vision, concerned, satisfied, possessive. His tongue darted out, licking my bottom lip, then came his teeth, nibbling. My slowing, post-orgasm heart rate picked up speed again. It only took a second for me to dive into the kiss with a groan. He tasted so good. Like nothing else. I didn't know if I'd ever get my fill.

Long minutes passed before he broke the kiss and slid out of me. The empty and lost feeling only lasted a second before he turned out the light, pulled me against his chest in a spoon, and covered us with the quilt.

I sighed. Being cradled like this felt way too good. I snuggled my ass against him and rested my head on his bicep. His other arm encircled my waist.

I touched the marks on my neck. As far as I knew, going through a mating ritual with a shifter was a deeper bond than marriage. I swallowed. I was only twenty-four. I wasn't ready to make a decision about being mated for life.

But even without his arm around me, I would feel the connection between us. What had started as a thin strand was now a corded rope. It bound us together, unseen but so very strong. Every time we made love, it got stronger. I'd made sure of that by biting him. Instinct had taken over again.

Having Kane's arms around me was nothing short of perfect. I didn't want to be anywhere else. Would I have any of these feelings if we hadn't started along the path of a mating ritual? Was I in my right state of mind?

I felt like myself, just...different. Changed. I didn't know what to think anymore.

Behind me, Kane's breathing remained steady. He wasn't asleep yet. I got the impression that his mind raced as much as mine did. What was he thinking about?

After long moments in the dark and silence, I finally asked the question weighing on my mind. "Have you dreamed about me?"

He tucked me more securely in his arms, his hand covering one breast, rubbed his chin on my shoulder, then grunted.

I wasn't sure what that meant.

20

KANE

I WOKE UP WITH A GROWL ERUPTING FROM MY THROAT.

Beside me, Brooke startled awake, hopping to her knees. "What? What is it? What's wrong?" Her head darted back and forth, her arms outstretched to the sides like she was prepared to do battle if we were threatened.

The cuteness of her actions calmed me some. Her hair stuck out in all directions, her skin flushed, and her pert, little breasts jiggled at the movement. It made what I'd dreamed about fade a bit.

This shared dreaming thing went both ways after all.

When she realized there was no danger, she dropped her hands, then pushed her hair away from her face. "What's wrong?"

Nothing. Everything. I tried to force the images out of my mind but couldn't. She'd been in heat. Loud music played in a club where everyone was dancing. She'd found a guy. Her hands were all over him. His hands were all over her. They were grinding in the middle of the dance floor, her butt in his groin, where everyone could see. He'd lifted her skirt, exposing the bare flesh of her ass...

Another growl ripped through me.

Her eyes widened. "Oh."

It wasn't the only memory of hers I'd dreamed about, but it was what woke me. I ran a hand over my head, and she watched me with a wary expression. "You dreamed one of my memories, didn't you?"

Pressing my lips together, I nodded once.

"I was afraid of that." She gathered the quilt to her chest, covering herself. Her lips parted like she wanted to say something else, then she snapped her mouth closed.

I'd heard of shared dreaming before, but it was rare. Most mated couples didn't experience this. It was especially rare since we weren't the same kind of shifters. Unheard of, really.

And I knew I shouldn't be getting jealous of someone in her past. That dude was long gone, but it didn't stop the possessive feeling that overcame me. It made me want to haul her underneath me, to make her pant and moan to make sure she knew we belonged to each other.

When I'd been inside her head, in her memories, I understood it was a regular pattern with her. Every time she went in heat, she'd search for a guy who would look like he could satisfy her for a few days. Sometimes they did. Sometimes they'd disappoint. But whatever happened, she'd do it again the next time with a different guy. She never had long-term boyfriends, never wanted to be tied down.

She was like her mother in that way, or so she thought.

I'd loved experiencing her other memories, even the ones that were sad. They allowed me to get to know her better, let me see how her mind worked. There'd been moments with her sister, ones full of affection, others tinged in jealousy. Her mother and sister both loved the whole camping, hiking, wilderness thing. Brooke often felt like the oddball. As a result, she'd gravitated toward the other things her mother liked: the makeup, the shopping, the partying.

There'd been memories of her running through the forest as

a bobcat, pure joy racing through her. It was something I'd never experienced, never remembered because of my blackouts. When Brooke shifted, her needs changed, but her mind remained intact. Living that from her point of view had been amazing.

But the dream about her hooking up with a random guy...

How many times would I be forced to dream about her curtailing her heat with someone else? I'd felt her desire, the burning need between her legs. The exhibitionist aspect of their dance had only fueled her lust. She hadn't cared who'd seen her ass in that moment. I dug my fingers into the covers at my hips, processing this new challenge.

Brooke studied me. After a while, her expression softened. "You're working really hard not to tear something in half, aren't you?"

I didn't answer while attempting to release my stranglehold on the covers.

She swallowed. "What's in the past is in the past."

I nodded once. I knew this, understood it deep inside, but it didn't chase away the possessiveness threatening to break free from my chest.

The quilt fell, her nipples pebbling in the cool air. "I'd like to go dancing," she murmured.

Another growl rippled through me, and she grabbed my hand.

"With you," she said, lifting my hand to her breast. "I'd like to go dancing with you sometime."

My palm settled on her warm skin, and her fingers tightened on mine, making me squeeze her breast. But the image of her dancing at a club, of everyone staring at her, wouldn't quit.

"It wouldn't matter if anyone was watching me," she said, moving slowly like she would with a skittish animal. Her knee lifted, sliding over my abdomen until she straddled me. "I'd only be looking at you."

The hot space between her thighs settled over my hardening cock. Without breaking eye contact, she grabbed my other hand.

"I think you'd like to watch me dance." Her eyes lit with both mischief and heat as she settled my hand on her other breast. "I'd only be dancing for you."

Teasing her nipples with my palms, a vision of her moving slowly to music filled my head. Her hips gyrated, her head thrown back. But there would be others there watching. Another growl emerged from deep inside me. I didn't want to share her with anyone else.

"It wouldn't matter who was there." She rolled her hips, moisture coating my hard cock. Her breath hitched when I pinched her nipples. "As soon as you felt like punching someone," she purred, "you could take me out back and fuck me in the alley."

I thrust upward.

"Or the bathroom." She rotated her hips again, adjusting until my strained cock pressed up against her entrance. "Or a dark corner." Her tongue darted out to lick her bottom lip. "Then we'd go back to dancing and do it all over again."

Images curled through me, echoing my emotions like a hot, living thing. I saw myself taking her from behind in a dark alley, like how we'd first mated. Rotating my hips, I slid inside her an inch.

Her breath hitched and eyes glazed. "I'd probably leave my underwear at home."

I couldn't hold back any longer. My hands dropping from her breasts to her hips, I held her immobile and thrust inside. We groaned together as she sheathed me. There was a moment where we held perfectly still, savoring the sensation of being fully joined.

The marks she'd given me tingled. She stiffened slightly, her eyes flying to those marks on my neck. For a second, she looked shocked, or horrified, like she was unsure of what had happened or how we came to be in the position we were in. I thrust my hips upward.

She gasped, her fingers flexing on my chest, then all the tension left her body. Rotating her hips, she closed her eyes and rode me until we both couldn't think anymore.

21

BROOKE

THE DAYS BLENDED TOGETHER IN A HAZE OF CONSTANT LUST FOR Kane. If it wasn't burning me up from the inside out, it simmered below the surface, ready to ignite.

It was this strange slice of time, like the rest of the world didn't exist outside of the cabin. Everything came down to the basics. We ate, we slept, we fucked. No, it wasn't just fucking anymore. That's what I used to do. With Kane, it had become something else. We'd become attune to each other. It wasn't only about release. It was giving pleasure instead of taking what I needed.

Serenity came from our routine. Food prep, laundry, I was starting to feel like a frontier woman. Before I knew it, I'd be making soap and churning butter. The thought didn't horrify me the way it would have before I came here.

There were some comforts as well. The subtle sounds of the forest were soothing. They calmed me in a way I'd never allowed. While the nights were cold, the cabin was warm, and the noonday sun banished the chill in the air. As long as I heated water on the pot belly stove, I could have a hot shower every day.

But no matter what tranquility I'd discovered being here, it made me sad thinking about how lonely Kane's life must have been before I arrived. He'd given up everything due to his fear of harming others.

I watched him now while I sat in the chair on the front landing, a coffee mug cradled in my hands. His shirt was off, and he'd cut a bunch of birch branches. They lay in a leafy stack next to him. Holding a knife in one hand, he stripped the smaller branches off, leaving behind long poles an inch or two in diameter. I had no idea what he was going to do with them.

The ambient quiet of the forest surrounded us, and I breathed the cool air in. My heat had peaked and now waned with each passing day. But it didn't stop my desire for the man in front of me. I couldn't seem to help myself. When we were near each other, I wanted to touch him. When we were in bed together, I wanted him inside me. If I'd gone home with the tattooed guy last week, I wouldn't still be with him now. I would have left him as soon as the threat of my heat had passed.

But I couldn't get enough of Kane.

I watched as he sawed some of the long branches into smaller pieces. His muscles bunched and moved as he worked the tool through the wood. Warmth curled in my stomach and spread into my thighs.

It was ridiculous, this need for him. Moving my hand to my shoulder, I touched the marks on my neck and swallowed. Mated for life. Oddly, now I was marked, a large part of me didn't mind in the least.

This isn't me.

But how could I say that when the part of me that was horrified I'd been claimed by a grizzly bear became smaller and smaller with each passing minute? I adored the way he made me feel, but this...this was complicated.

I didn't know what to do about it. My body, my instincts, my biology, told me to keep having sex with Kane. I liked him. I *more* than liked him. He was caring and sure of himself, a provider. My affection only grew every time I dreamed something about his past. It didn't hurt that he was hot as hell. Beards had never attracted me before now, but on him, it was perfect.

My brain, on the other hand, told me I should be panicking. What was happening here was serious, life-altering, and I'd had enough trauma with being abducted that I really shouldn't have life-altering decisions on the menu. The strange and new emotions rioting through me made me want to talk to my mom. She would have answers. She'd always been open and honest with me and Sabrina, especially when it came to sex.

This is more than just sex.

Swallowing, I watched as Kane secured some of the pieces together in a square. He didn't use nails, but some sort of notch construction.

Sabrina. I rubbed my chest. Sometimes the guilt of being free overwhelmed me and I became light-headed, my legs unable to hold me up. God, I hoped she was okay. I hoped she'd been able to break free. And if not, I prayed that when I finally returned to civilization, I'd be able to find her.

Even though Kane and I were isolated, contained in a bubble consisting of lust and sex, I'd planned what I would do once I returned to Detroit. I'd call the police and report my sister missing. I'd call her work. I'd call Frank to see if he'd heard from her, and if he hadn't, then I'd enlist his help in searching. He was one of those guys who "knew people." He wouldn't hesitate to help when it came to Sabrina.

Then, there was Kane's cousin. He might know something. Yesterday, Kane convinced me we needed to go there first, that his cousin's connection to the collar was the first thing we needed to exploit. It took me awhile, but I finally agreed. I didn't have a passport to take an international flight anyway.

After sharing his dreams night after night, I knew how Landon's involvement in this mess would hurt Kane. Despite the fact that someone had redesigned his collar for doing harm, I hoped Landon was innocent in the matter. Kane had so few personal connections, losing Landon would create a deep wound that might never heal.

Soon. We would get answers soon.

Nervous energy made me clutch my mug tighter. The thought of leaving this place hurt. Which was strange. I'd gone camping with Sabrina and Mom before, sure, but hadn't wanted to stay forever.

This place was different. I'd never felt so content or at peace before. Not even in my own home.

Like the wind heard my thoughts, it wrapped around me, calming my emotions. The trees swayed as I listened to that distinctive bird with its two-note song. The whipped cream clouds scuttled across the sky, blocking the sun every now and then. There was something magical about this place. My eyes returned to Kane. Or maybe it was the company I kept.

When he bent one of the longer poles in a U shape, I straightened. Tilting my head, I stared at the chair I sat on, then the one he was making. It was the same design.

He was building a chair. Who did that?

It got me thinking, and I surveyed his property. The cabin, the shed, the cold cellar, everything held the same quality in craftsmanship. Even the damn bed in the house. The table? No, that looked like it came from a store, the dresser and wardrobe too, but everything else?

The next time he turned to me, I gestured to the cabin. "You made all of this by yourself, didn't you?"

He nodded once.

An amazed breath huffed out of me. "You're a regular Dick Proenneke. You know that, right?"

His eyebrows lifted in question.

"He was this American who lived by himself in Alaska and made all his own stuff, a log cabin, tools, everything. He recorded it for years. It was this show on PBS. Sabrina and I used to watch it. He was like, 'Hey, I need a spoon.' So then he'd carve himself a spoon out of wood. It was kind of mesmerizing. I think the show was called *Alone In The Wilderness* or something like that. You remind me of him."

He shook his head at me.

"Well, you're hotter, but the principle is the same."

A smile curled at the corner of his mouth as he turned away and concentrated on the project. It was only a while later that he stepped back, arms wide in a ta-da fashion when it was complete.

I clapped. "You could sell tickets." I gestured to the forest beyond. "Everyone from miles around would come and watch you build stuff with your shirt off."

He tipped his head at me, shook it, and brought the chair up the landing to set it beside mine.

On an exhale, he sat, slapping his knees in satisfaction of a job well done. The new wood squeaked under his weight.

I couldn't help grinning at him. He was just so damn adorable. "I want to learn ASL." The words popped out of my mouth before I could stop them. The idea had sprung up during one of our dreams. I now knew a few phrases just from sharing his mind while we slept, but I didn't know enough to be fluent.

His eyebrows shot up into his hair line. His lips parted.

That look made my cheeks heat. "Will you teach me?"

From the intensity of his expression, I almost regretted asking, until his face softened, his eyes becoming warm, and he nodded once. The wind rustling the leaves on the trees echoed the twitchy feeling in my stomach.

Unable to bear his scrutiny any longer, I said, "All right, Dick, how sturdy do you think that chair is?"

His expression shifted into one of pure disgruntlement. Like *duh, of course it's sturdy.*

"You think so?"

He didn't condescend to answer again.

"All right, but if it breaks, don't blame me."

His eyebrows pulled together in a frown as I stood and closed the gap between us. The frown disappeared a second after I straddled him. The chair squeaked under the added weight.

I only wore his flannel shirt and nothing else. His hands were under it in the next moment, cupping my ass, roving up my spine then back down again. Urgency overtook me when we kissed, then we were both fumbling for the fly of his jeans.

The chair didn't break.

22

KANE

EARLY MORNING SUNLIGHT BOUNCED OFF THE LAKE AS THE SUN rose in the sky. I stepped out onto the porch with a mug of coffee in each hand. The tug in my chest told me I'd find Brooke at the end of the dock. Taking a step toward her, I stopped, hesitating.

She'd gotten up earlier than usual, rolling out of bed when the sun just began to brighten the sky. Usually, she slept late. Today there was a sadness to her movements, giving me the impression she wanted to be alone. That had been a couple of hours ago. *Should I leave her on her own or bring her coffee?*

Her heat had faded over the past few days, her scent returning to what it had been when she'd first arrived, not the bowl-me-over intoxicating entity it had become during her time. Even though her need abated, it hadn't quelled her sexual appetite. Not that I minded. All she had to do was look at me and I was ready for her. When she'd turned to me in the middle of the night, she'd licked the marks she'd given me.

Along with the recession of her heat came an influx of other emotions. She was more preoccupied and often lost in thought. Before it had been all about biology. Now she was more baseline.

What would happen once we left the solitude of my cabin must be weighing on her mind.

My hands tightened on the mug handles. This time between us was coming to an end.

The thought stabbed me in the gut even though it was understandable. She hadn't asked for any of this. If we'd met under normal circumstances, I wasn't the man a woman like her would choose to be with.

Should I leave her to her thoughts?

I stared at her slight form at the end of the dock. She'd wrapped a patchwork quilt around her body, a smudge of color against the blue of the water. In the end, the tug in my chest was too powerful to ignore. I could always bring her the coffee, then leave if she wanted to be alone. With purpose, I walked toward the lake.

She turned her head to me when I took that first step onto the dock. As I drew near, she scooted over to make room. The knot in my stomach eased, and I sank down beside her, cross legged, before passing her a mug.

"Thank you," she murmured, blowing across the top, then taking a tentative sip. Her gaze remained on the water, one arm wrapped around her knees.

We stayed that way for long minutes, sipping our coffee and staring out at the water. Brooke's silence weighed on me. I wanted to know what she was thinking.

Two loons slowly circled along the edge of the water, searching for fish. Once in a while, one would dive down, disappearing for long seconds before resurfacing several feet away. When they neared the rotor blade sticking out of the water, my hands tightened on my mug.

Finally, Brooke broke the silence. "I need to find my sister." Her voice was flat, her gaze glued to the scenic landscape. "Part of me thinks it's been too long already, that whatever those cougars had planned for her, it's done. That she's dead."

Her sadness cut me to the core. I leaned into her, my shoulder to hers.

"I have this guilt inside me too," she continued. "I'm here with you, safe, protected, and she could be—" She stopped speaking and hung her head. "I just want her to be safe too."

My hand went to her back, rubbing up and down, trying to give her what little comfort I could. As much as it appealed to me to stay hidden in these woods forever, there was no way I was going to let her deal with this on her own. We needed answers from Landon. We needed to go to Vancouver to find out what happened to the design of the collar and whether my cousin had sent mercenaries after Brooke, whether he had anything to do with that cargo plane, those other animals, and those hunters her sister referred to.

And after sharing Brooke's dreams night after night, Sabrina was as much my sister as hers. I wouldn't rest until the two were reunited.

Brooke let out a slow breath and leaned her head against my shoulder. I gave her a little squeeze, trying to ignore my rising panic. Over the past few days, emotion had built inside me. Along with my determination to help her find her sister came the understanding that once we found Sabrina, I'd have to let Brooke go.

The truth settled like a ball of lead in the pit of my stomach. I couldn't keep her. I cared for her too much to do that to her. If she remained with me, the potential I could harm her during one of my blackouts would always remain. I could lose control and she'd be the only one there to take the brunt of it. I couldn't put her in harm's way like that.

We were too different anyway. She lived in the city, loved going dancing at a club, and I loved the silence of nature. She liked being around others while I found comfort in my own company. How in the world would we ever make that work?

But she's your mate.

My animal shouted the same words every time I acknowledged that this thing between me and Brooke was temporary. Sometimes that voice roared. But there wasn't any way around it. Detroit was her home, and besides being a dangerous environment, living in a city held no appeal for me.

If I could, I would keep her here forever. The past two weeks had been the best of my life and I didn't want to lose her. The thought of separating from her sent actual pain throughout my body. But she had a life beyond this cabin.

I knew it was going to hurt. As mates living apart, we wouldn't be comfortable, but I hoped, over time, her discomfort would ease. I didn't care if mine did. If I ached this way for the rest of my life, it would be a small price to pay for the joy I'd experienced during our short time together.

After experiencing her life through dreams, I knew she'd eventually get over it. She always did. She never stayed with anyone long. As sick as the thought made me feel, in the grand scheme of things, I was just another guy who appeased her need for a time.

The bear inside me roared its disapproval.

I told it to shut up. I wouldn't force her to stay with me, couldn't no matter how much pain I experienced.

Beside me, Brooke's body slumped slowly into mine, her breathing evening out in the rhythm of slumber. Not surprising since she'd tossed and turned all night. Taking the mug from her hands, I set it aside, then scooped her into my arms to settle her bottom between my legs. It didn't take long for her to fall fully asleep.

We stayed that way for a long time, me cradling her, and her soft breaths tickling the skin at my throat. This is what I'd always remember, being like this on the edge of the water with her where the outside world didn't exist, didn't matter. Who the hell was I trying to kid? I'd remember *all* of our time together. Every precious second.

When the sun crested over the lake, I kissed the top of her head, bundled the blanket around her, and stood with her in my arms. The dock creaked under my footsteps. Keeping her tight against me, I walked up the small slope to the cabin.

Tomorrow, the plane would come.

23

BROOKE

At first, the sound of the plane was a quiet buzz, like one of the flies that liked to come at my head right after I showered. Then, as it neared, that light buzz turned into an all-out drone.

I stood on the porch and watched the float plane descend, an odd-shaped bird, mostly white with a stripe of blue. The floats skimmed over the water a few seconds before the backs of them hit. It stayed that way for a while, then the fronts lowered, the plane settling.

I'd never seen a plane land on water before. It was kind of cool.

After it hunkered down in the small waves, the engine became louder for a few seconds, then quieter. Finally, it rumbled its way to the dock.

Kane was down there already, a duffel bag beside him. He waved, and I saw the salutation returned by the person inside. John Clark. I knew his name and that he was human from Kane's memories.

When the plane slowed, sidling up to the dock, Kane tied it off with rope, first the front end, then the back. When John jumped out, they shook hands.

I straightened my shirt. Time to meet the bush pilot. I'd opted for my skirt, ballet flats, and G-string, but borrowed one of Kane's white T-shirts, tying a big knot at my hip so it fit better. My sequined top was already packed inside the duffel along with my toothbrush—the only other two belongings I owned right now.

Smoothing the front of my skirt, I made my way down the slight hill to the dock. The two men unloaded the plane. There were boxes of supplies, mostly food: fresh fruit and vegetables, bread, lots of canned goods, and non-perishables. Most of it would need to go back because we didn't know how long we'd be gone.

The newcomer froze with a box in his arms when he saw me. His eyebrows rose into his hairline. A blue baseball cap topped his black hair, and his features and medium brown skin highlighted his indigenous heritage. He set the box on the ground and pushed the cap off his forehead.

"Hi," I said, stopping a few feet away to give him a wave.

"Hello." His voice was slightly loud, the word clipped. "And where did you come from?"

"The sky."

He grinned and let out a whoop, slapping Kane on the back. "An angel. I knew it. You lucky bastard."

"It's Brooke, actually."

"Brooke, the angel. Got it." He extended his hand. "John Clark."

I shook it, his grip firm. "Nice to meet you."

When he dropped my hand, he went back to unloading the boxes like nothing was out of the ordinary, then froze again. He tilted his head toward the duffel bag. "I'm thinking I'm getting some passengers."

Kane nodded, and I said, "We need a ride to town," at the same time.

This time when he turned, he took in our surroundings with alert eyes. His gaze settled on the rotor blade sticking six inches out of the water. "You had some trouble?" he asked Kane with his eyebrows raised.

Kane passed him a note from his back pocket. I knew what it said. *Do you know anyone who'd be interested in taking apart the helicopter and keeping the parts as payment?*

John's eyebrows rose even more. "Not the same kind of list you usually give me." He took off his hat and wiped his brow before settling it back on his head. "Yeah, I might know a guy."

When Kane reached in his back pocket for another note, John grimaced. I knew what that one said too. *We need flight arrangements to Vancouver, not on a commercial flight.* I didn't have a passport or any sort of ID. I wouldn't be allowed on a commercial flight, even a domestic one.

John considered the paper with a frown. "You don't ask for much, do you?"

While he considered the request, rubbing his chin all the while, Kane sorted through the supplies, separating the perishables from the non-perishables. I stooped down to help but paused when Kane pulled three porn magazines out of the side of one of the boxes. I snorted.

His cheeks turning pink under his beard, Kane lifted the magazines in question toward John.

"Ah, yeah." John scratched the bridge of his nose. "Sorry about that. Didn't know you had company. Confiscated them from my nephew and thought you could use them."

When Kane would have tossed them in with the fruit, I put a hand on his arm. "Don't get rid of them on my account." I'd never been a prude and didn't care whether he got his jollies from looking at skin mags. He'd been by himself in the wilderness for years. What else was he supposed to do? "They're good tinder if nothing else."

For a second, Kane hesitated. Then, with a shrug, he tossed them in the box with the cans of soup.

When everything was sorted, Kane stacked two of the bigger

boxes one on top of the other and headed back to the cabin. I took the last smaller one and followed. We locked it all in the cold room, then headed back to the plane.

John had reloaded the other boxes filled with fruits and vegetables that would expire back into the plane by the time we'd stepped onto the dock.

"I can probably take you to Van," he told us when we stopped in front of him, "but I'll have to borrow my buddy's plane. Might work, though. We'll have to see once we get back to town. It could take a day or so."

"The faster the better," I said. The sooner we talked to Kane's cousin, the sooner we could find answers about my sister.

24

KANE

THE PLANE—A BEAVER—HUMMED LOUDLY AROUND US. BROOKE and I sat in the back seat side by side. We each wore headsets with ear protection and a mic so we could hear John if he spoke to us.

Brooke was rigid beside me. I took her hand. I knew she worried about her sister. It wouldn't be long before we landed. A trek that would have taken days and days of hard walking cross country only took a little over an hour in a plane.

Looking up at me, she tightened her hand on mine, then went back to staring out the window.

The landscape was a carpet of blue, green, and gray. The boreal forest took up almost thirty percent of Canada, cutting a swath right across the center, through the north of the provinces and practically all of the Northwest Territories and Yukon.

The plane dipped in a pocket of air, and Brooke tightened her hold on my hand. There were moments when it felt like the wind grabbed a hold of the little plane and shook it back and forth just for fun. I brushed my thumb over the back of her hand.

Another dip, and John began our descent. The glacier lake, Lac La Ronge, came into view, a massive mammoth of a thing. My lake was a drop in the pond compared to this one. It had over a thousand little and not so little islands speckled through it. The lower we went, the more of the town of La Ronge became visible. Buildings, mostly square, punctuated the shoreline. Roads ran up and away from the lake, disappearing into the trees.

The town—two towns really, La Ronge and Air Ronge, bisected by a river—was also connected to six First Nations reserves. The borders of the town and the reserves were almost indistinguishable except for where the pavement turned into dirt roads. Altogether, their populations amounted to about eight thousand people.

The floats hit the water, the engine droning loudly as John slowed the plane. Multiple docks stuck out into the lake in intervals, either connected to businesses or houses.

John's home was "downtown," a trailer-style aluminum building with one long dock. A bush pilot company had its base of operations two doors down. Four float planes, two Beavers and two Otters, were secured against a pair of docks coming out of their main building, an aluminum warehouse painted white— John's direct competition. He'd told me once they'd tried to get him to join the company, but he preferred to do his own thing, didn't want to work for the "white man" as he put it. He'd said it with a laugh, but I knew he wasn't joking.

The aircraft quieted as we floated toward the dock, then John cut the engine. He opened his door, hopped out, and tied off the plane. I got out first, then helped Brooke down with my hands on her waist before reaching inside for my duffel bag.

The town was quiet, but the strangeness of it pressed in on me. It had been years since I'd been here, with no other contact except John and now Brooke. Even though traffic only whispered from the road up the hill, the sound of it grated on me.

"What do you want me to do with your groceries?" John asked once he'd closed the door.

I looked at Brooke, knowing she'd answer. "Could you donate

them to someone who might need it?" We'd talked about it yesterday. I'd buy new veggies when I returned, whenever that would be. It all depended on how quickly we could find her sister.

"Can do." John pushed his cap back on his forehead. "I'll need to make some phone calls about that trip to Vancouver. Why don't you come inside?"

My hand on the base of Brooke's spine, I guided her after John as he led the way along the dock, up the stairs, then unlocked the back door to his building. At a width of about eighteen feet, it was one long, narrow corridor. We passed through a tidy living room and a modern kitchen, then we were in an office, the front door off to the left. A bedroom lay behind a closed door in front of us.

John threw his hat on the desk and picked up his cell phone. When I gestured to one of the lockers on the side, John nodded. "Yep, your stuff is still there." He tossed me a set of keys from the middle drawer of the desk.

The first time John flew me to the land I'd purchased on the lake, I'd left a box of things I wouldn't need along with emergency cash in case we ran into any problems with my accounts. Everything I purchased went through a third-party accountant. For a reasonable fee, John sent and received my mail, which he added to the cost of my supply deliveries.

I found the key marked with a six and opened the locker. My old wallet lay inside, along with a thousand dollars in one-hundred-dollar bills. Taking out five hundred, I tucked the wallet in my back pocket, then handed the brown bills to Brooke.

She stared at the wad, blinking. "What's this for?"

Suppressing a smile at her disgruntled expression, I tugged her outside and up the four steps to street level. La Ronge Avenue, the town's main street, wound its way along the shore of the lake. A public beach was situated a few blocks down, in the middle of what everyone considered downtown. No one would use it until the temperatures got hotter mid-summer. With a lake this size, a wet suit was almost needed any other time of the year, unless a person swam in one of the warmer bays.

Cars drove at a slow pace in front of us: white trucks, black SUVs, a blue beater blaring a 70s rock ballad out its window. Each sound slapped at me, and I tried not to flinch. I knew I'd get used to it. There weren't any traffic lights in this town, just four-way stops and the occasional yield sign. Still holding Brooke's hand, I gestured across the street at the pharmacy and a clothing store called The Burrow.

She curled the money into a roll. "Right." Then she glanced over her shoulder at John through the window, busy on the phone.

The dazed expression on her face worried me. I ran a hand up her spine.

"Sure." She tightened her hand around the money and sent me a forced smile.

After studying her a minute, I glanced down the street. There was a motel about three blocks down. I'd see if they had a room available. I signed *I'll get a room.*

She glanced at the motel, then at the money in her hand. "Motel. Got it."

Maybe I should take her with me? She looked lost right now, but we needed to make some sleeping arrangements before we found ourselves on John's couch for the night—if he'd have us. I ran my hand up and down her spine again.

She lifted her gaze to mine. "It's weird being in civilization again."

That was an understatement. She'd only had two weeks at my cabin while I hadn't been to town for years. I'd half expected the bear to have already made its displeasure known at the change in location, but he remained calm despite the hum of traffic in front of us. *So far so good.*

With a nod, Brooke waited for traffic to part, then started

across the street, her long legs bare, her blonde hair mussed. Our bond pulled tight against my chest. I watched for a moment, the urge to go after her making my fingers curl into fists.

With extreme effort, I headed down the hill and away from her.

25

BROOKE

I STOPPED ON THE SIDEWALK IN FRONT OF THE CLOTHING STORE AND stared at the five hundred dollars in my hand. When was the last time I'd held this much cash? Never. I made a fist around the money. He'd given it to me like it was twenty bucks instead of half a grand.

Turning my head, I watched Kane's retreating back. My chest tugged toward him, and my feet wanted to switch directions.

I tore my gaze away. Essentials, that's what I needed. Enough supplies and clothing to last me a few days. But what I really wanted was a phone. I'd almost tackled John for his cell. I just wanted to make a few calls, to reach out, but I understood finding transportation to Vancouver was important. If I'd seen a land line, I would have used it.

That last night in Detroit, all I'd had on me was a phone, my ID, one bank card, and forty in cash for the cab back home if I hadn't scored a ride. All of that had disappeared when I'd been abducted. I assumed the kidnappers still had it. They would know where I lived. They would have access to my contacts. I swallowed. Maybe buying a cell attached to my old plan wasn't a good idea. But then, how would Sabrina get a hold of me if she was safe?

I glanced up the street. Four young girls in a group, each with black hair and brown skin, came down the hill. One rode a BMX bike that looked too small for her, the other three walked. They held bright yellow grocery bags, one with a six pack of cola. Rap music played off one of their phones.

Normal. Everything was normal here. Just another day. It jarred me. I didn't know how long I stood there, staring at the everyday happenings of the town. It was like the past two weeks hadn't occurred. No one knew of my kidnapping or that my sister was in danger. No one knew I'd escaped. Life had kept trucking along without me, even though I'd felt like it stopped. The two weeks with Kane at his cabin had been a time bubble, and now everything felt real. *Too real.*

Tucking the wad of money into the back pocket of my skirt, I walked up the three wooden steps and into The Burrow. The scents of new clothes, plastic, and perfume swirled around me. Scents that were familiar but seemed like they came from another life.

The small space was about the size of the living room in my apartment. Four circular racks of clothes took up the center, then one rack down the side. It was mostly women's clothing, but there was one rack of men's stuff at the back. Beside it, one dressing room stall stood in the corner with a blue, wavy curtain.

The tug in my chest stopped, telling me Kane had gotten to his intended location. There was still a pull, it just wasn't moving away from me anymore.

"Hey, there," said the woman, a human, sitting on a high stool behind the counter. She looked a couple years younger than me, maybe around twenty. Her black hair was tied in a ponytail at the top of her head, the makeup on her smooth brown skin expertly done. She glanced at me once, her fingers scrolling through something on her cell. "Let me know if I can help you find something."

I stared at that phone, wanting to snatch it out of her fingers. A couple of calls, that's all I needed.

My feet moved toward the counter, ready to pounce. She lifted her head slowly as I neared, her friendly expression morphing into one that said, *you look a bit nuts.*

A black phone, a land line, was mounted on the back wall behind her. My heart pounded in my chest. With all my being, every molecule, I wanted my sister to be okay. Keeping my gaze on the phone, I put my hand in my back pocket. "Can I pay you a hundred dollars to make a couple of long-distance calls?" I slapped a hundred on the counter and put the rest back.

Taking the money, the woman hopped off the stool. "Whatever you need, lady." She moved out of the way so I could come around the counter.

My hand shook when I picked up the receiver. I'd always had a knack for remembering phone numbers. I dialed Sabrina's cell.

A mechanical woman's voice spoke before it rang once. *The cellular customer you are trying to reach is not in the service area.*

I hung up, hitting the switch in the cradle a little too aggressively. "Sorry," I murmured when I noticed the woman staring at me. I swallowed, then tried my mom's number. Sabrina had said she was in danger too.

It rang. My hand tightened on the receiver. *Please pick up. Please pick up. Please pick up.*

The call connected, loud music blaring through the line before a laugh, then my mother's voice. "Hello! Who's calling?"

"Mom." Holy shit, I basically shouted the word because the relief at hearing my mother's voice almost knocked me on my ass. "Mom, are you okay?"

"Brooke, honey. Good to hear from you. Of course I'm okay, better than ever!" She gave a whoop and the music kept pumping behind her. It sounded like a rave.

My jaw clenched. Sabrina could be dead and our mother was partying. "Where are you?" I raised my voice so she would hear me over the noise.

"Mexico! A seat sale came up, an all-inclusive package, and Luke and I thought, why not? It's fantastic. It's beach front and there are two pools, and it's so beautiful. I want to bring both you girls next time."

"Mexico," I repeated, my voice flat. I pressed my forehead against the wall. I didn't know who the hell Luke was, but that didn't surprise me. Natalie Covin burned through guys as fast as I did.

Or...as fast as I used to.

"I need help." On so many levels. I needed my mom, the strong parts. I needed to find Sabrina. I needed to figure out this mating thing. I *needed* my mom.

"It's going to have to wait until we get back, sweetie. Our flight isn't for another five days. You'll have to figure out whatever it is on your own for now. You're resourceful." There was a pause as a group of people cheered close to her. "Ask Sabrina to help. I think she was taking some time off."

My heart squeezed tight. "She's missing."

There was a pause on the other end of the line, but I could hear the music and other voices. Then my mother said, "I'm sure she'll turn up. You know how she likes to go on those week-long hikes of hers."

This was one moment when I wished my mom wasn't such a flake. *And I'm just like her.* "She's not on a hike."

More cheering and music. "You're worrying me here." At last, my mother's voice had left the carefree tone behind.

I squeezed my eyes shut, keeping the tears at bay. My mother was in Mexico. She couldn't help find Sabrina. When she returned home, she might end up in danger like me. Maybe taking a last-minute flight to Mexico had saved her from our fate. Maybe she partied in the safest place for her to be.

And if I told her the truth about the kidnapping, she would rush back and willfully put herself in danger to protect us. She was far away right now, safe, and needed to stay that way.

Opening my eyes, I forced my voice to brighten. "It's all good. I'll handle it. Don't worry about a thing."

"Are you sure, honey? You sound different." The music behind her stopped altogether, like she'd gone into a building.

"Positive. Just happy to hear your voice." Another understatement. Knowing my mom was safe took a burden off my shoulders. "What about," I said, closing my eyes. "What about seeing if you could stay longer?"

There was a slight pause. "You know, Luke and I were just talking about that and—"

"You should do it," I said, cutting her off. "You deserve a big vacation." My mom had worked as a receptionist at a doctor's office for longer than I'd been alive.

"Brooke. What's going on?"

I exhaled slowly and focused on the wood paneling of the wall. "I've just had a stressful couple of weeks is all." I almost groaned at the words and how true they were. "Everything's fine. I'll see you when you get back, okay?"

"Okay." Her voice remained hesitant.

"Have fun, Mom. I'll talk to you later. Love you." I hung up before I started to cry.

This time I set the phone in the cradle gently. I took one deep breath, then looked over my shoulder without meeting the woman's gaze. "Can I make one more call?"

"Go for it."

I dialed the number for my voice mail. The automated system prompted me for my cell number and when I got in, it announced that my mailbox was full. *Great.*

The first one was from Corey asking where I was. We were supposed to go partying the day after I'd been abducted. The next several were from my boss. Or, former boss. First the messages started out brusque, telling me to phone him or I was going to lose my job. Then there was the last two, both firing me. I didn't know why he felt the need to fire me twice, but the second one told me to come and clean out my locker or he was going to throw out my stuff.

The last one was from Corey again. It was a week later from her first, asking if she should file a missing person's report. I rubbed my temples. Corey wasn't the sharpest tool in the shed, but I would have assumed she wouldn't call the person who is missing to ask if she should report them missing.

Taking a deep breath, I made sure all the messages were erased in case Sabrina tried to call, then glanced at the shop owner again. "Sorry. Just one more." I called Corey's number. She didn't answer, but her voice mail picked up.

"Hey, Corey, it's Brooke. I'm okay, but I'll be out of town for a while. Not sure when I'll be back but if you haven't filled out that missing person's report with Detroit PD, you can leave it for now. Thanks. Talk to you soon."

I stared at my hand on the receiver. Should I fill out a missing person's report for Sabrina? Report our kidnapping? Should I do it here? Should I do it in Detroit? Could I do it over the phone? Would it help anything anyway? We were going to talk to Kane's cousin. Maybe that was still the best strategy.

Straightening away from the phone, I nodded to the woman and moved around to the other side of the counter. "Thanks."

"No problem." The woman's eyes had lost the *you're a nutjob* look and had gained a *your life is sad* expression. "Do you need help with anything else?"

"I'll pick out some clothes. Thanks." I walked through the racks, my movements robotic. There wasn't any underwear here. I'd have to find a new bra somewhere else. Not giving the garments much consideration, I grabbed a pair of jeans in my size, then a few graphic Ts. I made sure the jeans fit, then kept them on, same with the gray shirt that read *Beat It* across the front.

Rolling my old clothes in a bundle, I went to the front counter, allowing the woman to cut off the tags from the things I wore so she could ring them through along with the two other graphic Ts. A few purses and wallets were arranged on a shelf in the corner. I picked the biggest purse, a fake leather, square-shaped one.

"I'll use this for a bag," I said tucking my jean skirt, Kane's T-shirt, and the two new shirts inside. It bulged.

"Sure," the woman said, scanning the tag for the bag, then cutting that off too. Her eyes went to my neck.

Reflexively, I touched my mating marks. The neckline of this T-shirt was much wider than the one I'd borrowed from Kane, exposing the set of semi-circle marks completely.

My cheeks heating, I paid for my purchases and received some coins and a few bills left in change—a blue five, a purple ten, a green twenty. I slid it all into the inside pocket of the purse.

"What's this?" I asked when the woman passed me back the hundred-dollar bill.

"I have a long-distance plan. Your calls didn't cost me anything."

A small bit of light emerged through the gloom that hung over me. My throat tightened at the gesture. "That's okay." I slid the hundred back. "It was worth the money." Then I tucked my new, bulging purse under my armpit and left.

I stopped on the sidewalk, and the knot in my throat wouldn't leave. The tug in my chest told me to find Kane down the hill. He was taking a while at the motel. Maybe there was a problem and I could help. I let out a slow breath. He'd been making his way in life on his own for a long time. I didn't need to interfere.

With purpose, I turned toward the pharmacy. Time to get some essentials.

A hand shot out from between the two buildings and

clamped on my elbow. I let out a startled shriek and dropped the purse. A sweaty palm clamped over my mouth. I was yanked off the street, and my nostrils filled with the scent of shifter.

I tried to shout. The man clamped his fingers over my nose too. I couldn't breathe. With every bit of strength I owned, I struggled against him, kicking and clawing.

Something cold touched my neck, encircling it. Panic made me writhe. I started to shift, to tear away from him. *Click.* The collar trapped me. A familiar pain spiked through my head and into my stomach.

I screamed, the sound muffled beneath his hand. My body shook, then stilled, my vision blurred with stars.

"That's right," the rough voice said against my ear. His hand moved off my nose but stayed over my mouth. The sweet fragrance of aftershave mixed with what I now understood to be cougar scent. "Be a good kitty and relax."

He dragged me backward between the two buildings, my heels scraping in rough earth. The tug in my chest toward Kane intensified. When the separation was my choice, I could tolerate it. Now it was painful, like a limb torn.

The man's arm squeezed my ribs beneath my breasts. Then, to someone else, he said, "Keep it on low so she stays submissive."

A bone aching vibration quaked through my body, making my teeth clench and my shoulders curl forward. I couldn't feel the tug in my chest anymore. It hurt everywhere. I couldn't get away from it. They pulled me into an alley. Through the haze of pain, I saw the other guy. A shot of recognition went through me. He was the shifter from the airplane, the one with a trucker hat. The one who attacked Sabrina.

Rage burst through me, and I struggled with renewed force. I clamped my teeth on the hand in front of my mouth. He howled. I shouted for help as soon as his hand relaxed, but it covered my face harder than before in the next second. He squeezed me so tight I thought my ribs might crack. I couldn't breathe.

A car door opened. I was lifted inside and rolled into the back hatch of an SUV. The door slammed shut again before I could fight my way out.

With each wave of pain, my vision blurred. There weren't any handles on the inside of the door. I couldn't get out. I crawled to the front of the cargo space on my hands and knees. It was caged with bars like the owner had dogs. I rattled them.

"Let me out." I had to bite off each word. It hurt to speak, my teeth aching from the constant pain of the collar.

"Not going to happen," said the driver I'd bitten.

Both guys were dressed like construction workers with hard-hats and orange vests. They pulled them off and threw them into the back seat before the one guy started the SUV. Then he shifted into gear and we sped off.

I fell backward from the momentum, knocking my head against the hatch. More stars dotted my vision. Gravel spit from the tires.

"Did you see her mark?" He said it under his breath, but I heard him.

"Yeah."

"No one said she was mated."

The other guy didn't respond.

26

KANE

I was getting antsy. The separation from Brooke had become too long. The motel clerk in front of me was taking his sweet time registering us for a room. *Must be running on northern time.* Nothing was hurried.

The clerk set the room key on the counter in front of me a second before I knew something had gone wrong. It felt like someone reached into my chest and pulled out my heart. Brooke was in danger. My vision hazed red around the edges.

I turned and started running, almost breaking down the glass door of the motel in my haste. I charged up the hill, past the liquor store, the bank, the dollar store, the church, not seeing any of it.

I had one focus. Brooke. The tug in my chest told me where to go.

My fault. My fault. My fault.

My arms pumped as hard as I could move them, my legs eating up the distance in long strides. I caught her scent when I neared the clothing shop. I didn't pause when I saw the purse on the ground, clothing tumbling out of it. It held her scent too. I pushed my way between the buildings, following where she'd gone. I scented her fear and anger, and a growl erupted in my throat. The red crawled over my vision. My control slipped a little more.

I shouldn't have left her alone.

The alley was empty, but I turned left and kept running. I took a right on the next street, a back road that led to the freeway and out of town. My anger overflowed. I didn't know if I could catch up to them if they hit the highway. I'd need a car. I'd need to stop and turn back. Another growl ripped through me, adrenaline allowing me to pick up my pace.

As soon as I turned left on the next dirt road, I saw the black SUV and knew she was inside. When her scared face popped up in the back window, the red haze won.

The next step I took, I shifted. My clothes tore away from my body, my boots flung off my feet. Paws and claws hit the dirt.

27

BROOKE

I CLAWED AT THE HATCH TRYING TO ESCAPE. I HAD TO BREAK FREE. My life depended on it.

With the humming of the collar making me clench my jaw, I rolled onto my back and pressed my feet against the metal barrier between me and the shifters. It wouldn't budge. I kicked with both legs as hard as I could over and over again. I had to get out.

"Hey!" one of the guys yelled, and the pain in my body increased a second later.

I gritted my teeth and kept going. The metal barrier squealed with each kick. The bond in my chest kept getting stronger, empowering me. One last kick, the bolts holding the barrier in place bent, and the whole thing came crashing down. I clutched at the collar when another shot of pain went into my belly.

I needed to move quickly. Pushing past the pain in my body, I rolled to a seated position. A burst of movement made me focus on the outside world beyond the SUV's back window. Kane tore around the corner, his arms and legs pumping, his face a mask of pure rage. I gasped, my relief at seeing him so overwhelming it made the pain of the collar fade for a moment.

The driver stepped on the gas. I tumbled toward the back

door from the force, smacking my cheek against the back window. A burst of stars blinded me, the pain layered above the constant ache the collar delivered through my body.

Catching my balance, I straightened and pressed my hands against the window. Kane was running so fast, as fast as the car, his face full of stark desperation. In the next instant, he shifted, his muscular body bulking up. Shoes flew away from him. Fur ripped through his clothing, tearing the garments from his body.

I gaped. I hadn't seen him shift the first time. The display was as brutal as it was beautiful. A roar bounded toward us. His jaws snapped.

The car sped up, but it was no match for an enraged grizzly. He kept gaining on us until he ran abreast of the vehicle.

"Let me out!" I screamed, my gaze riveted on my mate.

Kane rammed it with his shoulder. The force knocked me on my ass, my head hitting the wall.

The SUV slowed for a moment, then sped up again.

"If you don't let me out, he'll rip you to shreds!" My throat was raw. My hands yanked at the collar.

Bang. Kane hit us again. This time it tipped to the side, two wheels lifting from the ground. I screamed, fear squeezing my chest. I wasn't buckled up. If we rolled, I'd probably break my neck.

Through the window, Kane hesitated, glanced in my direction, then picked up speed until he was more in front of the SUV than beside it. When he pushed up against us, I braced my hands on the floor.

Tires skidded. He kept pushing, then bounded away. I gritted my teeth when the driver hit the brakes. The car spun. I closed my eyes tight, waiting for us to roll, but we kept spinning, the momentum making my stomach clench.

We slowed, then everything stopped.

Bang.

I gasped and opened my eyes. Kane had jumped on the hood, his jaws open in a snarl of aggression.

"Jesus Christ," the one guy whispered.

They both had their hands up like Kane held a loaded weapon.

The bear roared again, spittle spraying against the windshield.

"Get out," the other guy ground out at me but didn't turn away from the sight before him.

I crawled through the opening I'd made in the back and reached for the door handle. As soon as I stepped out onto the road, my jelly legs collapsed. I stumbled a few feet away, then fell, gravel cutting into my knees. I gasped.

Kane roared again.

Even though I was free, the collar around my neck strangled me, sending a constant swell of pain throughout my body. I curled on my side and clutched at my stomach.

Glass smashed once, twice. The sound of grinding metal was followed by a loud crash followed by another. Windows shattered. He roared again, then the screeching sound of a door being ripped off its hinges cut through the air.

After a second of silence, I opened my eyes to see the SUV flipped into the ditch and two cougars running away. The bear's muscles bunched to follow.

"Kane," I gritted out through my teeth, the low rhythm of the shock collar making my jaw ache. I clutched at my neck, needing to rip it off.

He hesitated, then turned toward me, his muzzle frozen in a snarl. I could only clench my body against the pain. After a moment, he turned back to where the cougars had ran off. Was he going to leave me here like this?

"Kane!" This time my voice came out desperate.

He huffed out a heavy breath, then ambled toward me. I blinked slowly, willing myself to stay conscious. When I opened my eyes again, his wide paws were in front of me. Another breath left him, this one blowing my hair back from my face. He bent down, his nose to mine, and licked my cheek.

As much as I appreciated his affection, there were bigger things to worry about.

"Remote," I ground out between clenched teeth.

His eyes went to my neck. They narrowed. A growl rumbled through his body. His head turned sharply toward where the cougars had gone.

"Kane!" I was going to pass out if we didn't get this thing off me. We were in the middle of the road. There was no one else around to help. "Remote."

He focused on the SUV, and a wave of relief swept through me. He'd help. He wouldn't go after those cougars.

With my hands clutching the hot metal of the collar, I watched him stalk toward the SUV.

28

KANE

MY MATE NEEDS ME. MY MATE NEEDS ME.

The words repeated in my head as I approached the upside down vehicle. I needed to help her.

Broken glass crunched beneath my feet. Shoving my head inside the window, I nosed through the debris. Glass and more glass, some garbage, the cougars' clothes. *There!* On the other side of the vehicle through the broken window. I backed up a step, then walked around and reached to pick it up. My paws wouldn't grasp it.

Paws. I stared at them, comprehension slow to dawn. I was still a bear. A strange sense of novelty whipped through me.

It had been so long since I'd become aware during a shift, that I'd retained my sense of self while the animal took control. Usually, by the time I returned to myself, I was already back to being human, with only fragmented memories to keep me company.

I hadn't needed to think about shifting back in a long, long time, not since I was a kid. I remained motionless, processing. I didn't remember what to do.

A memory floated through my mind, one of Brooke running

through the forest as her bobcat, a shared dream. Shifting came so easy to her she barely thought about it. She only had to remember what her human body felt like, that she desired to return to that form. I tried to do the same. Nothing happened. I panicked, thinking I would remain a bear forever.

Brooke's groan of pain echoed toward me.

My mate needs me. The thought brought my focus to a pinpoint. Concentrating, I thought of my human form, that I needed to help Brooke, that I needed my hands to do that. Slowly, my bones shifted, my fur receded, my body became like sand through a funnel, one granule changing at a time. Then I stood naked beside the vehicle, panting from both exertion and shock. I'd shifted on my own, with my mind intact.

My hands shook as I stooped and picked up the remote. Straightening, I turned it off, then hit the release button.

Brooke gasped and I rushed to her side. She tore the collar away from her neck and threw it on the ground. Kneeling in the gravel, I gathered her to me, needing her close. I couldn't hold her tight enough.

She burrowed her face into my throat, her fingers clutching at my shoulders, her entire body shaking. "This was my fault," she said, her teeth chattering as she dug her fingers into my skin. "I called my mom. I checked my messages. They must have found me that way."

I shook my head and held her close. They wouldn't have found her that fast from tracking a phone call. They were already here, waiting. This town was the gateway to the north. They'd known she would have to come through eventually if she'd survived. I was an idiot to have left her alone. I'd failed her.

As I stroked her spine, my eyes went to the wreckage of the car. I'd ripped it apart, flung the door several feet away. I'd done that and barely remembered.

I was a danger to her. I'd known, but this reinforced it. At some point, I would harm her accidentally. There didn't seem a way to avoid it.

I cared for her too much to do that.

Despair clawing through me, I squeezed her to my chest and stood. Then kicking both the remote and the collar into the muskeg in the ditch where they wouldn't be found, I started back to town with Brooke in my arms.

29

BROOKE

IF I DIDN'T KNOW BETTER, I COULD HAVE SWORN I FELT KANE'S guilt like it was my own. We lay in our bed at the motel, safe, but he would not let go of his remorse for what happened.

We hadn't made it far from the where he'd flipped the vehicle over when a group of indigenous teenagers blasting rap music in a Ford Explorer pulled up beside us asking if we needed help. They might have wondered why Kane was butt naked, but they didn't ask as they gave him a blanket to wrap around his body and helped him find his wallet down the road. The town was small enough that they knew John Clark, and the teens gave us a ride to his place. Kane sat in the front passenger seat with me in his lap. All the rest of the teens had piled into the back except for the driver.

Once at John's, Kane dressed in clean clothes from his duffel bag. I could sense his internal turmoil and thought he still wanted to go after those cougars, but his need to take care of me must have outweighed the blood lust.

So I allowed him to take care of me.

Alone at the motel, he bathed me. He fed me. Warm under

the covers, he cradled me in his arms, his hands roaming over my body like he kept reaffirming I was well.

"It's okay," I said again, for the millionth time. "It's okay."

He buried his face in the curve of my throat, his beard tickling my skin, his arms tight around me.

We stayed that way until morning.

John's efforts of finding us a way to Vancouver off the books proved to be successful. He knew a guy with a bigger plane in a city south of us, and he'd arranged for him to fly up north the next day.

We had a day to kill in town before then.

Kane wouldn't let me out of his sight. Usually, that kind of possessive behavior would have grated on my nerves, but after the cougar incident, Kane's constant presence calmed me. We returned to the clothing store. There was relief on the woman's face when her eyes landed on me. Someone had found my new bag on the street and popped into the store to ask her if she knew who it belonged to. I was glad to have it back.

I was finally able to get that trip to the pharmacy, buying flip flops, deodorant, a hairbrush, toothpaste, and other essentials. The rest of the day was dedicated to making arrangements to get to Vancouver. Kane booked a hotel online using John's laptop.

Sitting in a restaurant on main street with a view of the lake, I dipped another fry in ketchup. "Why don't we call your cousin? We could ask our questions now and get a lead on my sister sooner. Or at least we could make sure he's in Vancouver."

His eyebrows twitched. I knew he'd already made sure his cousin was in the city. I thought Kane maybe didn't want to give Landon a head start if he was in charge of the mercenaries after me and knew Kane was coming. He didn't want his cousin to go underground. The guy was rich enough to do just that. We needed our questions answered, not to go on a cousin-hunting expedition.

When Kane shook his head, I took a bite of my fry, but my appetite had fled.

Every time I mentioned his cousin, a steely resolve settled over Kane. It made my stomach tighten with nerves. If it turned out that Landon had become a criminal, if he was in charge of those mercenaries, if he'd arranged for my sister and I to be abducted... I didn't know what Kane would do. After watching him kill four people at the cabin, then what he did to that SUV yesterday, I knew it wouldn't be pretty.

The main airport was situated about five miles north of town. The next morning, John drove us in his truck, and we parked alongside the brown brick building. His friend, Gordon, another human, met us out front. Introductions were made, handshakes given. At my insistence, it was decided Kane would be the only one on the passenger manifest.

I'd heard someone call the plane a King Air, whatever that meant. It was bigger than the float plane but quite a bit smaller than the commercial flights I'd been on, sleek with a blue and red stripe down the side. John had said Gordon owned a few different planes, and the mines up north would often hire him for last minute flights. Thankfully, he hadn't had anything scheduled when we needed him.

When John quoted the cost to us the day before, Kane hadn't blinked at the price. Apparently, dropping seven grand on a private flight barely phased him. From Kane's dreams, I knew he'd designed a lot of things that Landon either used in his tech company or sold to others. I'd never dreamed about a bank deposit to know how lucrative that might have been.

The King Air could seat about ten people in its gray leather single seats on either side of a central aisle. Kane and I sat in the front row with John and Gordon ahead of us in the cockpit. There was only a curtain to separate us, but no one bothered to pull it closed.

With the airport being so small, we didn't have long to wait. We were taxiing and taking off within minutes of buckling up.

I bought a couple magazines at the pharmacy but couldn't concentrate. Tension rolled off Kane in waves. With each passing mile, he became more and more rigid, retreating into a dark place. I didn't want him to go there.

"If none of this had happened, I wouldn't have met you," I said, my gaze fixed to the rigid set of his body.

I knew he heard me when he nodded once, but my words didn't alleviate his grim demeanor. If I hadn't fallen from the sky and found his cabin, he would still be by himself, avoiding all contact with the outside world. And I would have finished up my time with the tattooed guy I'd met at the bar.

I swallowed as a sudden sick feeling rose in my stomach. The thought of being with anyone else besides Kane made me physically ill. I couldn't picture it anymore. Me, who hooked up with a different guy every time I went into heat, couldn't picture myself with anyone except the man beside me.

How could I have changed so much in such a short amount of time? No one made me feel the way Kane made me feel—just by looking at me. Not only did he meet my physical needs, he met my emotional ones too. And no man, *none*, had accomplished that before him.

Setting the magazines aside, I reached across the aisle and rubbed the back of his forearm, feeling the corded muscles beneath the hair. Keeping my gaze focused on his hand, I interlaced our fingers. Mine were slender compared to Kane's, his thick and strong, with a light dusting of hair on his knuckles and the back of his hand. I tickled my fingers through his hair, feeling the bones and veins beneath, then lifted my gaze to gauge his reaction.

His eyes were at half mast, most of his earlier tension gone. He liked what I was doing. I stroked up his wrist, then back over the corded muscles of his forearm, petting him. His muscles flexed under my touch. I wished the aisle wasn't separating us so I could lean my head against his shoulder. I loved touching him as much as I loved it when he touched me. The thought made the mark on my neck tingle.

I kept hold of him until we landed in Calgary to refuel an hour and a half later. There was a lot of waiting involved as a smaller plane in a big airport—scheduled commercial flights took precedence. We taxied, we waited, we fueled up, we taxied again, and waited some more. Eventually, we lined up for takeoff.

Another hour and a half later, we had another wait, circling Vancouver International Airport and taking our turn among the larger airliners flying to the coastal city of two million before we began our descent.

As the plane taxied, any softness I'd fostered in Kane during the flight disappeared. His eyes turned hard, his mouth a grim line of determination. Kane was now a predator in the same city as his prey.

The plane parked. After we were completely settled, Gordon got out of his seat and opened the door, the stairs lowering to the tarmac. Kane picked up the duffel bag, and I got my purse.

Warm air blasted me in the face when I took that first step down. I wasn't prepared for it. My new jeans stuck to my legs, suddenly too thick and heavy. I'd been up north so long, I'd forgotten it was late spring everywhere else. After hearty hand-shakes and thank yous, we left John and Gordon on the tarmac and made our way through the airport to find a taxi.

Late afternoon blended into early evening. In some ways, the drive downtown seemed familiar even though I'd never been to Vancouver before. The freeways, the glass buildings, the construction crews fixing the roads all were things I would see anywhere. But it was a world away from a quiet cabin on a lake where my favorite sounds became the coos of the loons, the buzz of insects, and lapping water.

I glanced over at Kane. His eyes were fixed out the window. I touched his hand. His head jerked, and he looked at me with unfathomable eyes. Focused inward, I wasn't sure he was seeing the city beyond the window. I took his hand again, wanting him to stay with me. He didn't resist, interlacing his fingers in mine, but then his gaze returned to the outside view.

My heart thumped hard, nervous to let this version of Kane loose on the city. I knew he was angry at everything that had happened to me and had questions for his cousin. I wasn't short on them either. Landon could be the key to finding my sister. But I'd also seen Kane shift, twice, in an uncontrollable way. Would he lose it in the city? Our instincts made it almost impossible to shift in front of a human. We needed to protect our secrecy at all costs. Would Kane's need for retribution outweigh his instincts?

The entire taxi trip was taken in silence. Downtown towered around us, glass and steel. Kane's finger stroked the center of my palm every few seconds, but his gaze remained out the window.

Finally, we pulled up to a swanky hotel in the West End. The glass structure reached to the sky, more than forty stories high, and was situated right on Vancouver Harbour. Inside, the sparkly light cast by the crystal chandeliers shone of the marble floor of the lobby. The concierge treated us like royalty despite our basic clothing and lack of luggage. Check-in took only minutes with Kane's platinum credit card.

I examined his face as we traveled up the smooth elevator to the thirtieth floor, wondering at how he took this preferential treatment like he'd been born to it. From the memories I'd dreamed of his childhood home, I knew for a fact he wasn't. For a man who'd lived so simply for so long, he sure had expensive tastes at the moment.

Our suite had its own living room, floor-to-ceiling windows on two sides with a spectacular view of the harbor. French doors separated a jacuzzi tub and a massive king-sized bed from the rest of the space. Six of Kane's cabins would have fit inside. The luxury confused me. *All* of this confused me. We could have gotten a room at a budget chain and accomplished our goals.

The truth slapped me upside the head. Kane was rich.

Why had he been living in a cabin without a toilet or hot water? He could have built any kind of cabin he'd wanted up there and instead, he locked his food in a cold room instead of owning a proper fridge.

It finally hit me. *Punishment.* The way he'd lived, no matter how comfortable he'd made it, had become forfeit. Even though he'd escaped his Goldenlach Ridge with his life, he'd been punishing himself since. My throat tightened. He'd been denying himself any kind of happiness or human connection out there in the wilderness.

Thud. Kane dropped his duffel inside the bedroom, then headed back to the door. I could practically taste his blood lust. I understood his only intent right now was ripping answers from his cousin.

I dropped my purse and ran to block his way, spreading my arms wide in front of the door. "We can't go now."

It was nearing the supper hour. We'd traveled a thousand miles to get here. We weren't going to ruin everything now with Kane charging in there with death on his mind.

He stopped a few feet away and growled.

"Don't growl at me." I lifted my chin. "We're going to do this with calm heads because we need answers, not blood. I came here to save my sister, and if I can wait, so can you. We wait until morning."

When he took another step toward me, a deeper growl rumbled through his chest.

"If you're going to growl at me like that, you better have some-thing else on your mind than ripping your cousin's arms off."

The tension around us shifted, his red-hot anger changing into a different kind of heat. But his expression didn't alter in intensity with his brows lowered, his teeth bared, and his hands fisted at his sides. He took another step toward me, looking feral and ready to tear me apart.

I swallowed, liquid heat pooling between my thighs. Bear baiting probably wasn't the best plan of action. My heart thumped so hard I could hear it in my head.

He closed the gap between us in one stride, pinning me against the door, hands on my wrists. Hot breath cascaded over my temple. He caged me, grinding down and up until only my toes touched the floor and his erection wedged into the juncture of my thighs.

Every nerve in my body delighted in the sensations. Kane was in complete control, and I liked it. I couldn't move except to wrap my legs around his waist and bite the shell of his ear.

Another growl vibrated through me, making me buzz. An answering purr erupted from my throat. He ground into me, and the restriction of my jeans, the fabric between us, became too much.

"I need you," I whispered, answering his thrusts with my own. "I want you."

Warm lips took possession of mine, his tongue promising the things he'd do to the rest of my body. I gasped, excitement racing through me. Emotions washed over me, making it hard to breathe. Some were my own, the primal need. Others...they felt like they came from somewhere else.

The grip on my wrists loosened and I dug my fingers into his hair. He turned away from the door, allowing my feet to drop to the floor. My tongue grazed his neck on the way down.

Keeping my eyes on his fierce expression, I backed away, toward the open doors of the bedroom, unbuttoning my jeans and lowering the zipper at the same time. He stalked toward me like the predator he was, and my heart rate kept climbing.

The bed hit the back of my thighs. I broke his stare, turning away to crawl on the bed, displaying my ass to him. When I looked over my shoulder, Kane's half-mast eyes were filled with focused desire.

His clothes flew away from him, then he was there, his hands on my hips, his growl making me clench, and everything else faded into the background.

30

BROOKE

It took three more orgasms to make me believe he wouldn't go tearing through the city intent on killing his cousin. I knew I was using my body to get him to calm, but neither I, nor my body, minded in the least. Not when each encounter felt better than the last.

After our quickie on the bed, we'd showered together, making love against the marble tile of the wall. Then he'd taken me to bed and made love to me again. Even though it was slow and easy, there was an underlying desperation to his movements. I hadn't thought it possible to meet a guy with a sexual appetite to match mine.

Now I lay curled in his arms, the evening sun peeking through the thin curtains covering the windows. I lifted my head to read the bedside clock. It was only seven. And tomorrow we needed to be ready to see his cousin.

I rolled away from Kane, out of his arms, and stood. He sat up, alert.

"I want to buy a few things downstairs," I said, searching for my G-string amongst the covers. "Can I charge them to the room?"

He nodded, then stood, intent on going with me.

I was going to protest, to say that I could do a little shopping on my own, when the memory of those cougars snatching me off the street made me swallow. Right now, being joined at the hip didn't seem like such a hardship.

It wasn't only what happened two days ago that stopped my objection. Being next to Kane was where I felt the most content. When we were close, when we touched, the tug in my chest that connected us like a physical thing became a comforting cocoon. The tug became more insistent the farther apart we were, creating a pressing need to return to his side.

At some point, we were going to need to work out how to gain some space from each other. That moment just didn't happen to be right now.

Quickly, I got dressed and Kane did the same. The ride down in the elevator was as smooth as it was up. When another couple, dressed in a sequined black evening gown and a tux, stepped on from the tenth floor, the surreal nature of everything that had happened to me over the past couple of weeks hit me again. Life truly went on without me.

On the ground level, I headed straight for the women's clothing boutique. Beside me, Kane hesitated.

I stopped in front of him and took his hand. "Did you want to wait somewhere for me?"

He nodded, glanced around, then pointed to the bar where the stools that lined the counter had an open view of the hotel lobby.

"Okay. I'll try to be quick, then we can find something to eat." I couldn't resist leaning up and giving his cheek a kiss.

He blinked, then the corner of his mouth curled into a smile.

My heart swelling at that small expression, I squeezed his hand and headed toward the boutique. I hoped they would have everything I needed.

They did. It was perfect. They even sold undergarments. I

knew I should pick more practical things but couldn't stop from buying over-the-top sexy lingerie. Every time I picked up something new, I thought of how Kane would look at me when I wore them, the intense expression he would give me. I shivered.

Clothing wasn't the only thing I needed. When I asked the sales associates to help me track down some other items, they jumped to it. They didn't even blink at some of my odder requests, just phoned the concierge, who'd assured me he could take care of everything.

It paid to be inside the world of the richy-rich. Eccentricities were expected. Everything would be delivered to our room by six in the morning.

When I finally stepped out into the lobby, I found Kane with a half-drank pint of beer in front of him, his face in a glower, and everyone giving him a wide berth.

His expression cleared when he saw me. He stayed put as I advanced, and I didn't stop until I stood between his knees. His hand skimmed my hip to the small of my back, pulling me close. A sigh slipped through my lips. I'd known he remained close throughout my whole time in the shop, but standing next to him now gave me relief.

We had dinner on the third floor of hotel, an Italian place that made a simple carbonara perfectly. The view of the harbor made me think of the view of the lake during our first meal out together in La Ronge. Then, the decor in the restaurant had been simple and a little rundown. Now I was sure we sat in a five-star restaurant, its tablecloths a pristine white, the servers all dressed in matching brocade vests and collared shirts.

Throughout supper, it was almost like I could feel Kane's rage beginning to boil again. He became more closed off with each passing minute, his movements becoming robotic. I touched his hand, I made small talk, I asked him questions about Vancouver, where he'd been before. He used sign, but just gave me short answers. I thought it was more about him not wanting to talk than him trying to keep his answers simple because I was still learning. Nothing pulled him out of it, not even being together once back at our room.

When I woke up in the middle of the night, the space beside me was empty. The time on the bedside clock said three in the morning. The tug in my chest told me Kane had moved away from me, downward a few floors, but remained in the hotel.

What was he doing? I wouldn't be able to get back to sleep until I found out.

Sliding out of bed, I found my key card and put on the complementary bathrobe hanging in the bathroom. The tug in my chest led me to the fifth floor.

A weight room was encased in glass on two sides, giving a full view of anyone within. Kane was the only one there, running on a treadmill wearing a pair of athletic shorts and no shirt.

For long minutes, I watched him. The treadmill droned in a high-pitched whine, the sound carrying through the glass. It must be set to max from the way he was running so fast. It was almost hard to watch in its intensity—the same way he'd been running after me when I'd been trapped in the back of that SUV, right before he shifted.

My man. My bear.

My breaths became short. Possessiveness sliced through me like a blade, startling in its severity. I'd never felt anything like it before. If a guy I had in my sights at the club turned to another woman, I couldn't have cared less. If he didn't want me, then he wasn't worth my time.

But with Kane, I wanted all of him, and God help anyone who stood in my way. There was no stopping these emotions, and I didn't know if I wanted to. They kept escalating, consuming me.

Even though I could see him right in front of me and knew he was fine, the tug in my chest told me to go to him. I stared at the keycard in my hand. It was impossible to walk away. Swiping it, I stepped inside. The room smelled like sweat and Kane.

He must have scented me or felt the permanent tug between us, because he lowered the speed and glanced over his shoulder. As soon as it slowed enough, he jumped off. His breathing was labored, the sheen of sweat over his body glistening in the fluorescent lights. He took a drink from his water bottle, his eyes never leaving mine. Whatever focus he'd had on his run now switched to me.

I shivered and held out my hand to him. "I'm lonely. Come back to bed."

A sudden flutter of nerves danced in my stomach. Not because I knew what would happen once we made it back upstairs, but because I was offering him my hand. I'd never done that before with a guy. A prickle of apprehension snaked its way up my spine, but I didn't lower my hand, didn't give into my need to protect myself from rejection.

With our gazes locked, Kane took a towel from the shelf, wiped the sweat from his chest and neck, then tossed it in the bin on the wall. His hand clasped mine, and he didn't hesitate to follow when I tugged him along. Our hands remained joined until we made it back to the room where they became occupied with other pursuits.

31

KANE

THE KNOCK ON THE DOOR WOKE US AT SIX THE NEXT MORNING.

A towel wrapped around my hips, I answered with a frown, intent on growling at whoever it was. After taking Brooke to bed post-run, I'd only had a couple hours sleep.

Ever since leaving La Ronge, I'd been promising myself not to touch her. The more we sank into regular civilization, the more I understood she needed a fast-paced life. Brooke was made for cities and creature comforts.

As much as I wanted to take her back to my cabin to spend the rest of my days making her happy in simple ways, the more time we spent in the city, the more I knew it would never work. Once we found her sister, I'd go back to my solitary life, and she'd go back to hers, filled with shopping and people. The bear inside me was too volatile to live in a dense population.

The thought shouldn't have made me sick to my stomach, but it did.

Because of that, I'd vowed not to touch her, to keep my hands to myself and make this visit to Vancouver all about business. But every time she looked at me with those cat eyes of hers, my promise went right out the window.

I opened the door, glowering. Two hotel staff greeted me with hesitant smiles, then carried bags and boxes inside. They deposited them on the table beside the kitchenette and left without a word. When the door shut behind them, I stared, blinking at the massive mound of goods.

Brooke slunk out of the bedroom wearing nothing but a hotel robe. A cry of delight left her lips when she saw everything. "It's like Christmas morning." Smiling, she dove in. Makeup, shoes, hair products, smaller bags filled with tissue paper, everything got pulled out, examined, then set aside.

I'd wondered why she hadn't come out with anything from that clothing store after spending almost two hours inside.

Out of one of the larger, square shopping bags came a briefcase. A briefcase? I shook my head, wondering why she needed all this stuff. Not that I cared about how much she spent. It wouldn't even put a dent in the money I'd earned from working with Landon over the years, including the stocks I owned with his company, Urick Enterprises.

From the last bag, she pulled out two cell phones, one looking like it was the latest model, the other a low-tech flip phone.

"Burner phone," she said when I raised my eyebrows at her. "I didn't want to use my old number in case they could track me or my sister that way. But I need a way for her to contact me." Her expression hardened, erasing the joy she'd had from exploring all her purchases. "She'll try to check on me if she can. If she's safe."

I nodded. It made sense to get a disposable phone. My mate was good at thinking ahead. I jerked my chin at the other one.

She smiled. "This one is for you. I dreamed about how you used to text your friends and family all the time and thought you could use it."

When she extended her hand to me, I shook my head. I wouldn't need it. I wasn't going to be in town that long. As soon as we found her sister, I'd go back to my cabin.

Her smile fell. "But..." She stared at the box. Her hand twitched once before she lowered it.

Brow furrowing, she put the phone box back inside the bag. She wouldn't meet my gaze as she took out the charging cord for her phone and plugged it into the charging station in the side table near the couch.

Then, with two of the bigger bags in her arms, she headed to the bathroom. "I need a shower," she muttered over her shoulder. The door closed behind her with a click.

My chest ached. Her emotional withdrawal hurt, but I knew it was for the best. She had to know there was no way for this to work. Not with the beast waiting to break free permanently and Brooke needing civilization to survive.

Even as I said those words to myself, the bear inside me growled in protest. It didn't want to let her go.

Mate. Mine.

But I couldn't allow the bear to win. Not this time. Brooke's safety and happiness were on the line, along with anyone else's who would come into contact with me. The aching hole in my chest expanded.

I stared at the mess remaining on the table and ran a hand over my face. My woman liked to shop. I'd known it from her dreams. When she got together for a shopping date with her mother, they'd spend the whole day going around to different stores, having lunch and coffee breaks, making it a whole experience. I knew from Brooke's thoughts that those moments were some of her favorites with her mother.

On the other side of the bathroom door, the shower turned on. I remained immobile, staring at the shopping bags on the table. It took me long minutes before I moved, finding the room service menu in the kitchenette. After staring at it, I left, heading to the lobby to order.

The water was still running when I returned fifteen minutes later. That woman also loved her showers. Not that I could blame her for taking advantage of the room's amenities after being stuck at my cabin for so long.

God, how she must have hated it. I'd dreamed of her sitting on the dock once, and she hadn't been filled with disdain, only peace. But up at my cabin, she didn't have the things that had kept her happy before meeting me. The stores, the clubs, the dinners out, the excitement... I could offer her none of it.

I walked to the window and stared out at the harbor. No matter how much it hurt, I had to let her go. She'd had little choice in the initial mating and her heat had dictated the rest. Over time, the pain of being separated from my mate would fade. For both of us.

While I listened to the shower, I told myself these things over and over again, hoping at some point I'd believe it.

A half hour later, room service arrived on a rolling cart. I'd cleared the table and the server set it out before disappearing. To distract myself from the increasing pain in my chest, I arranged everything. I knew what Brooke liked from our dreams. Bacon and eggs, toast, a side of cherry Danish, coffee, and orange juice. I might have gone overboard, but I'd wanted her to have everything she loved.

I glanced at the bathroom door. The water had stopped, but she remained inside. I hoped she would come out before everything got cold. To keep her dish warm, I covered it with the silver dome. My stomach grumbled and I glanced at the door again. No telling how long she'd be. With a heavy exhale, I sat in one of the chairs and dug into the eggs. When I'd finished my plate, she still hadn't come out.

I was about to pour myself a second cup of coffee when the bathroom door finally opened. The sight made me jump to my feet, overturning my chair and dropping my mug in the process.

Gone was the mate I'd come to know over the past two weeks. In her place was a business woman in a navy pantsuit with a bright white dress shirt underneath. The blonde hair that usually spilled everywhere like it had a life of its own was tamed in a neat twist at the back of her head, not a stray curl out of place. She wore glasses, *glasses*, and behind them was a face that belonged in a boardroom. Arched eyebrows, red lips, cheekbones that looked like they could cut glass—she'd sculpted her usual softness into something else. How had she done it?

If I hadn't seen her go into the bathroom myself, I would have thought a stranger had walked out.

A small smile twitched on her lips at my reaction. She spread her arms and did a little turn. "What do you think?"

The dress pants hugged her bottom and made her legs look longer than they were. I wanted those legs wrapped around me. I wanted to pull the pins from her hair and make it tumble around her face. I wanted to tear open the front of her shirt with my teeth and see what she hid underneath. I wanted to whip those sexy glasses off her face and make her eyes roll to the back of her head.

My body poised to pounce. The rational side of my brain told me to hold back. I'd convinced myself that our separation would be for the best, and now I wanted to paw at her like a wild animal. The two halves of me battled, their needs equal in strength. I wanted to keep her safe. I also wanted to take her in my arms and make her scream with pleasure.

Seemingly oblivious to where my thoughts had gone, Brooke walked toward the table, her focus on the food. But when she met my gaze, her eyes were filled with heat. Maybe not so oblivious.

"Thanks for ordering breakfast," she said, sitting down in the chair opposite mine to pour herself a coffee. "I'm starving."

I knew I should sit, act like everything was normal, but I couldn't stop staring at her.

After a while, her cheeks colored. "I wanted to look professional to meet your cousin." She took a sip of coffee.

Right. Landon. The anger, the rage, I'd been trying to smother over the past day boiled up inside me once again. With jerky movements, I set my chair back to rights and picked up my coffee mug from the carpet. As soon as I sat, I poured myself a second cup, knowing I glowered, but couldn't help it.

A part of me couldn't believe that Landon had betrayed me, either by selling my collar design to another company or bastardizing so much of it on his own. But my cousin had always been about business, about making money and climbing to the top. Landon had moved away from Goldenlach Ridge without looking back. I'd known he wouldn't return while his sights were focused on penthouse suites and beyond.

But during everything I'd gone through, Landon had my back. Why would he betray me now? For the money? Over the past five years, had Landon turned into everything we despised, enough to send minions after young women? None of it made sense.

"We'll get answers," Brooke said from across me, calling my attention. Her eyes were concerned and she'd taken my hand. I hadn't noticed. When she squeezed my fingers, I did the same to hers.

Yes, we'd get answers. And we'd find her sister. And then...

Uncertainty hung over the table for the rest of the meal. When we were done, Brooke went to her new phone. While I watched, she tried her sister's number.

"It still says she's out of the service area." Her brow wrinkled with worry, she punched in another number. "I'm going to leave the number for this burner phone direct to her voice mail." After a few long seconds, she spoke. "Sabrina. Call me." Then she recited her new number, complete with a Vancouver area code.

When she hung up, her breath hitched. "Please be okay," she said to the phone, gripping it tight.

Unable to stop myself, I pulled her to me, wrapping my arms around her shoulders. I wanted to tell her everything was going to be okay, but I wasn't sure that was true. A lot could happen in two weeks.

After my shower, I dressed in my best shirt and jeans. Brooke took one look at me, scowled, and told me to take my shirt off. It wasn't for a quickie. She found an ironing board and iron in the closet and set about taking out all the wrinkles.

I didn't think I'd ever seen a woman iron something before. The domesticity of it made me grin, but my amusement didn't last long.

It was time to see my cousin.

32

KANE

THE CLOSER WE TRAVELED TO URICK ENTERPRISES, THE MORE THE edges of my vision hazed red. I fisted my hands, willing the sensation to fade away. I needed to keep it together for Brooke. We needed to find her sister.

The taxi dropped us off in front of a towering building, one of many glass and steel skyscrapers that reached for the clouds in downtown Vancouver. Forcing a measure of calm, I held the tall door open for Brooke and took a breath, trying to keep my composure. After a light touch on my arm, she strode ahead of me toward the main receptionist's desk like she'd been born with a briefcase in her hand. Even with my ironed shirt, I still looked like the hired help compared to my mate.

Brooke's heels clicked against limestone tile. She held a card out before we'd stopped in front of the woman on her high stool overlooking the tall black and gold desk.

"Kane Baird to see Mr. Urick," Brooke said, her tone short and clipped.

The woman took the card with a raised eyebrow. All it had on it was my name, nothing else. Where had Brooke gotten it from?

"Do you have an appointment?" the receptionist asked, barely giving the card a glance.

"Mr. Baird doesn't need an appointment." Brooke said it in the voice reserved for unintelligent children.

Looking like she was trying not to roll her eyes, the receptionist picked up the phone and dialed. A moment later, she said my name, then waited. When someone spoke to her on the other end, she straightened like a buzzer went off under her butt. Her eyes shot to us. "Yes, he's standing right here with his assistant." A second of silence, then, "Yes, sir."

Hanging up the phone, she said, "Mr. Urick is up on the thirty-third floor and will see you now." She gestured to the elevators behind her.

"Thank you," Brooke murmured, her expression unchanging from its serene state, like she'd expected that response.

We made our way to the elevators and stepped on the first one that opened up. We were alone in the car.

"That was fun," she said, her serious expression turning into a grin.

I might have agreed with her, except the more I thought about the upcoming encounter, the more the red haze swelled. The urge to rip off my cousin's arms kept climbing up my throat.

I was only vaguely aware of Brooke pressing the button for the correct floor, didn't see her stop in front of me until she took my hand. My gaze focused on her face, and I drowned in her tawny cat eyes. There was concern there, but something else too. The rhythmic stroke of her thumb on the back of my hand was supposed to calm me, but it wasn't working. The closer the elevator climbed to Landon, the more the red haze took over.

Keeping hold of my hand, Brooke rose on her tiptoes and placed a kiss on the corner of my mouth. My heart rate lowered, the haze receding. When she rocked back on her heels, I kept my gaze on hers, letting myself sink into the depths of her eyes.

A tone above us dinged, signaling the thirty-third floor.

Brooke dropped my hand, and we strode out into a world of glass walls. A desk spanned the foyer, a receptionist behind it with a phone to her ear. She lowered the receiver when she saw us coming.

"Mr. Baird to see Mr. Urick," Brooke said, her voice back to its short and clipped professionalism.

The receptionist stood and gestured to the door on the left. "This way, please," she said, using her keycard to pass through the first door. A long hallway was bracketed by tall doors. The glass walls allowed us to glimpse the business people inside, who glanced at us briefly as we walked by, then returned to their phone calls.

We were led to the last office. The receptionist knocked twice, then opened the door to a space sheathed in windows. There wasn't a lot in the room, but it was the only one without glass walls to the other offices, offering a certain amount of privacy. A central, glass-topped desk took a major portion of the middle, a flat-screen monitor and keyboard sitting to the one side. Tropical plants were placed strategically around the room.

I barely saw any of it, my gaze entirely focused on the man behind the desk.

A flash of disbelief crossed my cousin's expression. "Well, this is a surprise. If I'd had some advance warning, I could have cleared my whole day. When they said you were downstairs, I half-expected an imposter."

His words were faint in my ears, like they came from far away. My entire focus tunneled to the man who had put Brooke in such a dangerous position. Wanting her to take the lead, I stood stock still as she stepped forward to introduce herself.

Landon stood, extending his hand. "His assistant," he repeated, the words muffled from the roaring in my ears. Landon's appreciative gaze ran up and down Brooke's body.

A growl ripped itself from my chest.

Landon raised an eyebrow. "More than an assistant. Got it."

He sat at his desk and folded his hands in front of him, serene. "You didn't come all this way for nothing. What can I do for you? Did you bring me another design?"

The jackass was acting like nothing was the matter, that he hadn't become some evil overlord in his skyscraper plotting to hunt down women. His nonchalance made my jaw ache to rip into him.

Through the red haze, I saw Brooke open the briefcase and take out her collar. She dropped the remote, then the heavy piece of metal on the glass surface. *Whack.* A shard flew to the side.

Good. Because I really wanted to break some shit on Brooke's behalf. Starting with Landon's face.

"Where did you get this?" His posture suddenly stiff, he picked up the collar with both hands.

"From around my neck," Brooke replied, her voice calm.

Images of her stumbling into my cabin, starving and afraid, only made me seethe more. The rage kept coming, building, as I thought of my mate being in pain. Of being hurt.

The conversation between Brooke and Landon continued, but I didn't hear any of it. I kept thinking of Brooke in danger. Red covered my entire vision. That collar had ended up on Brooke's neck because of my cousin. Every instinct in me told me to protect her, to eliminate the threat.

I would have Landon's blood in exchange for Brooke's pain.

A growl emerged from my chest. Brooke and Landon snapped their gazes to me.

Through the red haze, Brooke's eyes widened. Her lips moved, forming my name. She must have said it aloud, but I didn't hear it. The roaring in my head was too loud.

A flash of movement. Landon vaulted over the desk, putting himself between me and Brooke. The act of aggression, separating us, sent my protective instincts through the roof.

The shift came over me, my claws, my teeth. A tearing sound

echoed off the glass windows. My bear wanted out. It yearned for blood as much as I did. I couldn't stop it.

Landon took a couple steps back, his arms spread wide. He said something in warning over his shoulder—to Brooke. My cousin was telling my mate to get out of here for her own safety, protecting her from me.

My mate.

I would never hurt Brooke. I only wanted my cousin's blood.

I waited for Landon to shift and fight like a bear.

But my cousin didn't shift, not even his claws or canine teeth. His eyes remained steady and guarded. I swayed back and forth, wanting to attack but holding back because Landon hadn't shifted yet.

Brooke came out from behind my cousin.

"Don't. He's dangerous like this." Landon's words came from a great distance as he stepped in front of her again.

She ducked under his arm. "He won't hurt me."

"Are you sure about that?"

"Yes." She turned her head to the side but kept her eyes on me. "Leave us for a minute, okay?"

Through my haze, I saw Landon hesitate, then give a small nod before moving to the door. My instincts told me to go after him, to tear into him and relieve the rage inside me, but then Brooke was there, filling my vision. Her eyes never left mine as she swayed with me, always blocking my view of the door where Landon had gone.

"Kane, focus on me." She put her hands up, like I held her at gunpoint. "Listen to my voice. Smell me." She extended her hand forward. "We're in a public place."

Inhaling her fragrance, I rubbed my face against her skin. My staccato heart rate slowed as her familiar scent calmed me. She was here in front of me, safe. There was no danger. The red edges of my vision began to fade.

"You need to shift back," she murmured, stepping closer.

Shift? I shook my head to clear it. I hadn't shifted, had I? I looked down at my body. My muscles bulged beneath my shirt, fur tearing through the fabric. Long claws stretched from my fingers, and my teeth were sharp in my mouth.

I was neither a bear nor a man, but stuck as something in between.

This had never happened before.

I'd never stopped a shift midway.

Blinking fast, I stared at my hands. The red around my vision receded a fraction but not completely.

When we were in La Ronge, when those two cougars took Brooke, I'd been able to shift back on my own. Because my mate needed me.

My mate needs *me*. We came here for answers. My rage pushed that necessity aside.

Staring at my hands wasn't willing them back into human form. A frustrated breath huffed out of me, making a stray hair on Brooke's forehead twitch.

The last time I'd shifted, Brooke's memories focused me. Her running through the woods, the desire to return to human, all those things facilitated her transformation. I concentrated on those memories again.

"Kane?" she asked, her hand on my cheek.

I nodded once and focused on her eyes. They pulled me in, their yellow color a pool of concern and caring. Swallowing, I remembered Brooke's memories like they were my own. My bones shifted, my fur receded, my body became like sand through a funnel, one granule changing at a time.

When my hand returned to being fully human, I touched her cheek like she held mine. Closing her eyes, she leaned into the connection.

My eyes burned as emotion welled up inside my chest, so hot I thought it might scorch me.

I pulled her to me, needing to feel her against my body. It

wasn't just about being mated. It was *everything*—her strength, her intelligence, her fearlessness in the face of what had happened to her. Her courage in facing me during one of my shifts. We may have met in an unusual circumstance, the odds against us, but she was my perfect match. My perfect mate. I loved her.

I loved her, and that was why I needed to let her go. I wouldn't allow myself to hurt her, to put her in danger again. A defeated sob worked its way up into my throat, pain shooting to my limbs when I thought about separating.

Because when I shifted, I lost all sense of self.

The second I had that terrifying thought, realization hit me like a hammer to glass. The bear hadn't subverted me completely. Not this time. I hadn't fully shifted. Even though it had taken a minute, I'd rationalized. I remembered everything about the incident, the look on Landon's face as he tried to protect Brooke, her words to me, Landon leaving. I hadn't blacked out.

I remembered part of my last shift too. When Brooke needed me after those cougars had abducted her, I made the decision to stay with her instead of chasing after those fuckers. I'd returned to my human form so I could help her with the remote.

I'd had coherent thoughts. I could shift and retain my control. With practice, I might be able to master it. I wasn't like my father who now lived as a bear. I wasn't like my grandfather who'd been put down for hurting others.

Brooke had made that possible. There was no way I could let her go now just because I couldn't adjust to her lifestyle. Not in a million years. She made me whole, a sensation I never thought I would experience. I'd move mountains for her.

My torn shirt hanging off my body, I hugged her to me. I stroked her hair, her back, her shoulders.

"I love you," she murmured against my chest.

My whole body froze.

Her arms squeezed me tighter. "I know it's probably something you don't want to hear, but it's true." She pressed her face to my sternum. "I know I'm probably not what you'd want in a mate long-term, but I can't help the way I feel. And I...I just wanted you to know that."

She didn't think she was something I'd want in a mate long-term? Disbelief making my movements slow, I leaned away from her and took her elbows in my hands. At first, she resisted the separation of our bodies but then tilted her head enough to look up at me. Tears welled in her eyes.

"I'm sorry. I shouldn't have said that."

I kissed her to make sure she wouldn't apologize for loving me ever again, pouring every emotion I had for her into it— thankful. So very thankful. Her memories had helped me control the beast inside me. Her calm tempered me. Her presence in my life made me a better person.

I couldn't stop kissing her, couldn't stop the emotions churning and swelling inside me.

I love you. I love you. I love you.

She gasped, her breath catching in my mouth, then tore her lips from mine. "I can feel you."

I shook my head, not understanding. The bond between us? It had been there for a while now.

"Your emotions." Shaking her head like she wanted to clear it, she whispered, "I can feel them. They're so strong now."

I stilled. *Yes, there.* Our bond had grown exceptionally powerful over the past few minutes, and there were new things there. I felt her hesitancy, her love...her everything.

33

BROOKE

I COULD HARDLY BELIEVE IT. HIS EMOTIONS CAME TO ME AS CLEAR as day—love, gratitude, peace, concern... Each had a different flavor, melding into each other, but I could feel them all. The emotions passed from him to me through our bond, a bond that now connected us from head to toe.

My heart raced. Sensing his emotions was like coming home, like everything was perfect in the world even though it was far from it. The impressions I'd been getting from him before, where I'd understood what he was feeling, I'd thought I'd imagined them.

But this... He loved me. He didn't want to let me go.

My arms squeezed him tight against me. Nothing had ever felt so good. Nothing. Not even sex. This connection we had, it meant everything. And there was no way I could ever give it up. Not without a fight.

I poured every bit of love I had for him through our bond. I closed my eyes and thought of all those special moments we had together at his cabin, how much I loved being there with him, how I loved the calm and tranquility of the place, how I would give anything to go back there again and recapture those quiet moments between us.

He gasped, then held me tighter. His lips pressed in my hair. I felt impressions of myself, of me sitting on the dock or him just watching me sleep. I felt his joy at being able to take care of me, to make me dinner and hold me. Every new emotion made moisture pool in the corner of my eyes. His feelings were so beautiful, his intent clear. It was like some sort of song we were singing to each other, our own melody.

We were going to make this relationship work. I believed it with my whole being. We could split our time between his cabin, my place, wherever. It didn't matter. As long as we were together, nothing would get in our way.

I didn't know how long we stayed that way. It could have been hours. When, at last, I lifted my head, Kane's eyes were glistening too. Lifting my hand, I brushed at the corner of his eye. He smiled. I did too, a goofy smile that made my cheeks hurt. This bond between us was more powerful than anything I'd ever experienced.

Behind us, the door opened. We turned together. I'd forgotten where we were.

Landon stood at the door, hesitating. Kane stiffened, but this time, the tension in his body remained manageable.

"Since I didn't hear any roaring or screaming, I thought perhaps all is well?" Landon phrased the statement as a question.

"Yes," I replied, my arms tight around Kane. Not because I thought he'd attack—his state of mind remained calm—but because with our emotions so raw, I needed him close. When his hand skimmed down my spine, a purr rumbled through me.

Landon held a bundle of clothing in his arms. "Thought you might need these." He extended his hand. "Workout clothes."

When Kane glanced down at himself, I felt his shame. Not only was his shirt torn, but his jeans had split down the sides as well. His regret stabbed me. I also knew he wouldn't allow it to happen again. I could feel his control, and his recognition that our bond made him stronger.

He reached for the bundle with jerky movements. He was angry at himself. As he ripped the remains of the torn shirt off his body, I crossed my arms over my chest.

"That's the last time I'm ironing a shirt for you," I muttered out the side of my mouth.

Kane paused, flashed me a quick grin, then pulled on the sweatpants.

I shot Landon a quick look as he moved to his chair on the other side of the desk. Despite the businessman's unruffled exterior, I could see the worry in his expression, his eyes alert like he expected Kane to lose it again. And if he did, he would do what was required to stop him.

The calm Kane and I had achieved between us told me that wouldn't be necessary.

The moment I'd laid eyes on Landon, he'd given off an air of authority and self-importance. His short brown hair was thick, a light dusting of scruff on his jaw, and his coloring was different than Kane's, more olive-toned, perhaps from some Mediterranean ancestry. He'd changed from Kane's last memories of him, become stronger, maybe even a little taller, if that was possible. While Kane's strength was bulky, Landon was lanky and hidden expertly beneath an expensive suit. Everything in the office was designed to exude wealth and power, and that was echoed in Landon's demeanor.

Kane straightened. The clothes were a bit tight on him, highlighting his muscular form. I took his hand.

Landon gestured to the two chairs across from him at his desk, and we sat, keeping our hands joined. Some of Landon's pompous air had melted away. Instead, he stared at us with speculation, assessing.

"I think we need to start at the beginning," he said, his fingers steepled together in front of his chest. "I understand whatever brought you here is important." He tilted his head toward Kane. "I'm not going to pretend that you popping up after five years isn't significant." Then he stared at me, his eyes missing nothing. "With him being on edge like this, I need to ask, are you in danger?"

I swallowed. "Yes. My sister and I."

"American?"

I nodded once and he made a motion with his hands for me to go on. My lips were dry and I pressed them together. "Some people abducted us and used these collars. I got free. My sister didn't. I need to find her."

He kept my gaze, and I had the impression of multiple wheels turning in his head all at once. Whether that was a good or bad thing remained to be seen.

He looked at Kane. "Tell me more."

Kane began to sign, slowly at first, then faster as he sank into the story of us. I only caught some of the words, but understood he told Landon about the animals on the plane with me, that I came from Detroit and, with the flight path, was probably headed somewhere even more northern. He told him about the cougar shifters, the helicopter, and the tactical guys. There was anger in his movements, but he didn't lose control.

When Kane finished, Landon stared at us for long minutes. "It's not my plane, but I know someone who could track flights from that day, find out where it was headed."

Hope speared inside me, and I realized then that I'd tried not to hope too much ever since landing in Vancouver.

Landon reached for the collar on his desk. Picking it up, he balanced it like he considered its weight. "And this isn't our design. It isn't what we did with yours," he said, nodding at Kane. "There might be some similarities, but there are also major differences."

Kane twitched. I stroked my thumb along the back of his

hand. "I don't know if we can believe you," I said, my gaze unflinching as I stared at his cousin.

Landon watched us, his eyes lighting on our joined hands, then our faces, bouncing back and forth like a tennis match. After a long minute, he stood with my collar in hand. "Come with me." His smooth gait took him around the desk and to the door.

Stooping to pick up the briefcase I'd set on the floor, I snatched the remote off the desk and popped it back inside. Landon held the door open, allowing us to proceed ahead of him. When we passed the receptionist's desk, he said, "Clear the rest of my day."

We stopped at the elevator, and once the car arrived, we all got inside. Landon pressed the button for the seventeenth floor.

I tucked myself into Kane's side. His arm circled me, pulling me close. Our emotions ebbed and flowed within our bond while my mind raced. In a way, I was relieved if Landon didn't turn out to be the one behind our abduction. I didn't want that permanent scar between the two cousins. But if he wasn't the one behind it, then this trip might have become a dead end.

My breath caught in my throat. To come all this way for nothing... I didn't know what I would do. I needed to find Sabrina. When I leaned my head against Kane's chest, he rubbed a hand up and down my back.

The elevator doors opened. Landon stepped off first and we followed. This level didn't have the polished "office" feel the other had. This floor was more sterile with florescent lights and a tile floor.

A heavy metal door with a narrow window closed off the space ahead of us. Landon swiped a card, and we entered a long, narrow hallway lined with more windowless doors, unmarked. When we reached the end, he swiped his card on another keypad and the door opened into a lab.

A half dozen people stared as we entered. There was one

"clean" area behind glass, but otherwise, the people working there were wearing lab coats over semi-casual attire.

With a jerk of his head to the side, Landon led us over to a workstation where collars like mine were lined up on the surface. Some hung from hooks on the wall, each one a little bit different from the next.

A low growl emerged from Kane's chest. I tightened my grip on his hand.

"This," Landon said, taking the last collar off its hook, "is what we've done with the design. There are similarities—I see them too—but what you showed me isn't the same."

He balanced the two, then set them side by side on the table. The one he'd taken off the wall was segmented, like it would move fluidly with the person wearing it instead of being one immovable circlet like mine. The metal was also slimmer. It would be easier to hide under a high collared shirt.

The more he stared at the two designs, the more he scowled, the first crack in his polished demeanor.

Kane signed a question, and Landon's eyes flicked to us then back to the collars. "We didn't design it to be used with a remote."

From what we saw, he was telling the truth. None of the designs were paired with remotes, and they each looked designed for comfort.

"May I see it again?" he asked me.

I set the briefcase on the work surface to open it up and give the remote to him.

"This frequency gauge?" Landon ran his thumb over the square button. "A shock element?" He asked the question to Kane, who growled and nodded at the same time. "We never did that either," Landon said, his frown becoming fierce. "It wasn't even remotely on our radar. We did add a tracking device, but honestly, that was a given." He set the remote down and picked up both collars and held them side by side. "Plus, you can see another designer had a hand here. It's like they started off with the same prototype we did but ended up somewhere completely different because they didn't have the same goal."

"And what was your goal?" I asked, taking the one his company designed from him to examine it more closely. I knew how much Kane had intended from his dreams, but I wanted to hear it from Landon.

His gaze went to my mate. "The same as Kane's from the beginning." He shook his head. "I have to admit, it's not a priority for us to develop. It's a small market, and the design is too expensive." His voice lowered. "Rabid shifters aren't a high-yield investment. I developed it as a favor to you." Grimacing, he set the collar on the work surface. "Production on it has stalled. I get more use out of your other designs."

I stared at the collar in my hand, then the ones on hooks on the wall. "If my collar started out with the same prototype, how did someone else get Kane's original plans?"

Landon's lips pressed together, his features hardening. "I don't know."

Kane gestured to the people in lab with a sweep of his hand.

"One of your employees betrayed you?" I asked.

Landon shook his head. "No. No way. Everyone here is loyal. There were two shifters working on it in the beginning, but anyone else who had a hand in the design thought it was for animals."

Setting the newer design down, I took the first prototype off the wall, the one identical to the collar in the bottom drawer of Kane's desk at the cabin. "Where did the two designs split from each other?"

Landon tipped his head side to side, thinking. "About four years ago, that third design on the wall. Those first couple of years, we worked on it a lot, but I haven't done anything with it in a while. This version," he said, picking up the newest design off the table, "is the final one. It's done. It works."

I looked at Kane, understanding the next question in his eyes because it was mine as well. "Did you have any disgruntled employees who worked in this lab four years ago?" I asked Landon.

He stiffened. That made Kane tense too.

"Who is it?" My heart raced.

Landon shook his head like he couldn't believe it. "No. Not possible. She wouldn't have stolen from me." From the way he said it, it sounded like he was trying to convince himself, not us.

"She?"

His gaze became distant. "I lost track of someone, Jolyn." He looked at Kane, his features pinched. "Do you remember her from Goldenlach Ridge?"

Kane shook his head.

"She was the one...the one you saved that day when you were kids. The one Tom was beating up."

A fragment of one of the dreams I shared with Kane surfaced in my mind where a girl with red hair was straddled by the boy Kane hated, the one who was eventually responsible for his throat injury, the one Kane killed.

"I thought she'd left because..." Landon shook his head like he didn't want to continue the thought. "Good news. If it's her, then I already have someone trying to track her down. When I have answers, you will too."

Kane twitched.

"Who do you have tracking her?" I asked before he could sign the question.

Landon crossed his arms over his chest and leaned against the worktable. It looked like he was trying to appear calm, but I could tell from the way tension rolled in his body that he wanted to punch something. It kind of reminded me of Kane.

With his gaze fixed on Kane, Landon said, "I've got Walker tracking her. Or, at least, he's supposed to be. I haven't heard from him in a couple weeks. He isn't returning my calls."

I knew who Walker was from Kane's dreams, the skinny

cougar who lived in the trailer park on the outskirts of their town but had been deployed overseas in the military.

Kane signed another question, his emotions becoming discontent.

Landon shrugged. "He needed a job, some sort of direction." He raised a hand before Kane could object to him using Walker as an underling. "You haven't been around, Kane. You didn't see him when he came back. He wasn't the same. His time overseas fucked with him. I did him a favor." His face stark, he ran a hand over his head, mussing his perfectly groomed hair. "I've given him something to do other than contemplate a bullet."

Kane glanced away, and I felt his shame. He hadn't been here for his friend, and he didn't know how to fix it. Taking his one hand in both of mine, I tugged him to me, offering comfort.

"This," Landon said, gesturing to the collars. "This is my fault. I had a breach and I'll take care of it."

"I need to find out where they've taken my sister." My chest tightened painfully. "I need to get her back."

Landon nodded. "I can understand that. I'll do whatever I can to help, with tracking the plane and anything else. And I'll let you know as soon as I've found something or when I hear from Walker." He picked up my collar. "Can I keep this? I'd like to find out as much about the design as possible."

When I looked to Kane, he nodded once. "We're okay with that."

The tension in his body easing, Kane's gaze bounced around the rest of the lab, never settling.

"You can take a look around if you like," Landon said to him. "You'll see a couple of your newer designs in prototype production."

After a brief hesitation, Kane ran a hand down my spine, then strode off, looking at the different things the employees were working on. They watched him with wary expressions. And while my mate prowled around, I realized Landon was watching me. I raised my eyebrows.

"Kane has mating marks," he said quietly.

My cheeks heated. Kane's dress shirt had concealed them, but his borrowed T-shirt did not. "Yes," I said, lifting my chin.

His eyes went to my throat, but I knew mine weren't visible underneath my shirt. I'd checked before leaving the hotel.

"What do you know of Kane's past?" he asked, his eyes going to Kane across the room then back to me.

I didn't see a reason to lie. "Everything." And it didn't matter. What was in his past didn't change how I felt about him.

Tucking his hands into the front pockets of his suit pants, Landon leaned against the work surface. "Then maybe you could tell him what he won't hear from me."

The statement made me tense, but I remained quiet, too curious to object.

"The authorities in Goldenlach Ridge aren't after him. They haven't been for years. He doesn't need to remain in exile because of what happened the day he left." He paused like he was unsure if he should continue, like he wasn't sure if I really knew everything.

I nodded for him to go on.

"That woman was dead before Kane trampled her during the fight. The coroner's report proved that. Tom's dad buried everything because he knew it was his kid's fault. I think he'd known Tom was the one behind all the recent tourist disappearances from the start." He ran a hand over his face. "Kane wouldn't believe me when I tried to tell him years ago. Maybe he'll listen to you."

Swallowing, I nodded. "I'll tell him." Someday. Not today. There was too much other shit to process.

Our next moments were silent as we watched Kane across the room. He picked up some sort of tool and gestured to a workstation. The employee moved out of his way so he could sit.

He was in his element here. It was like he wanted to play. It brought warmth to my chest, banishing some of the cold dread I felt at not having leads on my sister's whereabouts.

"Kane's a lucky man," Landon murmured, his voice bordering on wistful. I might have replied, except a ring tone I was not used to sang from the briefcase beside me. I froze, my stomach squeezing painfully. I only gave one person my number.

34

KANE

THE SECOND BROOKE'S PHONE RANG, I JUMPED TO MY FEET. Meeting her shocked stare across the room, I strode away from the workstation where the engineers collaborated on one of my 3D multi-sensor transmitter ideas. Since sending my first thoughts last year, they hadn't made as much progress on it as I would have thought.

But as soon as that phone rang, all thoughts of transmitters went right out of my head.

She held the phone away from her, like it was something that might explode. The screen read "unknown number" and her hands shook as she pressed the green icon to answer it and put it on speaker phone.

Please don't be a wrong number.

"Hello?" Brooke's voice shook, her nerves and fear slapping at me. I ran my hand down her spine, trying to give her some amount of comfort no matter who was on the other end.

"Brooke. Thank God you're okay."

"Sabrina."

When Brooke's knees collapsed, I caught her to me, my arm around her middle, her back supported. I took the phone too so she wouldn't drop it. The relief pouring out of my mate made me heady. A large part of her had thought her sister dead.

Her entire body shaking against me, Brooke swallowed, her throat clicking with the effort. "Where are you? Are you okay?"

"Yes. I'm okay for now."

I took note of the "for now" part of that sentence as my eyes flew to Landon's. He'd heard it too.

A moment of silence on the line, then, "When I heard your message... God, Brooke, I was so worried about you. Are you somewhere safe?"

Fingernails squeezed into my forearm. "Yes. I'm protected."

"Thank God. What about Mom? Have you heard from her?"

"Yes, she's okay. She's safe." Brooke said, her voice shaking. "Where are you?"

There was a bang and another voice, a man, and he didn't sound happy. Brooke and I tensed at the same time. My hand tightened on the phone.

"I don't have a lot of time to explain," Sabrina said, and I heard the strain in her tone, the panic. "I got free, but I have some things to take care of."

Brooke straightened against me. "What things? We can help. Just tell me where you are."

"No!" Sabrina's voice came out a bark. "I don't want you anywhere near here. If you're safe, you stay safe. I'll contact you again when I'm done with this."

"What is 'this'?" Brooke was practically shouting now, her anger and frustration washing over me in a tidal wave. "Sabrina, you're scaring me."

"Just know I'm okay. I've got to go. I love you, little sis." The call disconnected.

"No," Brooke whispered, her hands gripping my forearm tight.

We were both so relieved Sabrina was alive and well, but from that phone conversation, would she stay that way for long? I tried not to dwell on the fact that it sounded like Sabrina was saying goodbye for the last time. The same dread echoed to me through our bond.

Brooke turned her face to me. "How can we help her if she won't say where she is?"

Turning her so she faced me, I hugged her. I sent her my belief that we'd find her together. A sob shuddered through her body, and I pressed my lips against the top of her head.

Our emotions flowed back and forth between us until I couldn't be sure who was feeling them first. It had all started in Detroit. That's where her sister pulled Brooke from the club, where those men snatched them from the street. Someone in Detroit would know something. We needed to go there to find answers.

There were no longer any questions between us. We were doing this together. There were no other options.

"We need to fly to Detroit." She pulled away from me to look up at my face. "I don't have a passport, though. How do we figure this out?" A fierce frown puckered her brow.

"I can help with that."

Landon's voice broke through our internal conversation. I'd almost forgotten he was there.

"I have a private plane and connections with the American embassy here in Van."

A small portion of tension eased from me and Brooke at the same time.

"But I think I need to go with you," Landon added. "The last time I heard from Walker, he was in Detroit."

We both stiffened at this revelation. Everything that had happened was connected. We just needed to find out how.

Landon nodded his head to the phone I held. "If we give that to my people, they might be able to track where your sister was calling from."

I passed it over without reservations.

Finally, we were getting somewhere. The phone, the flight, the new direction. Satisfaction hummed through both of us, two companion emotions echoing each other in perfect harmony. We were going to make this work—us, our relationship, everything. We could live at my cabin, here in Van, or in Detroit. It didn't matter, because wherever we went or whatever we did, it would be side by side.

And we were on the road to finding Sabrina. No matter what obstacles we saw before us, we would conquer them together.

EPILOGUE
SABRINA

Back to the beginning...

Flood lights lit up the building all around the perimeter. An eight-foot, chain link fence went around the whole thing, a twelve-foot swath of grass between it and any building. Nowhere to hide and only one way to get in, through the gate manned by a guard house and two guards. Other guards walked around the perimeter.

I lowered my binoculars, contemplating. It was like a mini prison. Was it keeping people in or out?

How the hell was I supposed to get inside? There was no hint as to the happenings within. If that missing couple was inside, then I had no idea how to get them out. If I contacted the police at this point, would they even be useful? I'd only run into roadblocks with them ever since those two went missing in my park.

As a park ranger, I'd tracked many hikers who'd gotten lost on the trails and led them back to their campsites. But the disappearance of this particular couple was completely different. For one, they were bobcat shifters like me. Shifters didn't get lost. Not when we could follow our scents back home. And two, when I'd followed their trail, it had disappeared at the highway. All their belongings had remained at the campsite. I couldn't believe they'd hitchhiked and moved on. They'd been snatched.

Without a lead, the police had stopped looking. Without a lead, I had started digging into their lives, trying to figure out the reason behind their abduction. They'd been missing for two weeks now. If it was a random act of violence, then I would have hit a dead end. Instead, my off-the-books investigation had brought me here, to the Fort Knox of warehouses on the outskirts of Detroit. The woman had worked for the company that owned the place. What did they do here?

A twig snapped behind me and I spun around. The next instant, a hand clamped around my throat. The binoculars dropped to the ground as I pawed at the fingers gripping my windpipe.

I smelled shifter, predator, as I tried to take a breath.

Shrouded in darkness, a man's face took up my vision. His features were veiled by the shadow of his cowboy hat. "Look what I've caught," he said with a Texas accent. "Another kitty for the hunters to skin. You've been poking where you shouldn't. Have you told anyone where you are? Your sister or mom perhaps?"

I wanted to shift, but with the lack of air came the lack of energy. I needed to break free first.

Something moved behind him. Another guy. No, two more. They were all shifters. Their scents overwhelmed me. They were feline, but not a bobcat. They had a heavier scent, maybe mountain lions.

My brain told me this as my vision blackened. He was choking me to death. I put all my energy into shifting my hands, clawing at him, trying desperately to make him release me.

Something streaked through the night, ripping the hand away from my throat. A brutal, feline scream rent the air, followed by another. The sounds of a full-on brawl came at me through the dark.

I couldn't see anything but moving shadows, but what I heard made me back away. I didn't know who any of these shifters were. The urge to flee overrode everything else.

Without a backward glance, I ran.

Twigs and bushes scraped at me as I took off. I ignored the twinges of pain and pushed on. I needed to get as far away from here as possible. They knew about my mom and sister. I needed to warn them. Stumbling toward where I parked my car on the highway, I grabbed my phone.

By the time I tumbled into the front seat of my car, my mother's number was already ringing. It went to voice mail. "Call me. It's important."

I hung up as I careened onto the highway in a spray of dirt. Then I texted Brooke knowing she didn't usually answer calls. *Where are you?*

I kept driving toward the city limits, waiting for my sister to respond, my heart racing more and more when she didn't. Finally, my phone dinged with a text. *Blackguards!*

Relief that my sister was okay made my hands shake on the steering wheel. It was a Friday night, and it didn't surprise me that Brooke had named one of her favorite dancing spots. Another text dinged.

Are you off work for the weekend? Join me! There are so many hot guys here. You'd have your pick!

Being invited to go dancing grated on my nerves more than usual after almost having the life choked out of me. I didn't know what I'd stumbled onto, but those shifters meant business. They would have killed me without thinking twice about it. My fear for that missing couple grew.

I needed to get Brooke to safety. I texted back.

On my way.

Thank you for reading! Did you enjoy? Please add your review because nothing helps an author more and encourages readers to take a chance on a book than a review.

And don't miss book two of the *Goldenlach Ridge Shifters* series, CAGED FURY, available now. Turn the page for a sneak peek!

You can also sign up for the City Owl Press newsletter to receive notice of all book releases!

SNEAK PEEK OF CAGED FURY

Darkness shrouded the trees surrounding the warehouse, keeping me cloaked in shadows. The quiet sounds of the woods tickled my senses as my heart beat an accelerated rhythm. I used to live for this shit.

What the fuck was going on in this place? Guards circled the structure, flood lights illuminating the space between the barb-wire fence and the building—a mini prison. My instincts told me it wasn't good. What had Landon gotten me into?

The human woman I was tracking, Jolyn Mahn, was a ghost. When we were kids, she'd been quiet, but it was kind of hard not to notice her with her bright red hair that spiraled out in every direction. But now, she was either very good at existing in the shadows or someone had killed her and gotten rid of the body. If that was the case, Landon was going to be pissed.

I'd done some research, found her service record. She'd joined the Canadian army four years after me even though she was only a year younger, but she hadn't seen as much action. As soon as her four-year contract had ended, she'd moved to Detroit, then disappeared. That was this past year. No record of employment, no activity at the apartment leased in her name, no travel trail, just *poof*. Gone.

Because she'd turned into a ghost, I'd focused on her brother. All of us had grown up together in Goldenlach Ridge, a town nestled in the Canadian Rockies. Emerson Mahn was the same age as me, and I remembered him as a nerdy, little kid. If he had some contact with his sister, then I could pinpoint her location, let Landon know, and go nurse a beer at my favorite bar in Vancouver until the next time he had a menial chore for me to do. I knew he gave me these odd jobs to keep me busy, but, it had seemed personal for him.

I didn't know what thing he had for the woman, and frankly, I didn't give a flying fuck. He could moon over and screw whoever he wanted. When I found her, he'd send money direct to my account—money I barely touched. More importantly, once I found her, I'd return to that barstool with my name on it, maybe convince Landon to go to the shooting range again, or allow him to finally take me golfing like he's been pestering me.

But right now, Jolyn Mahn remained a ghost.

Which was what led me here. In tracking her brother, I'd found the listing for this property in a roundabout way. It was strange. For one, no one was supposed to be here. According to city records, it was abandoned, slated for demolition. But someone went to the effort of the guards, security gate, flood-lights, and barbed wire fence. It definitely wasn't condemned.

Snap. I tensed, listening. Someone walked through the woods a couple meters away. Annoyance rippled through me. I should've heard them sooner.

I stilled. A feminine, feline scent slammed into me like a physical thing. *Shifter.* It made every hair on my body stand on end. My heart galloped in my chest, and I developed the sudden need to go to her, wrap my arms around her body, and *claim*. A growl began low in my chest and worked its way through my throat. I bit it off before the sound could escape.

I stepped toward her without thinking, about to reveal my position, when I shook my head and forced myself back into my hiding spot within the bushes. *What the hell is happening?* Every instinct I owned wanted me to touch her, to take her. I was getting a damn hard-on, and I couldn't even see her properly. Nothing like this had ever happened to me before, and I didn't understand it.

Gritting my teeth, I clenched my hands into fists, willing myself to stay put. It didn't stop me from inhaling deeply as she passed three steps away from me, so close if I reached out, I'd have her. My hot blood pumped through my veins. I couldn't even recall why I was here in the first place. All I wanted was the woman in front of me.

I slowly exhaled, trying to keep my shit together in the face of this unexpected need, her intoxicating scent. *Peaches and cream.* She didn't notice me, her gaze on the warehouse. I shifted my eyes to see her better. Her long brown hair was swept up into a ponytail, curling slightly as it cascaded down her back. Dark wash jeans and a blue plaid shirt clad her petite form.

She kept going down the hill toward the warehouse, only stopping by the outer chain link fence. Even though we were shadowed by trees and bushes, she was way too close. My instincts to protect her came from the same place as the need to claim. I wanted to rip her away from that fence and take her from whatever danger lurked behind the walls of that warehouse.

She stared at the building for a long minute, then lifted binoculars. When she lowered them, she ran a hand over her head, agitated, like she was deciding what to do. If she made a step toward the warehouse, I'd have to stop her. There was no way she could get inside without being seen.

Another twig snapped, this one from her other side. She'd distracted me so much, someone had snuck up on us. *Fuck.* What the hell was happening to me? Why was I acting like such a rookie?

She spun around at the sound. A man gripped her by the throat a second later, pressing her against a tree. Fury snapped through me so fast it blinded me for a moment. I stood, my instincts telling me to attack, to protect what was mine, when I realized there was more than one person out there.

The scent of shifters swamped the area, and I recognized them as my own kind. Three cougar shifters surrounded her in a loose circle. Every muscle in my body bunched, ready to fight. My instincts warred with my training. I wanted to charge forward and rip out the man's throat for touching her, but I also needed to stay concealed, to find out more about what the hell was going on.

"Look what I've caught," said the one with his hand around her throat. He wore a cowboy hat and spoke like a Texan. "Another kitty for the hunters to skin. You've been poking where you shouldn't. Have you told anyone where you are? Your sister or mom perhaps?"

Hunters? Primal rage ripped through me. When the one in the trucker hat adjusted his crotch like he was getting turned on by what his friend said to her, I couldn't contain myself any longer.

I ran and shifted, my cells morphing in a flash of heat, one molecule at a time. With every sense enhanced, the world brightened around me. Canines lengthened and muscles realigned, ripping my clothing from my body. My fighting screech tore through my throat. I attacked the one touching her first, my teeth tearing into his shoulder. In the next instant, he shifted, the flesh knitting back together in a horror show suture. Before I could launch again, another shifted, only the third remaining human.

The woman's footsteps retreated into the distance. She ran away through the forest, not even bothering to be quiet about it. A shot of betrayal made me stumble. I didn't know why I would've thought a woman I'd never met before would stand beside me while I took on these fuckers. It was safer for her to run. But it stung anyway.

Story of my life... Everyone always left me in the dirt while they moved on.

The pair of cougars weren't letting up, charging over and over again. I got in a few good bites, but so did they. I shifted partway, healing the gashes. Snarls cut through the night. Claws came at me from every direction. I tried to stay in front of them. This wasn't the first time I'd been outnumbered, and I usually came out on top.

I knocked out one with a kick of my hind legs and was turning to take down the other cougar when something jabbed me in my ass cheek. I whipped my head around. A hypodermic needle stuck out at an odd angle from my rump. To have that syringe at ready and in hand... They'd planned on using it on the woman.

A new wave of fury crashed over me as my movements slowed, my muscles lethargic. My paws wouldn't hold me up. My knees were made of rubber. It was all slipping away.

But at least the woman was free.

"Find her," was the last thing I heard before my vision blackened.

Don't stop now. Keep reading with your copy of CAGED FURY.

Don't miss book two of the *Goldenlach Ridge Shifters* series, CAGED FURY, available now, and find more from J. E. McDonald at www.jemcdonald.net

Abducted and stripped of her shifter abilities, Sabrina faces certain death. Unless...

Captured, caged, and brought to an unknown location, Sabrina Covin is controlled by a deranged doctor and sociopathic businessman. She only has one chance of escape, but that means she needs to put her trust in the person whose tortured screams reach her through the walls. Can she count on him as an ally or will this tormented soul become her biggest enemy?

Walker Hayles is no stranger to being held captive. Former military turned freelance investigator, he might have been doing a friend a favor, but it landed him in a whole heap of trouble. What he doesn't expect is the woman who got him abducted in the first place to come to his rescue. Or that his shifter instincts tell him they are fated mates—instincts she doesn't seem to share.

When the pair make a break for it, will distrust and resentment lead them right back in the hands of the enemy, or will they find solace in each other's arms?

All reviews are **welcome** and **appreciated**. Please consider leaving one on your favorite social media and book buying sites.

Escape Your World. Get Lost in Ours! City Owl Press at www. cityowlpress.com.

ACKNOWLEDGMENTS

This was such a fun book to write, and I wouldn't have even come up with the idea without my editor, Heather, inspiring me. I'd never thought to write a shifter book before, but with her influence, and a trip up north, the idea of two sisters being abducted and one of them being dropped into the great Canadian wilderness came to me. Sometimes brains just need a break, and mine was telling me to embrace something that wasn't wholly Wickwood related. But don't worry, the Wickwood Chronicles are not even close to being done yet!

I need to thank my husband, Marcel, for all his advice and expertise about living in Northern Saskatchewan. He was born and raised in the town of La Ronge, and his opinions were invaluable. He also didn't balk (too much) at some of my more absurd questions, like how to get rid of a helicopter. I hope my love for this beautiful and rugged place came across in the book. Northern Saskatchewan is one of my family's favourite places to visit and go camping.

I have to again give my beta readers a HUGE thank you. Bevin, Caryn, and Melodie, your really are THE BEST. I don't know what I would do without you. And thank you for encouraging me to write book two RIGHT NOW because you needed to find out what happened to Sabrina. Her story is coming soon!

Thank you to everyone at City Owl Press/Mystic Owl, especially Tina, Yelena, and Heather. I'm so excited to be a part of this new endeavor and I look forward to this imprint flourishing in the years to come. And the cover artists! Oh my! Thank you Mibl-

Art. I could stare at this cover for hours. You really outdid yourselves.

A special shout out to my fellow authors at City Owl Press/Mystic Owl. You are all such a supportive and fantastic group of individuals. A special thank you to Melissa Sercia, Wren Michaels, Ashley R. King, and Gabrielle Ash for all your kind words and encouragement.

Thank you to my publicist Mickey Mikkelson at Creative Edge Publicity. Your love for your work shines through and I've appreciated every opportunity you put in front of me.

And thank you to the all readers and reviewers out there. Thank you for being excited for something new like the Goldenlach Ridge Shifters, and thank you for being excited about the next Wickwood Chronicles book. Your enthusiasm makes it all worthwhile!

Thank you to all my family and friends for being so supportive. You're my biggest cheerleaders and I appreciate that more than words can say. Love you all.

ABOUT THE AUTHOR

Photography by Zehra Rizvi

J. E. MCDONALD was born and raised in Saskatchewan, Canada, The Land of the Living Skies. As a child, she was either searching the clouds for identifiable shapes, or star-gazing way past her bedtime. She's an anti-morning person who wakes up at 5am to write. Needless to say, coffee is a morning requirement. She cut her teeth watching Star Trek, James Bond movies, and reading the Harlequin novels her mother left in the bathroom—which resulted in an extremely skewed sense of sex education by age eleven. All of these factors contribute to her love of writing paranormal romance with humor, mystery, and lots of spice. J. E. resides in Saskatchewan with her husband and three daughters.

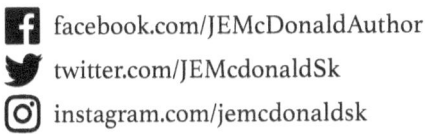

facebook.com/JEMcDonaldAuthor
twitter.com/JEMcdonaldSk
instagram.com/jemcdonaldsk

ABOUT THE PUBLISHER

City Owl Press is a cutting edge indie publishing company, bringing the world of romance and speculative fiction to discerning readers.

Escape Your World. Get Lost in Ours!

www.cityowlpress.com

facebook.com/YourCityOwlPress
twitter.com/cityowlpress
instagram.com/cityowlbooks
pinterest.com/cityowlpress

www.ingramcontent.com/pod-product-compliance
Lightning Source LLC
Chambersburg PA
CBHW020650030726
47498CB00002B/445